W0016710

WICKED LUCK

BY: SHANNON L. MAYNARD

Wishing you wicked good luck—
Shannon L Maynard

CLEAN TEEN PUBLISHING

For my five beautiful girls who amaze and inspire me every day.

THIS book is a work of fiction. Names, characters, places and incidents are the product of the author's imagination or are used fictitiously. Any resemblance to actual persons, living or dead, business establishments, events or locales is entirely coincidental.

NO part of this book may be reproduced, scanned, or distributed in any printed or electronic form without permission. Please do not participate in or encourage piracy of copyrighted materials in violation of the author's rights. Purchase only authorized editions.

WICKED LUCK
Copyright ©2014 Shannon Maynard

All rights reserved.

Cover Design by: Marya Heiman
Typography by: Courtney Nuckels
Editing by: Cynthia Shepp

ISBN: 978-1-63422-066-8

For more information about our content disclosure, please utilize the QR code above with your smart phone or visit us at

www.CleanTeenPublishing.com.

Dax

DAY ONE: THE ARRIVAL

I ADD ANOTHER STICK TO THE FIRE AND LAY CLOSE TO the flames, wondering what other nineteen-year-old guys with a normal life are doing at this very moment, or what I'd be doing if an ocean didn't separate me from modern civilization. Eating cold pizza for breakfast? Maybe downing a Coke before heading out to catch some early morning waves? Or if I were lucky, I'd be sitting on the beach in San Diego next to a beautiful girl, waiting for the sunrise.

It's fun to imagine for a while and then the thrill becomes unpleasant, like riding a roller coaster over and over until you make yourself sick, so I shove those thoughts aside to conjure up my favorite memory and the one that usually puts me to sleep. But tonight, it's no use because the storm has left me restless. I grab my guitar and step outside the cave into the cool night air.

Black clouds smothered the sky earlier like angry, clenched fists, but now the moon peeks through the softening billows and an eerie calm settles over the island. Propping myself against a rock, I inhale the crisp scent of wet sand, seaweed, and salt, a refreshing change from the suffocating atmosphere of most days. I manage to strum only one verse of a song before something in the distance catches my eye.

1

About two-hundred yards out in the water, a faint, yellow light blinks every few seconds. For a minute, I stop playing and stare to be sure it's really there, then my guitar is abandoned to the side of the cave and I stumble over the rocks in a rush to get to the beach. I stand at the water's edge to study the light, and a burst of excitement catches fire inside my chest before I quickly extinguish it.

No one is coming to rescue me.

The floating object is too small to be a boat, and I decide the best thing to do is sit in the sand and wait for the mysterious, flashing light to get to shore.

The minutes tick by at an annoying pace, and I can't take the suspense. The surf is lapping at my toes and in the dim light of the moon, I can now make out a small mass bobbing with the rhythm of the swells and realize it might be a person. Instinct kicks in, and I'm gone. My legs thrash through the tide before I dive into the water and swim out to get a better look.

A surfboard floats on the surface of the water next to a girl. Her hair covers and mutes the flashing beacon in the life vest, but she's not moving and my stomach rolls. She's probably dead.

I lift her chin and check for a pulse. She's unconscious but alive, and now a new worry unfolds. The sun will be coming up soon, and I have to get her to shore and inside the cave where she'll be hidden from view. I position the surfboard between us, pull her on top from the opposite side, and then paddle as fast as I can to push the board to shore. Using the surfboard like a spine board, I drag it across the sand to the rocks before I notice the leash tangled around her leg. It takes a minute to set her free and when she moans, I glance up to see her eyes flicker open and then close.

She feels light when I pick her up in my arms. There's a hint of a smile on her lips as I carry her to the cave and lay her down near the fire. I drop to my knees beside her and brush the hair away from her face. Other than the massive contusion on one side of her forehead, I don't see any other visible injuries.

"Hey. Can you hear me?" I ask, but she's not responsive. I check her pulse again. Ice grips at my chest until I find her heartbeat, slow and steady but faint compared to when I'd first felt it in the water. I lean down and put my ear to her mouth to check for breathing. Nothing. Did she just stop breathing or is it so shallow I can't tell? *Damn it!*

Yanking the life vest off with trembling fingers, I fumble to remove the chain of a necklace twisted so tight around her neck that a chafe mark is visible. I listen for her breath again. Still nothing. She's so limp—so fragile and delicate that I worry I found her too late. *Noooo.... don't freaking die on me.*

I'm trained to ignore the adrenaline coursing through my veins and I start mouth to mouth, pausing to place my shaky hands on her chest and stomach for any signs of movement. *Come on. Breathe.* I repeat the process, trying not to think too hard about my lips touching hers. It's been so long since I've been around any girl other than my stepsister Roxy.

The girl's eyes flutter and she coughs up a small amount of water. She's managed to keep her eyes open and she's trying to speak, so I lean closer, but no words come out. Blinking, she then focuses on me with the most beautiful eyes I've ever seen—green with flecks of blue—and the color reminds me of the water in the lagoon that glistens in the afternoon sun. I smile at her and sigh with relief, but I'm so fixated on her eyes that I don't pay enough attention to the confusion and alarm spreading across her face. She tries to scream, her voice hoarse and desperate, and I reach up to gently touch my fingers to her lips.

"Shhhhh. Don't scream," I tell her. "It's okay now,

3

you're safe. And alive."

I'm not sure if the last part is to reassure her or myself, but my words don't seem to comfort her because she's still crying. *Why is she still crying?*

"I know you've hurt your head, but are you injured anywhere else?"

She doesn't answer me, and now her breathing is short and rapid. If she doesn't calm down, she's going to hyperventilate and pass out again.

"Can you hear me?" I ask again.

She's pale, her lips are chapped, and her fit of crying is taking more energy than she can spare. I know she's dehydrated and weak—possibly in shock, and she must have a concussion. If only I can get her to calm down and drink some water. I start to ask if she's thirsty, but something about the way she's glaring at me makes me stop.

She looks horrified, and I can't figure out what could cause her to look so repulsed by me. I used my knife to shave yesterday and convinced Roxy to cut a few inches off my hair, but now I wonder if her less-than-perfect trim left me looking like some sort of mad scientist. I self-consciously run my fingers through my hair and smile at her again, but the look she's giving me is twisting my insides. I'm used to that look of disgust from Roxy, but not from a complete stranger. Especially a girl.

She won't stop crying and for the first time since being on this island, I feel totally helpless. I don't know what to do. She's inconsolable, and I'm positive if she had the energy, she'd hit me and then run away. She stops long enough to try to say something, but then her eyes close and she's quiet. I curse under my breath and check her pulse. It's faster and stronger, and now I can see the steady rise and fall of her chest, but she's cold. I add some wood to the fire and take off her Vans and socks to place them close to the flames. Very carefully, I roll her onto her side in a recovery position and scoot against the wall to watch her.

There's an uncanny resemblance to Roxy, but this girl is much prettier. She's the kind of girl most guys dream about. She has thick lashes that fan high cheekbones, and her features are arranged in such a perfect way that make-up might cheapen her natural beauty. My eyes follow the length of wet waves of brown hair that cling to her shoulder and arm, but then I can't stop my eyes from gliding down the rest of her—along the curve of her hips and across her long, bare legs.

I close my eyes and sigh. She reminds me of a girl I met at the beach when I was nine; the one I can't seem to stop thinking about. I remember how the ocean breeze blew her long, wavy hair back from her face to expose cat-like eyes that watched me intently and hung on my every word. She didn't talk much, just acknowledged my words with a nod of her head or a smile. That smile. It was genuine and warm as the sun, conveying all the words her mouth refused to say.

The memory of that day has kept me sane and puts me to sleep almost every night. My eyes open to study her again and I laugh quietly to myself, because I've imag-ined a million times in my head what that girl would look like now. And if I could create someone to fit my fantasy, this girl would be it. I'm fighting the primal urge to touch her—but not as a necessity like before. I want to run my fingers across her skin to see if it feels as flawlessly smooth as it looks. Being stranded on an island for three years has left me too much time to fantasize, and my thoughts wan-der out of control. Irritated, I jump up and walk outside to clear my head.

The sun has managed to chase away the clouds, so I comb the beach for signs of other people and spot a large, orange trunk. I discover it's an inflatable life raft, and I can barely contain my emotions because I'm exploding with excitement. I want to jump up and down—whoop and holler—scream at the sky. Of all the times I've attempted to conjure up an escape plan, one important element has always been missing from the equation. A boat. Because venturing out in the Pacific Ocean with a canoe would be a suicide mission, so this life raft is a dream come true. If only something catastrophic would happen to leave the points of the inlet unguarded, maybe it would be possible to take Roxy and this girl and leave the island. Then I could finally go home.

'*Go home and do what?*' my subconscious asks, poking fun at the thought. I could sell the story of my time spent stranded here to anyone willing to pay, and then find somewhere to live and even finish school. But I'd be lying to myself if I didn't admit a good part of my time would be spent searching for *her*, even if it meant living homeless under the San Diego Pier.

The lifeboat case is heavy, but I drag it through the sand and up to the cave. After checking to make sure she is still breathing, I decide to walk along the beach and see what else I can find.

I come across a briefcase and another surfboard and then see something else on the shore in the distance, so I leave them and jog to retrieve the other item. It's a backpack. I sling it over my shoulder, picking up the briefcase and board on my way back to the cave.

I put everything next to the other surfboard and my guitar, but she's still asleep, so I sit down and unzip the backpack. I'm surprised at the condition of everything inside—dry and in one piece. The backpack and briefcase are both high end and obviously waterproof. I toss out a collection of empty plastic water bottles and shove random items to the side until I find what I'm looking for.

I pull the purse out to see what's inside, hoping she doesn't wake up suddenly and catch me snooping through what I assume is her property. There's some gum, a phone, keys, sunglasses, a bottle of aspirin, an envelope, and a tube of some lip stuff, but I spot the wallet and open it. Her driver's license is in plain sight, and a smile spreads across my face at her picture. She is beautiful. My eyes drift to her name and almost pop out of my skull along with the curse word that flies out of my mouth.

Ava.

That's insane. What are the freaking chances of that? This girl—having the same first name as the girl I met on the beach when I was nine. The one I've spent countless hours thinking about and trying to find.

No way. No way! It's stupid to even think this is anything but coincidence, because there are other people in the world named Dax, and they're not me.

Maybe this is a sign. A pep talk from heaven in the form of a fluke accident to let me know I should just accept my fate, forget about risking an impossible escape, and then let *my* Ava go and try to be happy with a substitute. Because finding *my* Ava is really the only reason I want to leave this island.

Or maybe I've finally lost it, and this girl lying in front of me isn't even real. It could happen. Just like a guy stranded in the desert that wants water so bad he imagines he really sees it. My stepmother was certifiably crazy and Roxy's right there, teetering on the edge of insanity, so maybe I've lost it too, and this is what happens when people go mad. Their wildest dream becomes a mirage.

I look at her license again. She just turned eighteen, and she's from some town in Colorado. I heard they do all kinds of extreme winter sports there, so maybe she paid a lot of money to fly halfway across the world and try extreme surfing. That would explain the surfboards, but not how she ended up here in the middle of the Pacific Ocean. Unless she was on a helicopter, and it crashed in the storm while trying to drop her down by a gigantic wave where she planned to surf into shore undercover to rescue me.

Ha! Leave it to me to turn this scenario into some twisted version of a James Bond movie. This girl looks the part—physically fit and stop-in-your-tracks stunning, but that's where it ends. For some reason, I can't picture her with a gun. But hey, a guy can always dream. She moves a little and groans, so I replace the wallet and shove the purse in the backpack before zipping it shut. I move to her side to tuck the life vest under her neck, worried that the cause of her discomfort is more than just the bump on her head.

After tending to the fire, I check out the surfboard. This feels like Christmas morning because I just got everything I wished for all in one day—a hot girl, a surfboard, and a life raft. A quick glance reassures me she'll be fine, so I grab the short board and run to the water to try it out. I only go one time because the waves aren't that good, and I'm worried she'll wake up alone in the cave and freak out again. But judging from her reaction to me before, maybe her waking up alone would be better. I can't help but smile on the way back to the cave. This is the best day I've had in over three years.

The briefcase is locked and I know I can probably break into it, but that'll have to wait. The castle is too far away. It's not a real castle, just a large cave with rooms hidden beneath a waterfall that I've turned into a secret hideaway. And the thought that I now have someone to share it with makes me smile.

As soon as she wakes up, I'll run to the tree house and get some food and more fresh water, but not unless I'm sure she'll stay put. Her being discovered by either one of the tribes that inhabit the island wouldn't end well. How am I going to introduce her to Chief Anwai anyway? Tell him she's a mermaid? Once again, she's nailed the beautiful and enchanting part, and if I could convince her to walk into the village without any clothes, it would definitely be believable—*if* Chief Anwai had ever heard of mermaids.

I laugh quietly, but she doesn't move.

Convincing the chief to let her stay might be easier than introducing her to Roxy. That conversation makes me cringe. What will I say? *Look, Roxy,* and point to Ava. *God took pity on me and sent me a better version of you. She's hot, she can surf, she has the same name as the girl of my dreams, and the best part is... she doesn't hate me like you do.*

At least, I hope she likes me better than Roxy does. I haven't looked in a mirror for three years, but girls dug me in California so I'm not too worried. I know I was never the best-looking guy at school, but I definitely wasn't a mutt.

A tune forms in my head that I hum to myself. I need to try it on the guitar, but it will have to wait until morning because a whole night without sleep is catching up with me. I tuck the backpack under my head for a pillow and close my eyes to ponder the possibility of a future with the beautiful girl that lies just a few feet away.

THE AWAKENING

*D*YING WAS NOT LIKE I THOUGHT IT WOULD BE AND DE-
spite being born on the wrong side of luck, I tell myself this wasn't supposed to happen. Maybe that's
why there were no smiling angels holding a welcome ban-
ner or a bearded man dressed in white guarding a pearly
gate. There wasn't even a crowd waiting with my dead
parents to greet me with open arms. And I'm sure I died,
because the world seemed too calm and beautiful in an
unrealistic sort of way—exactly how I've always imagined
heaven to be.

I knew I was finally dead when I found myself floating
through a tropical forest filled with thick greenery in the
dead of the night. My feet barely touched the ground, and
I reached out to welcome the tickle of leaves on my wrists
and watch the moonlight shimmer off the drops of dew
hugging my skin. The short journey led me to a lagoon
where Preston, the love of my life, stood in waist-deep water that reflected the stars, beckoning me with my favorite
smile.

I tried to go to him, but a long vine wrapped itself
around my leg while my arms hung useless by my sides,
making no effort to untangle the menacing vine that kept
me hostage in its grasp. Preston rushed to me and gently

freed the vine before scooping me into his arms. I smiled up at him as he carried me through the water and into a cave where he laid me down on soft, cool sand.

I wanted to ask him if we were dead, but just like my arms, my lips seemed unwilling to move. Leaning down to kiss me, he pressed his lips firmly to mine. He pulled away and then quickly kissed me but his lips felt wrong—forceful, not gentle, but maybe because I was distracted by the strange burning in my throat and a heaviness that weighed down on my chest and made it difficult to breathe. My eyes drifted closed, and I waited for his next kiss.

Even in death, his lips seemed so real as he pressed them to mine. He brushed the hair away from my face to kiss me and I fought to open my eyes, not wanting to miss that tender moment. Because Preston loves me—even though there was nothing tender about that rough kiss and his heavy hands that rested on my stomach and chest, drawing the heat from my scorched lungs as I struggled to fill them with air. I forced my mouth open to say his name, but the words turned to warm liquid that spilled out over my lips and down my chin.

Then I blinked to remove the blur obscuring his face and realized Preston's dazzling green eyes turned blue, and his short, dark hair had transformed into golden waves that dangled just above his brow. A stranger had replaced my perfect Preston, and what started off more pleasant than a dream suddenly twisted into a nightmare I couldn't escape. I screamed in hopes of scaring myself awake, but there was still no sound—and everything wrong simply stayed the same.

I started to cry but breathing was difficult, which seemed to be the fault of the stranger. I wanted to reach up and push him away, but my arms were too heavy to lift. His mouth moved like he was speaking to me, but I didn't care and his words got lost behind the panicked screams in my head. If only I could have moved, I would have run out of the cave and back to the safety of Preston's arms. I tried to cry out for him, but my voice failed me and once again, complete darkness closed in around me.

I thought I'd be lost in the dark forever, but now the soft chords of a simple melody are pulling me back. A collection of harmonious notes strummed from an acoustic guitar floats on the air, and I strain to hear the tune being drowned out by a crackling noise much louder and closer. Am I still alive?

I force my eyes open and stare at the dark shapes of rock above me, shiny from the moisture that clings to them. The air smells damp and cool and my eyes dart around, but I see nothing familiar. Flickering light from a fire dances on the wall, playing a game of cat and mouse with tiny embers as they jump into the shadows.

My whole body hurts. I turn my head slowly to see past the fire and notice an orb of brightness revealing the entrance of the cave, but I remain motionless, trying to make sense of my surroundings as confusion and then fear creep over me. The last thing I remember is getting on the plane with Preston, and now I'm alone in a cave. But wait—I'm not alone, because I can hear music.

I sit up swiftly, ignoring the nausea and searing pain that shoots through my forehead.

"Preston!" I yell, but my throat is raw and my desperate cry comes out sounding weak and unfamiliar.

The music stops. Dizziness threatens to overtake me and the room swirls, so I lie back down. Quick steps approach in the sand and I hold my breath, waiting for Preston to appear next to the stranger standing over me, but the seconds tick on. My heart sinks. The stranger who replaced Preston earlier wasn't a dream at all, but a reality worse than any nightmare I could ever have. Preston really isn't here.

"You're awake," the stranger says softly. His blue eyes hold a flicker of excitement.

The need to speak is there, but I choke up. I fight back tears and try to muster the courage to ask the only question that matters. Where is Preston? I struggle to sit up again, but he puts a hand on my shoulder.

"Take it easy. You have an enormous bump on your head." He smiles and laughs a short laugh. "I thought you were dead when I found you. Good thing I know CPR. I guess that job as a lifeguard finally came in handy."

I look away from him, frantically searching the room for any sign that Preston has been here.

"Are you looking for this?" the stranger asks, reaching in his pocket. He holds up my necklace. Dangling from the bottom is the familiar silver, heart-shaped locket covered in an ornate design, alongside a silver key with '*The key to our hearts*' engraved in small script down the side.

"So you won't forget us while you're away at college," my mother had said while fastening the clasp around my neck. That was the day before she died.

The stranger drops the necklace into my extended palm.

"I hope you don't mind, but I had to take it off," he says. "There's a scratch on your neck from where the life vest rubbed against the chain."

A tear escapes and trickles down my cheek. I pry the locket open and look at my parents' pictures, water damaged but still intact. The death of my parents was hard enough, and the thought of Preston being dead terrifies me to the point I'm seconds away from exploding into a major meltdown. I force myself to not make any assumptions about Preston's fate and search my mind for a clue that might help find him, but my head is fuzzy as if someone stuffed it with cotton while I was unconscious. I can't recall anything about the last twenty-four hours—or maybe longer—and the only person who may be able to help is a couple of feet away, studying me intently.

The stranger sits on a small log next to where I lay, wearing nothing but a pair of khaki cargo shorts and a choker made of woven twine with a small sand dollar hanging from the end. He looks close to my age, eighteen or nineteen, lean but muscular, and his tan skin is a nice contrast to his tousled blond hair.

I wonder how long he sat in the same place earlier, watching and waiting for me to wake up. A hundred questions are on the tip of my tongue, but I don't trust myself to talk without bursting into hysterical crying. Maybe if I just try harder to think, a logical explanation for how I ended up in a cave with a stranger might appear in my foggy brain.

"So did you drop out of the sky from a helicopter—like one of those extreme sports kind of people?" he asks, and then pauses, waiting for me to answer. "I don't see why you'd want to get dropped down into the middle of a storm just to catch a decent wave. I mean, I love to surf too, but I'm not insane." He glances at my shorts and tank top. "And a wetsuit probably would have been a better choice."

He stares at me with a smirk on his face, waiting for a response, but his lame attempt at humor is grating on my nerves. I turn my gaze to the ceiling above me.

He continues talking. "I hope you don't mind, but I tried out your surfboard."

My mind struggles to catch up.

"And this morning, I found another one further down the beach. I was totally stoked. There must have been someone with you, right? Or did you bring an extra board in case you broke one?"

My eyes flash his direction, but I don't have the patience to tell him the surfboards aren't mine, or that they were in the luggage compartment of the plane because

Preston planned to go surfing when we got to Australia. I grit my teeth—afraid of what might happen if I open my mouth. He stares at me for another second, realizing I'm not going to answer.

I don't move or acknowledge him. I'm too busy screaming inside my head. *What happened? Where is Preston? Think! Where is Preston?*

He sighs. "You speak English, right?"

I don't know why, but I don't respond.

"Wait. Are you—?" He snorts. "Never mind."

He thinks I'm deaf. That's almost enough to make me laugh at him, but that would give me away. My eyes move to the wall of the cave and what I really want is to tell him to go away. It's unfair to be angry with him, but I hate him for not being Preston. I hate him for not *finding* Preston— only me and a couple of stupid surfboards that belong to Preston and his co-pilot, Kirk. But most of all, I resent him keeping me hidden from view in a cave, where Preston doesn't stand a chance of finding me if he's looking.

The stranger stands up and starts to walk away as if he read my mind, then pauses and turns back around.

"Anyway, if you can hear me, my name is Daxton Miller, but you can call me Dax. I'll be your rescuer for the evening, and now I'm going to go find some food."

He laughs and then uses his hands to imitate feeding himself, and I wonder when he read *Sign Language for Cave Men 101*. If he weren't so cute, he'd look like an idiot.

"Stay here though. It's sort of dangerous out *there*," he says, pointing outside, "and your—head." Now he points to my forehead. Next, he picks up a bow and quiver full of arrows and slings them over one shoulder, then holds his index finger up to let me know he'll be right back.

I wait for him to leave, and then calculate the distance from the opening of the cave. The exit is only about ten feet away, but judging from what happened earlier when I sat up, an escape plan doesn't look promising. I want to yell Preston's name again, but I refrain for fear Dax will hear and come back to my side—the last place I want him to be. My fingers explore the lump on my head and I wince at the pain, but I still have no knowledge of how it got there.

Irritation rips through me. How long have I been unconscious, lying hidden in this cave? For all I know, Preston is looking for me right now, and I cling to that little bit of hope. I need to find him, but something tells me Dax will never agree to let me leave in my current condition. Now the cave seems more like a prison than a place of protection, and my irritation blurs into rage. I know I should drop the act and talk to him, but ditching him seems like a much better plan.

I always have a plan. For most people, that would be a good thing—but for me, it's a ridiculous habit because my life never goes as planned. Part of the bad-luck jinx I was born with. I do it because making a plan gives me something to hope for, despite the slim possibility of success. I didn't plan to get on a plane and end up who knows where, in a cave with some stranger. But I did plan to spend the rest of my life with Preston, and in two weeks, we had planned to run away to Europe. But now he's missing.

Even my plan of moving to California to escape my past didn't pan out so well, because some things are just too hard to forget. But Preston made it possible to smile again.

I have to find him.

3

Dax

HIGH NOON: WORTH THE RISK

I'M RELIEVED THAT AVA'S STILL HERE WHEN I RETURN to the cave with some water and berries, but her eyes are closed and she hasn't moved at all. My heart leaps in my chest, and I freeze to watch for the rise and fall of her stomach. Each time I see movement, doubt makes me think I've imagined it, so I kneel next to her and place my ear by her nose. Warm air coats my cheek and clears the paranoid thoughts from my head.

I pull up a small log and sit, conflicted on whether I want her to wake up and catch me sitting here studying her. But I can't help it. To see a real girl after so long is like being reunited with a fluffy wad of cotton candy at the annual fair—forgetting how good the real thing is until a pinch of the wispy sugar melts on my tongue so fast I'm craving more.

It's not like I'm one of those guys who think of women as an object to devour. I'm simply enjoying this moment and reminding myself of all the little things that make girls likeable, since Roxy is proof that all girls aren't made of sugar and spice and everything nice. Besides, there's not much else to do unless I snoop through more of her things.

The backpack beside me grabs my attention and stares at me with two pull-tab eyes and a zipper mouth. I try to ignore it, but the thing grows in my peripheral vision and waits for me to rationalize the decision in my mind. *Why not?* I can start by looking for medical supplies.

Quietly, I slide the bag close. Underneath the purse I went through earlier, there's a sketchpad and some colored pencils, a magazine, some book with a buff vampire guy on the front, some clothes, an orange, a box of granola bars, and... a journal.

Jackpot.

It's hidden on the bottom under everything else in hopes of not being discovered. The sketchpad is a safer bet if I get caught, but my eyes are fixed on the leather-bound journal that suddenly feels heavy in my hand while guilt and fear battle with my curiosity.

Idiot! I know this is a very bad idea because Roxy caught me reading her diary when we were kids and that ended badly. It's not like I was going to use the info against her or make fun of her hopes and dreams; I just wanted some insight to what kind of thoughts were spinning around in that hamster-wheel brain of hers.

She got crazy mad and every entry after that (yes, I peeked) consisted of morbid drawings of me missing body parts after encountering various forms of violence, or detailed writings about every embarrassing or annoying habit I ever had, including a few that didn't even exist. Now the memory makes me smile. There was actually a time when I worried about the content of that journal getting out and preventing me from being seen by prospective girlfriends as anything but repulsive.

But I guess some lessons are never learned because a quick glance at Ava's sleeping face gives me the encouragement I need to open the front cover. I catch a pressed red rose that starts to slip from inside and replace it, then lift the book to sniff the faded floral scent before turning the page. A neatly written journal entry stares back at me.

June 1

Dear diary...blah, blah, blah blah. Dr. Blevins claims this stupid journal will help me express the feelings I've pent up inside for the last two weeks. I think she assumes I'm angry because I don't like to talk about what happened. I'm not. I just figure what's done is done and no amount of talking or sharing is going to change that. Mother always nagged me to keep a journal, but I never saw a need to remind myself of trivial things I spend most days trying to forget. But now I'm being forced to despite my stubborn resistance. I've decided to just get this over with so next visit I can hand the journal over like an obedient student, let her read my thoughts, and make of them what she will.

Looking back, I realize I wasted most of that precious day and threw away valuable time that can never be replaced. I think I slept in until noon, exhausted from the stress of my high school graduation the day before, and remained in my pajamas until I went to bed again at midnight. The only things I accomplished all day were finishing a marathon of chick-flicks and a pint of Ben and Jerry's, like some lame attempt to rebel against seventeen years of spending each day practicing, organizing, studying, and doing everything right to meet the perfect-daughter expectation held by myself, not my parents. I am a classic case of Only-Child Syndrome according to Mrs. Blevins.

Anyway, the shrill chime of the doorbell startled me awake, and I contemplated not answering. The glowing digital numbers on my alarm clock said 2:23am. I'd only been asleep for a couple of hours so I closed my eyes again, cursing the neighborhood kids I thought must be pulling pranks on their unsuspecting neighbors in the middle of the night. But after the third chime and a round of impatient knocking, I finally got up.

I flung the door open, hoping to catch the little punks in action, and expected to see the trees in the front yard draped with garlands of toilet paper. Instead, two officers stood in the dim glow of the porch light. I scanned the street, looking for any signs of thug-type activity, but as soon as the officers asked to come in, I knew it was something much worse. I told them my parents weren't home, but I realized from their lack of response the information was something they already knew.

Six hours earlier, my parents left our small town of Glenwood Springs to drive to Denver, a larger city four hours away to catch a flight headed to Mexico. I'll admit I was more excited about staying home alone for a week than I was for them, and I even wished they'd be gone longer, which makes me think of my father telling me once to be careful what I wished for.

My heart beat wildly as the officers sat down in the two chairs across from me where I sat on the couch. The younger one, Officer Wilson, fidgeted with a pamphlet he held in his hand. He wouldn't look at me, only at Officer Sanders, who I recognized as a parent of a girl on my school soccer team. He cleared his throat quietly before speaking.

"Your parents have been in an accident," he said gently.

I spoke before he could say any more. "So you're here to take me to the hospital, right? Let me grab my shoes."

"No, Ava," he said before I could get up, and those two words felt heavier than a cinder block on my chest. Officer Wilson covered his mouth with one hand and stared at the floor. Officer Sanders continued. "I'm sorry, but your parents didn't survive."

The sentence hit me like a bag of cement to the gut. The air whooshed from my lungs, and a pinch grew inside my chest. Stunned, I looked at Officer Wilson, whose wet eyes confirmed the harsh news his partner just delivered. I think I asked them what happened. They informed me as gently as possible that my parents were killed when my dad lost control of the car and careened off a cliff a few miles outside of town.

I sat on the couch completely numb, not hearing anything after the initial news of my parents' death. I could see Officer Sanders' mouth moving, presumably giving me advice for dealing with the trage- dy and offering his condolences the best he knew how. Officer Wilson sat the 'How to Deal with Death' pamphlet on the coffee table in front of me, the same one he'd been fidgeting with moments before I heard the devastating news.

I felt trapped in a terrible nightmare, one where you scream inside your head to wake up but your eyelids seem too heavy to lift, so you wait out the torture until eventually your eyes pop open and you lay still as your pulse slows and everything returns to normal. Only this was a nightmare I couldn't wake up from. And nothing will ever be normal again.

"Is there someone we can call for you?" Officer Wilson asked, but I didn't answer.

In that moment, I realized that I didn't have anyone to call. My mother homeschooled me until my freshman year when, after a series of quiet arguments between my parents behind closed doors, my father won and I was allowed to attend public school. I never knew the exact reason my mother had been so against it, but after overhearing her mutter words like, "unsafe" and "risky" before being shushed by my father during their private disagreements, I chalked it up to her over-protectiveness. The compromise was that I almost never attended social activities unsupervised with the exception of one school dance and sports practice after school, which put a screeching halt on my social life.

I don't think she trusted people in general, and she didn't allow me to participate in the popular forms of social media like Facebook because of her fear of sexual predators and identity thieves. She even went so far as to keep my picture out of the yearbook and school paper to satisfy her paranoia. So no sleepovers or parties meant no close friends, and I have no relatives to speak of since my mom's only sibling, a sister named Vivianne, died the year I was born. My dad was an only child like me, and both sets of grandparents passed away when I was young. The obituary for Veronica and Dale Starr shouted to the world what I already knew. The only living survivor is me.

I peek up at Ava and wonder if grief drove her to do something insanely stupid to end up here. I can relate to being parentless. My mom took off when I was three and left me with my dad because she thought a boy needed a father figure. At least, that's what she told him, but I know better.

My parents met at a rock concert when my dad was a freshman in college and she was an aspiring actress. They had a short fling before they decided to get married in Vegas one fantastic weekend, both too young to realize they had nothing in common besides their taste in music. A year after I was born, my mom decided she preferred to be a free spirit than the housewife of a soon-to-be architect, so she left. She sent an occasional postcard telling us where she was the first three years, and then we never heard from her again.

It wasn't until I got a little older and read the backs of the postcards that I figured out she was just a groupie who left her plain husband and only child to chase the dream of being some rock star's wife and traveled around the world in search of the next big party. My dad married Roxy's mom when I was five, and although I wished I'd gained a stepbrother instead, it was good to see my dad happy again.

I turn the page to read the next entry.

June 3

Here goes my second entry. Shocker. I know. But Dr. Blevins luuuved that I'd written something last week. I half expected her to put on a party hat and whip out some blowouts and horns by the way her face lit up when I showed her the page. I must admit I felt better after I wrote it, but is it weird that I prefer to talk to a piece of lined paper instead of a real person? She asked me to write something else before our appointment tomorrow, and I planned to show up empty-handed until last night. If I didn't know better, I'd think Blevins was best friends with my current enemy—fate. When I informed her I would only write about significant events in my life, which are normally few and far between, she smiled and said in her calm, robot voice, "Perfect, Ava. But I'm sure you will find much significance in the weeks to come. This is a new chapter in your life, one that will bring many great things to share."

So now I'm playing the game of fate like a game of chess, with Blevins officiating. Fate moves in and calls checkmate, so I have to find some way to deal with it. I'm definitely being outplayed. Fate's first move was the death of my parents, and now the secret I discovered last night has caught me off-guard again.

I'm not sure what made me decide to go in the attic last night. I might have gone sooner if my mother's friend from work, Mrs. Hansen, hadn't been hovering over me like a bumblebee. I must have given the officer her name that night because then she was here, offering to stay with me for a few days and make sure I was all right. Days turned into weeks, but yesterday, I finally convinced her I was sane enough for her to return home.

I waited exactly five minutes after she left, just in case she forgot something, and then I ran upstairs two steps at a time. I guess I needed closure, a break from the grief that had completely consumed me. I just wanted to be alone and sit among my parents' things.

I hesitated in front of the retractable pull-down stairs that led to the attic, a place full of treasures and memories of forgotten times. My mother's familiar voice cautioning me to climb the stairs carefully was absent, replaced with the creak released from each step under the weight of my feet as I climbed the stairway. The air smelled damp and musty, mixed with a faint hint of cedar and mothballs. Small bits of light peered in from the octagon-shaped stained glass window, casting an auburn glow and illuminating what was once my playroom.

My eyes fell on the big, cedar chest full of gowns my mother wore to black-tie events before I was born. I spent hours as a child twirling around in those dresses and admiring my reflection in my grandmother's large, oval mirror that still stands in the corner.

A smaller trunk full of purses and handbags sat pressed up against the bigger chest, the way a small child clings to a mother's leg in fear of separation. It saddened me to see the film of dust that covered them, undisturbed for the last ten years. I was searching for more memories when I noticed the cigar box, looking out of place among my parent's things. Light beams stretched in from the window like long, bony fingers, pointing it out to me from across the room, yet I'd never noticed it before. Curiosity drew me closer, and I pulled the box from a top shelf, where it sat next to my father's old college books.

I blew a thin layer of dust off and lifted the lid. At first glance, the old photographs looked like duplicates I'd seen in our family album. Most of the pictures were of my mother and Aunt Vivianne together, but then I came to a few of Vivianne with a man I'd never seen before, and one with her holding a baby. These were definitely not in our family album. In these pictures, my aunt's long, blonde hair was cropped short and dyed black. She was almost unrecognizable.

Below the pictures, I found clipped newspaper articles describing the graphic details involving my aunt's controversial and mysterious death. When Mother mentioned that Vivianne died in an accident the year after I was born, I assumed she meant a car accident. But she died from falling off a bridge, and the controversy seemed to be whether she jumped on her own. The articles said she left a suicide note, but an unreliable witness surfaced who said he saw someone else on the bridge with her before she jumped. From what I can tell, the mystery still remains unsolved.

I found two official-looking papers at the bottom of the box. Unfolding the top one, I saw my birth certificate, but the name on the line where my mother's should be was replaced with Vivianne's name, and the line where my father's should be was blank. The birth certificate was completely different from the one surrounded by footprints and pink ribbon, arranged neatly in my baby book sitting on the bookshelf downstairs.

The second paper was an adoption certificate complete with Mother and Father's notarized signatures, testifying as proof to its validity. They adopted me from Vivianne almost a year before she died.

I removed a stack of letters Vivianne wrote to my mother, each one stored neatly in the original envelope. They were dated starting shortly after I was adopted and ending one day before Vivianne's death. I read through them one by one, looking for clues that would lead me to the truth. But there was nothing. No information about the reason behind Vivianne's decision to give me up, or the reason my parents had hidden my adoption from me. In fact, there was no mention of me at all, as though I didn't exist. The peace I went to the attic in search for was replaced by the burden of an unspoken secret. And last night, my parent's secret became mine.

Being orphaned at eighteen is overwhelming. Lonely. I want to move somewhere new and find a way to forget about the accident. Any place has to be better than staying in the same house I've lived in my whole life where time seems to have stopped mid-tick. My dad's briefcase still sits by the front door, and the newspaper from that morning waits to be read on the floor next to his recliner. The glass of water my mother drank from before she woke up for the last time still remains on the side table next to her bed.

The one place I love as much as my hometown is San Diego. Besides, California seems to be the place most people go to start over and leave the past behind. And this is my plan. I haven't thought long and hard about it. I just woke up this morning and decided to leave Glenwood Springs to head for San Diego. Mrs. Hansen has agreed to watch the house until I am ready to come back and deal with my parent's things. In exactly two days, I'll board a plane and hope my bad luck curse doesn't follow me to San Diego.

Ava

PAST NOON: THE ESCAPE

*D*AX HAS SET A BOWL OF BERRIES AND A CUP OF WATER beside me, but he's not here. I drink some water and pop some berries in my mouth before the thought catches up to me. *Dax isn't here.*

Crawling to the entrance of the cave, I hold up my hand, shielding my eyes from the blinding sun to have a look around. I can see his head bobbing around in the distance as he jumps from one rock to another near the water.

This is my chance.

The beach is not far below, but the large boulders separating me from the sand is a problem—a virtual obstacle course I'll have to maneuver through at a snail's pace before I can reach the safety and camouflage of the tropical forest.

I ease down the first rock and focus on the next, ignoring the little specks of silver dust obscuring my vision. If seeing stars is the worst thing to happen during my escape, it will be a miracle. One by one, I leave the boulders behind and near the white sand. The last drop is the biggest. A normal person would jump the last few feet but with my vision being off, I don't trust my balance, so I roll onto my stomach and dangle my legs over the edge, searching for a foothold to help me climb down. My cheek rests against the warm rock before I lift my head to look behind me and see movement in the distance.

Dax is coming back.

I pull myself up and crawl behind a nearby boulder to watch. He goes to the opposite side closest to the water and hurries up to the cave. I wait for him to disappear inside the entrance before standing to survey the situation. There's no time to find a better spot. I swing my legs over the edge again and hug the large boulder while my feet scramble to find traction with no success.

Dax rushes out of the cave and pauses to search the area below him, and I panic. I let go and fall awkwardly on my back with a soft thud in the sand. The fall wasn't graceful, and I know he's seen me because he's rushing down the rocky slope. I can't let him catch me or he'll drag me back to the cave.

I run up the beach, but he reached the sand faster than I thought possible and is coming after me in a full on sprint. The bump on my head pounds with searing pain and I blink repeatedly, trying to clear the double vision causing me to see two of him and everything else. I stumble and sway to keep my balance, positive I look like a drunk running slow motion in the sand. I'm weak, out of breath, and Dax is closing the distance between us, so I dart into the trees and thrash through the thick maze of blurred green with my hands out in front of me, hoping I don't run smack into a tree.

The ground cover makes running a little easier, and I go until I can't anymore, then stop and turn to look behind me. There's no sign of Dax. I sigh with relief and then grip the sides of my head to stop the world from spinning, trying to catch my breath.

After my vision clears, I swivel around to keep running and freeze. Five feet in front of me, Dax stands with arms crossed. I didn't even hear him approach. He puts a finger to his lips to signal my silence and then points into the forest, covering the entire perimeter surrounding us. Next, he points to his eyes and then to me. Now he raises his brows to ask if I understand.

Is something out there? I glance around and when I look back, he's nodding slowly to confirm my suspicions. The word dangerous bounces around in my brain, and when I finally catch hold of it, the memory clicks into place. Dax told me not to leave the cave... because he said it was *dangerous.*

He must see the panic register on my face because his serious expression falls into one of amused satisfaction, making me wonder if this is his plan—to scare me back to the cave with him. He holds out his hand for me to take it. So. Not. Going. To. Happen.

Throwing him a smile that only lasts a millisecond, I spin on my heels and walk away from him. I can only assume I'm heading back to the beach and the cave because I have no sense of direction, so I veer left but get no more than a few steps before his hand clamps down on my arm to spin me around. I jerk free and take off into the trees, knowing I don't stand a chance of outrunning him but hoping he might give up and let me go. No such luck.

He grabs me from behind, but I kick and hit his arms with my fists as I struggle to break free, feeling dizzy and on the edge of fainting from sheer exhaustion. He pulls me to the ground with some kind of wrestling move, him on his back and me on my back on top of him. His leg is wrapped around both of mine and my wrists are held by one of his hands while his other hand clamps down on my mouth. I can't move. I can barely breathe. All I can do is marinate in my anger that I wish could radiate off me and burn his skin.

"Ava. Stop it!" He hisses the words into my ear. "I am not the enemy. There are worse things than me out here and if you don't be quiet, very bad things will happen."

I don't care. If I scream, maybe Preston will hear me. I inhale in preparation, but his hand presses down harder to muffle my attempt.

"Do you have a death wish? They'll hear you!" he says.

Maybe he's not lying about something being out there since he's scolding me through gritted teeth in an attempt to keep from yelling. I can't see his face but I know he's annoyed, and that gives me some satisfaction.

"Please," he whispers. "I'm trying to help you. You need me."

I need him? No. I need Preston.

We lay perfectly still for a few seconds, and then I feel him relax his grip. He rolls to the side, lifting his head and saying in a hushed voice, "I'm going to let you up. Behave, or I'll... I'll kiss you." His light smirk and narrowed eyes threaten to make good on his promise if I don't keep quiet.

My temper flares, and I want nothing more than to punch him in the mouth. I am clearly losing this battle, so I surrender and nod quickly in compliance while secretly plotting his future demise. He stands and pulls me up, then signals his plan of us returning to the cave mime style while I glare at him.

The walk back to the cave is shorter than I expect, which only adds to my irritation. I didn't make it far at all. Storming to the deepest corner of the cave, I huddle against the wall with my arms curled around my knees and watch him bring me the water and berries.

"Water," he says louder than necessary, the way people do when talking to someone who's deaf or someone who doesn't speak English. As if saying the word louder will somehow break through the language barrier.

He hands me the cup containing fresh water. "Drink."

I'm dying of thirst and snatch the cup out of his hand, taking big gulps until the water is gone.

"Eat," he tells me and holds up the bowl. His talking in one-syllable words like I'm a toddler is beyond annoying. I can't take it anymore.

"I speak English, and I can hear you just fine," I say in a sharp tone. I think he'll get angry, but I couldn't be more wrong. He doesn't even act surprised. *Is he smirking?*

"Well now, we're getting somewhere. I guess this really is my lucky day." He clears his throat self-consciously, like he wishes he'd kept the last comment to himself, and takes a sudden interest in the sandy spot between his feet. "What's your name?"

He's sitting on the log by the fire and looks up to watch me eat. I want nothing more than to squelch his excitement, so I ignore his question.

"How dare you threaten to kiss me," I say.

His brows rise for a split second before an amused grin tugs at the corner of his mouth. "Don't flatter yourself, princess. I was only trying to shut you up. As a general rule, kissing's only fun when the other person kisses you back."

"Somehow, I don't believe you wouldn't enjoy it."

He refills my cup with water from a wooden pitcher and then sits back down before responding.

"Now that you mention it, I might have to agree with you, considering I haven't kissed a girl in years."

He offers a smile to make peace but as far as I'm concerned, we're still at war.

"So, are you going to tell me your name?" he asks when I don't respond.

"Ava Starr," I say without taking my eyes off the bowl.

"Ava?" He pauses. "That's—an interesting name."

This all-too-familiar comment in reference to my name is something I've heard numerous times before. Now it hits a nerve. "So is Dax," I snap, and then continue eating.

"Ava, about what I said earlier... there are—"

"Where am I?" I interrupt.

"We're on an island. I call it—"

"Where?"

"I'm not sure exactly. I think it's a small isle somewhere in the middle of the Pacific Ocean. But what I was trying to—"

"You're not sure? That's great. Well, do you know how I got here?"

He runs his fingers through his disheveled hair and then picks up a stick to stoke the fire.

"No. I found you early this morning. It was still pretty dark but I couldn't sleep, so I walked outside the cave and saw the light flashing on your life vest. You weren't too far from shore so I swam out to get you." He lets out a short laugh. "That's when I found the first surfboard too. The leash was wrapped around your ankle a bunch of times, so I untangled it and brought you to this cave, but then you stopped breathing. I was worried you were going to die on me, but then you came to and freaked out. You were hysterical for a couple of minutes before you passed out again. You don't remember?"

I shake my head. That's weird. How did I end up with a surfboard from the storage compartment of the plane? Did the plane crash? My mind is going in a hundred different directions.

"What else did you find?" I ask, looking at him intently. "Besides the other board."

"Well, I found some more stuff not too far from where—"

"Like what?" I interrupt again. I'm not normally impatient, but he acts like time doesn't matter—like he has all the time in the world. To me, time is running out.

"Like I was saying, I found another board, a life raft still in its case, a backpack, and a briefcase."

He gets up and walks to a crevice near the front of the cave, then returns with Preston's black briefcase and sits it beside me.

"Do you recognize this?" he asks with a proud smile, as if he's done something important by finding it.

I nod. "Where's the backpack?" I ask softly, trying not to look at Preston's briefcase that's causing a lump to form in my throat.

He points to the backpack on his left, close to where I'd been laying when I woke up.

"I used the life vest to prop up your head and used the backpack for myself. As you can see, there's a shortage of pillows."

He grabs the backpack and tosses it in front of me. I should laugh politely at his attempted humor, but my next question weighs heavily on my mind.

"So you didn't find any *people*?" My voice cracks a little, and I hope he doesn't notice. I stare at the bowl of berries, but now I've lost my appetite and set it to the side.

"No. And I walked up and down the beach." He pauses. "I guess you weren't alone then."

I swallow and blink back tears.

"We need to get help. I have to find them—I have to find Preston," I tell him.

"Who's—?"

"Do you have a phone?"

He starts to laugh but stops, silenced by the horrified expression on my face.

"Uh, no. I don't have—. I'm sorry. I should have clarified. This island is—very primitive. There's no electricity or plumbing."

Staring at him, I try to decide which of the million questions in my mind to ask next. I think he will notice my obvious distress but once again, he proves me wrong.

"So what's up with the briefcase?" he asks. "Please tell

me you're a spy or something, or a secret agent?"

His assumption annoys me for only a second before I fall apart. I lie on my back and cover my face with my hands, not wanting him to see me cry, but it's too late. He moves closer and touches my shoulder.

"I'm sorry." His voice is sincere and full of remorse.

"Please, just leave me alone," I say between sobs.

He pauses, and then I hear him take a few steps before speaking. "I'm going back down to the beach to find us some dinner. Please don't go anywhere this time. Seriously. It's really dangerous. I'll be back in a while, and we can talk some more."

The hurt in his voice makes me feel bad for being so rude. What is wrong with me? Unleashing all my pain and frustration on him is unfair. He saved my life, and now I'll have to apologize before thanking him.

I force myself to face the reality of the situation. I'm alive. But Preston, his co-pilot Kirk, and Anna, the flight attendant, are all missing. If the plane crashed, there's a possibility they may not have survived. But I'm not alone. I'm on an island—who knows where—with a stranger I just met. And I rudely told him to go away. He probably wishes now that I didn't speak English.

I stop crying long enough to notice the pounding in my head. After unzipping my backpack, I'm shocked to see that everything inside appears to be dry and intact. My parents bought it for me to use on a raft trip for school last year, and the fact that it's waterproof and stuffed with three empty water bottles from the flight must have kept it afloat.

I rummage through the items until I find the bottle of aspirin. I swallow one after taking inventory of how many are left, and then slip the bottle back into the bag.

At least I have my drawing pad if I get really bored, along with plenty of reading material to use as handy excuses for ignoring Dax. I've already read the entire book and magazine, but he doesn't know that. And I can always write in my journal until I run out of pages. Speaking of, I should write in it now. Maybe I'll mail the stupid thing to Dr. Blevins for a Christmas present when I get off this island. That would prove once and for all that my luck is more than just bad.

I dig to the bottom and feel around for the journal, but it's not there. Where is it? I pull the items out one at a time until I'm left with the empty backpack. *Ugh.* Did I write in it on the plane? I must have had it out when whatever catastrophe landed me here. *Great.*

One less distraction.

The items get shoved back in my backpack one at a time. I start to shove the envelope with my paycheck and notice the top is torn open. The check is crammed inside with half of it hanging out like someone shoved it back in a hurry. I don't remember opening it. Dax must have snooped through my things and opened it himself.

Part of me wants to storm down to the beach and confront him, but I'm so tired and hungry that I'm not sure if I'll make it past the entrance of the cave. There's an orange and some granola bars, but I decide to save them for when I successfully ditch Dax, even though my stomach rumbles fiercely in opposition. Sitting requires too much effort, so I collapse onto the life vest and feel the pounding in my head increase.

Everything seemed to come together so easily when I first moved to California, but it fell apart like a knit sweater with a loose thread. My life has a way of doing that. Unraveling until there's nothing left but a pile of yarn, waiting for me to weave the remains back together. If I hadn't taken that stupid job, I wouldn't be in this predicament now. But that would also mean I never would have met Preston. I picture his perfect face to distract me from my growling stomach, but my pleasant memory is interrupted by the faint rumble of Dax's uncontrollable laughter, carried up from the beach and into the cave. My irritation spikes but is quickly replaced by morbid curiosity. We are stranded on a stupid island. What could possibly be so funny?

Dax

TWILIGHT: THE COMPETITION

CAN'T BELIEVE SHE HATES ME SO MUCH SHE TRIED TO run away. And now she probably hates me more since I threatened to kiss her, but the expression that crossed her face made the threat well worth it and proved once and for all there was nothing wrong with her hearing.

I've been sitting here for at least half an hour since I caught the fish, but I plan to give Ava plenty of time to cool down before I break the news about the island. Man, she's going to freak. I'm still surprised she didn't ask. I think she's so concerned with finding Parker—Preston—whatever his name is—that she's lost her grip on reality. I started to ask who he was, but then I remembered the journal. There must be plenty of info about him in there, and I intend to find it. I pull the small book from the side pocket of my shorts and lean against a rock, where I have a good view of the cave in case she tries to sneak away again.

June 5
The funniest thing happened yesterday in the coffee shop at the San Diego terminal. A middle-aged man in a suit sat down at the table to my left and asked if I was looking for a job. He sipped his coffee and his eyes jumped back and forth from my face to the help wanted section of the newspaper I was reading. I remembered my mother's

childhood warning about talking to strangers and briefly contemplated moving to another table before I smiled halfheartedly and nodded in response. Of course, I'm old enough to talk to him, but I have to be extremely cautious now that I'm in California alone. Anyway, he sensed my reluctance and said, "I know where there's a great job that would be perfect for you," and I wondered what job description I fit from a glance.

He was well dressed and for a second, I thought maybe he could be a talent scout for a modeling agency or the film business. Even the not-so-good kind of film business. The horrifying thought made me blush. I asked what kind of job before my imagination got the best of me, and then braced myself for the answer. "Line Hostess," he said, but then his phone interrupted our brief conversation and he jumped to his feet and gave me an apologetic look.

He reached into his jacket pocket to pull out a business card and then whispered away from the mouthpiece. "Oceanview Aviation. Here's a card. Stop by if you're interested and tell George that Brad sent you." Then he hurried away. I don't know the first thing about aviation, but it sounded exciting and perfect for keeping my mind off the past few weeks, so I took a taxi straight there.

Large plants and contemporary furniture filled the lobby, and floor-to-ceiling windows exposed a ramp full of large jets, positioned neatly on the other side of the glass. A slim blonde behind the counter greeted me while the brunette next to her helped a pilot. Both girls topped the high end of the Richter scale for beautiful. The blonde made a quick phone call before directing me to the stairs across the lobby.

George's office was at the top of the stairs, and he jumped up from his desk when I entered and extended his hand. I handed him my resume and was shocked to see him give it a two-second glance before he tossed the ivory paper haphazardly into one of the piles on his desk. He leaned back in his chair with his hands steepled finger to finger in front of him. "You're hired," he said after he asked a couple of basic questions. I'm still in shock. I guess looks are more important than a 4.0 GPA.

Oceanview is a gas station for private aircraft, mostly private jets with a customer clientele of the rich and famous. They offer other services, but my job consists of luring the planes to visit his FBO instead of the competition on the opposite end of the airfield. Wave to the pilots, entice them to pull in, then guide the plane to a parking spot and greet them with a smile.

When I told him I needed to find somewhere to live, he shuffled through some papers on his desk until he found a scrap piece of paper. He scribbled the address of a rental house owned by his friend and handed it to me, then picked up his phone to inform the front desk I'd be borrowing the crew car until I found one of my own. Reaching into a box near his desk, he handed me uniforms consisting of bright-colored tank tops and told me to wear short shorts. He sent me on my way with a handshake and his eagerness to see me today.

Filling out paperwork and getting a security badge consumed my entire morning but after lunch, things got a lot more interesting. I found myself posing in front of a small plane with a fancy paint job while a photographer with a French accent took my picture for a calendar that Oceanview hands out to customers every year.

Can you believe it? Twelve months filled with pictures of female employees posed on various airplanes to lure pilots in to buy fuel and maybe talk to their favorite 'girl'. I'm not sure what irritated me more the uninterrupted gaze of the creepy, dark-haired guy leaning against the building in an Oceanview uniform, or the fact that George failed to mention anything about a calendar and that I'd be the feature girl for the month of April. Seriously, the fact that I'm required to carry a sharpie around to sign autographs definitely should have been mentioned in the job description.

After my shift, I went upstairs to thank George for the lead on the rental and let him know I rented the house. When I exited his office and turned the corner into the hallway, I couldn't avoid plowing into six feet of trouble resting against the wall right outside the doorway. The same guy who'd been watching me all day like it was part of his job peered back at me with sinister brown eyes. His lips were set in a firm line with just a twitch of a smile at one corner, and his black hair was slicked away from the sharp features of his narrow face. He couldn't be more than a couple of years older than me, but his stark appearance made it difficult to guess his age.

He'd obviously been eavesdropping. I told him sorry and attempted to walk around him, but he pressed away from the wall and matched my step with one of his to block my path. "Are you?" he asked with perfected sarcasm. "Sorry for not watching where you were going—or sorry you didn't bump into me sooner?" Ewww. Then his eyes slowly scanned the length of my body. Double ewww. George came to my rescue when he told the guy to come in. I took a deliberate step back, allowing him to pass through the doorway into George's office and actually caught myself staring at him, bewildered by his last comment. George introduced us.

His name is Sergio and he's a personal mechanic for one of our customers. After George told him my name, Sergio stroked his chin with his hand and the large, fang-bearing serpent tattoo on his arm seemed to come alive when he said, "Ava... what an exotic name." I wanted to roll my eyes but somehow refrained, but my dumb feet seemed frozen in place as if I needed his permission to leave. Thank goodness George's phone rang. He said, "See you tomorrow, Ava," before picking up the receiver.

I hastily took my cue to escape the uncomfortable meeting, but not before glancing at Sergio and hearing him mumble "And tonight in my dreams." Triple ewww. He threw me a wicked wink that I pretended not to notice. I think I'll enjoy this job as long as I don't run into him too much. I just hope he's not one of those guys that will offer his assistance, claiming he has nothing better to do, and cause the hours to drag on as he and his ego infringe on my bubble of personal space. Please fate... don't let that happen.

I glance up at the opening of the cave and feel guilty. Not for reading her journal, because this is the best entertainment I've had in three years. But I've been gone longer than I planned. She has to be starving and might regret telling me to go away. Or maybe not. There's nothing about Preston yet and I'm running out of time, so I flip through a couple of pages until I find what I'm looking for—the entry beneath a border of hearts and flowers doodled whimsically around his name at the top of a page.

June 20
Best. Day. Ever.
Today started out like any other day except it was hotter than usual, and my fingers tugged at the tank top clinging to my skin. I used the magazine clutched in my hand as a poor substitute for a fan and squinted through my sunglasses to make out the plane in the distance. As usual, I turned the golf cart around, flicked on the flashing beacon, then peeled my legs from the vinyl seat to stand at the edge of the taxiway and start my routine of smiling and waving like a princess in a parade. I directed the plane to a parking spot and waited for the door to open.

The single passenger in his sixties exited first. His white hair matched the color of his expensive-looking suit, and the crocodile-skin shoes he wore were polished to a high shine. Of the multiple rings on his fingers, the horseshoe full of rhinestones stood out the most. He stepped off the plane, acknowledged my greeting with a nod, and then paused to light a cigar he held between two stubby fingers. I started to remind him of the no-smoking policy on the ramp, but the cloud of arrogance surrounding him said he knew the rules and they didn't apply to him. He exhaled a ring of smoke from his mouth and glanced at me one last time, challenging me to say something, and then he stepped into the waiting limo.

A flight attendant named Anna greeted me next, and I wondered if that could be me in ten years. A flight attendant seems fitting for someone without a lot of people to miss. She handed me the leftover catering tray of caviar, fine cheese, and crackers, so I hurried to place it in the cart, turning to ask the pilot my usual questions, but my breath got caught in my throat.

Forget cute. At the bottom of the stairs was six feet of sizzling hotness. An amused grin crept over his lips, and he pulled his sunglasses down to peer at me over them with green eyes that stood out in contrast to his dark brown hair, and not a hair was out of place. Suddenly, I couldn't remember my own name or what I'd planned to say. I froze, feeling more foolish as each second ticked by, and I wondered if my being mute was the reason for his smirk. I opened my mouth to speak but before I could form the words, he said, "Well, well, well. Looks like Georgie hired himself some new eye candy."

I thought he was talking to me, but the copilot bounded out of the plane on cue to look me over with an impish grin and waited to hear my response. The distraction was enough to snap me back to reality. The pilot glanced at my name tag, still smirking, and said, "Ava, is it? Or should we call you Miss April?"

And I said, "Only if I can call you Mr. Gulfstream." As soon as the stupid words escaped my mouth, I regretted them, especially when he raised a perfectly arched brow. The heat must have gotten to my brain. The co-pilot, whose name is Kirk, burst out laughing and stepped forward to extend his hand. Freckles dotted his nose and his red, curly hair glistened from an overuse of gel. He didn't even look old enough to be flying a Gulfstream.

The pilot stared at me over his glasses, but I avoided his smolder and looked at his name tag instead—PRESTON—and the name fit him well. He appeared to be in his early twenties—tall, slim, very well built, with his crisp, white shirt tucked neatly into black dress pants tailored to perfection. The musky scent of his cologne fogged my brain, and I suddenly found myself picturing him in a TV commercial, buff and bare-chested in front of a mirror, applying aftershave to his freshly shaved skin.

He is visually perfect. There were never any guys at my high school that looked like that. It seemed a little late for my 'welcome to Oceanview Aviation' spiel, so I quickly asked how many gallons of fuel he'd like and when he smiled back at me, his smooth lips exposed a perfect set of teeth—as if I expected any less.

He told me to top it off, and then asked me to have the front desk page his boss for him. When I agreed, he said, "His name is Mr. Pitts... first name is Harry." Kirks' snickering should have clued me in, but I was mesmerized by Preston's smile and realized my mistake one second after the words left my lips into the walkie-talkie, requesting a page for Mr. Harry Pitts.

Sergio and the line techs fueling the plane doubled over in hysterics. My face flushed, and then I got mad. I spun around to face Preston with vicious intentions, but the moment my eyes came in contact with his supermodel face as he chuckled to himself, my irritation dissipated and was replaced again by embarrassment. "See what I have to put up with?" Kirk said, and I wanted to say something clever but the response part of my brain sat empty as if someone deleted the file. Mustering a smile, I climbed in the cart, speeding away to wave at another jet preparing to land in the distance, and I wondered how someone so hot could be so obnoxious.

Later this afternoon when they got ready to leave, I asked Preston if there was anything else I could get them (protocol for the job), and he said, "Actually yes," and felt around in his pocket. "I think I left the keys to start the plane at the front desk. Would you mind grabbing them for me?" Kirk peeked his head around the tail of the plane and, of course, I politely agreed and headed for the lobby.

After not seeing them on the front counter, I looked in the pilots' lounge, then walked back to the lobby and scanned the couches, end tables, and finally the floor. The girl working the front desk finished helping a customer, then looked at me quizzically and asked what I was looking for. I told her the pilot from Hotel Charlie lost his keys to start the plane, and then I got down on all fours to look under the couch. She called my name to get my attention, motioning me to come closer, and then she whispered, "Airplanes don't need keys to start."

Yeah. Well, I was forced to look at Preston and Kirk when I directed them out of the parking spot. Preston gave me a wink before slipping on his sunglasses, with a smug grin plastered to his face that was irritatingly handsome. Kirk shot me an amused smile and waved as they taxied away.

As if the humiliation of Preston's pranks weren't bad enough, Sergio decided to grace me with his presence after the plane turned onto the taxiway. He held out his palm. In the center sat a crisp bill folded into the shape of an airplane. He told me we each got a five-dollar tip, but Preston told him to make sure I got that specific one.

I reached for the origami plane, but he moved his hand so fast I swiped air. The line techs behind him snickered, and I folded my arms firmly across my chest and glared up at him. In a slithery snake voice, he told me that Preston said to make sure I got it, but "he didn't say I couldn't make you earn it first." I told him with a flat smile that I just did. Sergio studied my face, and a wicked sneer crossed his lips before he promised to give the tip to me later tonight at his place—after going to dinner with him. Glancing over his shoulder, I saw the line guys waiting eagerly for my response. I told him to keep the stupid tip and use it to rent himself a date for tonight at Babes-R-Us.

His entourage whooped and hollered with amusement at my shutting him down, but his smile vanished and he clenched his jaw. He looked mad. For a split second, I worried about the repercussions of my comment, but he seemed to regain control of his emotions and tossed the money plane at my chest before he turned and walked away. I unfolded the five-dollar bill and right in the middle, Preston had scribbled this message in sharpie.

~A donation for Ava's training fund!

I'm laughing so hard that my gut actually hurts. Worried Ava can hear me, I glance up at the entrance to the cave. She's not glaring back at me, so she must be asleep again. The smart thing would be to replace the journal while she's asleep before she discovers it's gone, but now I don't know if I can. I have to read more.

I don't even know this Preston guy, but I like him already. Not sure why she seems to like him so much though. He's obviously got the looks of a Greek god, but he served her a hefty portion of humiliation and mockery, which in my mind should dock him some points in the looks department. But noooo... *I have to find Preston*, she said, right before she told me to go away. Huh. Maybe the reason she doesn't like me is that I'm too nice.

What was I thinking, trying to be her knight in shining armor? I rescued her from drowning, risked my own life to save her from a suicidal escape, and fetched her food and water, only to have her hate me because I'm not him. And now I'm sure that's the reason, because last time I checked, I wasn't that bad looking. I'm tan, fairly buff, and have managed to keep up my personal hygiene despite being stranded on an island. And I love a good competition, but this is just weird. I am competing against a guy that's MIA and probably dead, but for some reason, I still feel like the one with a disadvantage.

Preston

DAY ONE: THE MISSING

*T*HE LOOK ON AVA'S FACE AS SHE FLOATED AWAY IN THE water is stuck in my head, haunting me and refusing to go away whether my eyes are open or closed. Telling myself I made the right choice is the only thing keeping me from going ape crazy, that and the fact that Anna has kept Kirk's undivided attention since we made it to shore.

I did what I had to do, but my damn loyalty to being responsible has finally crossed the line and taken my heart and sanity with it.

"Preston?" Kirk says, for like the twelfth time this morning.

I continue to ignore him, the same way you tune out the morning alarm, fighting to treasure your thoughts for a few more precious moments before the incessant pestering snaps you back to reality.

"Hey, Preston?"

Shut up! My fingers tighten around the short hair on the top of my head until the pain draws me away from Kirk's nagging. I close my eyes and see Ava's face, eyes wide in shock and horror when she realized I didn't jump in after her. Her expression is one I've seen many times before and one that, up until now, I'd always taken pleasure in making appear—usually following one of my witty

45

comments or pranks that preyed on her susceptibility to being so naïve. I couldn't help it. She was so unbelievably gullible. The word should have been printed on her name tag right under her name, in parenthesis.

I first saw that look the day we flew into Oceanside and I'd asked her to page 'Mr. Harry Pitts'. One eye roll and I was hooked. I even sent her on a wild goose chase for keys right before we left in hopes of seeing it again.

I wonder if she recognized our tail number over the radio one week later when I requested to land, and if her heart fluttered with anticipation or with dread. Pathetic, I know. But now, I'll never know.

It was the little things that shocked her the most, and maybe that was why I found her so intriguing. Big info came as no shock to her at all, like when I told her Kirk and I were known in the aviation industry for being the youngest pilots to fly a Gulfstream, or when she found out Mr. C was my boss and a wealthy businessman with no shortage of power and greed. She probably wouldn't have batted an eye if I'd whipped out a cape and told her I was a superhero with special powers.

But my simple request for a ride to the hotel that day was enough to send her into shock, and that was evident on her adorable face.

I could almost see the panicked thoughts whizzing through her brain, probably wondering if she'd be capable of driving a car with me sitting close to her. When we met, she could barely remember her own name.

I remember being surprised that she managed to pull the van up to Hotel Charlie without taking out a wing as nervous as she looked, then I watched from the cockpit as she loaded our bags into the back of the van while I finished with the plane. I could tell her plan was to pretend not to care about my existence, but that disintegrated the moment I came up behind her and took the last heavy bag from her hands to place it in the back of the van.

"Bought any stock in sunscreen yet?" I asked, fighting back a smile, and then, "I'm thinking you might be their biggest customer."

She kept her back to me so I wouldn't see her blush and faked the importance of rearranging our bags.

But then her reply shocked me.

"I haven't really had time to buy any stock because I've been too busy searching for unicorns, keys to start airplanes, and other things that don't really exist."

I laughed out loud and was proud that she'd stood up to my antagonizing. An amused grin tugged at the corner of my mouth when I said, "Well, Miss April, it's always good to stay busy," and then I winked before climbing into the van.

I secretly thought about betting Kirk as to how many traffic laws she would break in a short jaunt to the hotel, but instead, I played the sick game all by myself, knowing exactly what to do to keep her flustered long enough to complete my challenge.

Five.

That was how many she broke. I would have guessed seven or eight if I'd bet Kirk. She caught herself speeding twice and made a quick glance in the rearview mirror before applying the brakes. She also made California stops at all three stop signs in what I assume was a rush to get us out of the car ASAP.

I sat in the seat directly behind her and let Kirk sit in front. He made small talk about her job and just when I thought she might start to relax, she glanced in the rearview mirror to change lanes and her eyes caught mine. My arms draped over the seat beside me and my sunglasses were pulled down to watch her in the mirror with a smug grin. My stare was relentless. Her face flushed but before I could thoroughly enjoy the satisfaction of my success, Kirk yelled, "Look out!" and her foot slammed into the brake.

The car in front of us had slowed to make a turn, and she was inches away from a rear-end collision. I would have felt awful if I had actually caused her to wreck, but damn, that was fun. Kirk's laughter broke the tension. I slid my glasses back up where they belonged and then leaned forward, resting my forearms on the back of her seat. My face was right next to her flaming red one. I offered to drive and pointed out that we were all too young to die, but at that moment, I think she might have welcomed death.

I asked if I could take her to dinner to make up for my obnoxious behavior the week before, and she paused long enough to make me wonder what kind of debate was going on inside her head. She finally agreed, and I lifted her hand to place another twenty-dollar money plane with a carefully written message in the palm of her hand.

~A donation for Ava's traffic school fund

The thumping snaps me back to the present.

Thump... thump... thump... thump... thump. The tiny ball bounces off the wall and into Kirk's palm before being tossed again to a precise spot for the millionth time.

"Can you please stop?" I say between gritted teeth.

Kirk stops for a whole three seconds before he throws it again.

"Someone's a little grumpy," he says to Anna, and her eyes drop to avoid making contact with either of ours. She won't take sides. "You're just jealous you don't have a toy in your pocket to keep you entertained," he says carefully in an attempt to make me smile.

"Hmm. Well, you wouldn't have a toy either if I hadn't given you fifty cents to put in that stupid machine, a decision I deeply regret right now." He catches the ball and pauses to look offended by my comment. "I need some air," I tell them and jump to my feet.

"Hey! We have strict orders not to go outside. Remember? Preston!" Kirk calls after me, but it's too late.

Screw the orders. I'm a master at following orders and look where that got me. Besides, I'm just going outside in search of fresh air to clear my conscience, even though I know that won't be possible for a very long time.

Ava

TWILIGHT: THE BEARER OF BAD NEWS

AX'S FOOTSTEPS INTERRUPT MY THOUGHTS, BUT I KEEP my eyes closed and pretend to be asleep. I hear him walk closer to retrieve the log, so I sneak a peek when he walks away. He sits down by the fire to cook two fish at the end of a stick and still doesn't realize I'm awake so I watch him, hoping the shadow from the sloping wall will hide my face.

I'd been so upset and angry that he wasn't Preston, that I hadn't really looked at him. Wisps of wavy, blond hair kiss the top of his lashes and frame his vibrant blue eyes, and the muscles in his arms and chest are well defined. No wonder he had no problem pinning me down in the forest. He seems kind and sincere, and now I feel even worse for how I've treated him. I've stared too long, and he turns his head to glance at me. My weak smile doesn't draw one from him, and I worry that he's angry.

I sit up to drink the rest of the water with shaky hands. Propping the stick on the rocks that surround the fire, he retrieves the pitcher sitting behind him. He walks over, fills the cup, and then sits the pitcher next to me.

"Thank you," I say, looking up at him through my lashes. "I'm sorry I was rude before."

He stares at the ground in front of me, but then his mouth breaks into a smile. For the first time, I notice his dimples. I must be forgiven.

"It's fine. I understand," he says. "Besides, I got a little over anxious. I don't ever get visitors." He spins around, retrieves the fish, and then sits back down on the log.

"So where are we again?" I ask. The smell of the fish makes my mouth water. He places them on a large palm leaf to remove the skin and small bones.

"I call it Daxton Island." His mouth twitches at the corner. "But the official name is Lamarai."

"I've never heard of it," I say.

"Of course not. And those who have wish they hadn't. It's a very small island somewhere off the coast of New Guinea, I think."

"Then why do you live here?" I ask, and then blurt out the obvious question. "And who lives here besides you?"

He slides the fish over to me, and it tastes incredible.

"I don't live here by choice. I ended up here when my family's boat capsized and sank when we hit some rocks in a storm. After a while, we figured no one was coming to look for us, so we made the best of it. There was no other choice, besides not living."

"So your family's here, too?" I swallow the last of the fish and wonder why he isn't eating, but before I can ask, he slides his towards me.

"You eat it; I already ate." I think maybe he's saying this only because he saw how fast I devoured mine. He picks up a stick and pokes at the fire. "My stepsister's name is Roxy, and she lives here. Roxy and my stepmother were below deck when we hit the rocks. They came up on deck just as a huge wave hit us and capsized the boat. It happened so fast they didn't have time to grab life vests. We all ended up in the water. Roxy couldn't swim so my stepmother insisted my father save Roxy first and told him she'd be fine.

It took both of us to get Roxy calmed down and when we turned around, my stepmother was just... gone. She didn't make it to shore, and we never found her."

He stares at the flames as their shadows dance on the wall behind him.

"That's terrible."

"Yeah, it was."

"So your father's here too?"

"He was—until he died about a year ago."

"Oh no. I'm so sorry. I lost my parents too. They died four months ago in a car accident."

Dax doesn't say anything else, and I wonder if he's waiting for me to distract him from a memory like mine. His face is filled with sadness and maybe a hint of regret. I know this pain, and I'm all too familiar with his look of remorse—wishing there was some way to turn back time. After a minute, I muster enough courage to press on with my questioning.

"So it's just you and your sister? Where is she?"

My voice breaks his trance, and he lets out a short laugh. "*Step*sister," he clarifies, and he seems thankful he isn't related to her by blood. "And there are others." He glances at me and hesitates, like he's choosing his words carefully and trying them out in his head. "There are two tribes that live here—the Lambai and the Anwai. Neither tribe likes outsiders. They consider them to be evil spirits, or ghost demons."

Ohh...kay. Is that who he was referring to in the forest?

"So they aren't friendly?"

"Not really. I don't consider people that want to eat you for dinner very *friendly*."

I stop chewing and force myself to swallow. "Are you saying we're on an island with a bunch of cannibals?" I enunciate each word.

He offers a slow nod in response, and my heart skips

a beat as I come to a startling conclusion. The palm leaf with the fish falls from my hands, and I jerk backwards. The back of my head smacks against the cave wall, but the hurt is nothing compared to the relentless beat of pain in my forehead.

"If that's true, then why are you still alive... unless you... you are one of them!" I say, and I'm horrified at the thought. Is he keeping me in this cave for himself—like a prisoner—to fatten me up?

I assess the distance to the entrance of the cave and wonder if I can make it without passing out first. Two things are in the way of my escape path, the fire and him. He reaches for me and I jump, flinching away from the touch of his hand. He slowly recoils his hands to a surrender position.

"Ava," he says softly. "I'm not going to hurt you. I promise. Just let me explain. Please?"

I stay pressed against the damp wall and wrap my arms around my knees. My eyes stay fixed on him. "Why are you still alive?" I ask again through clenched teeth.

"After we swam to shore, we waited out the storm under a tree, and then after it passed, my dad and I got busy making a shelter. Roxy was too distraught. There was another storm coming, and my dad wanted us to have somewhere safe to stay before he went off to explore the island. The Anwai tribe found us; they saw my dad gathering materials and followed him to the beach. We were taken captive and hauled back to their village where they were going to kill us... and eat us for dinner, but one member of the tribe convinced the Anwai chief not to."

"How?" I ask, impatient to hear the rest of his story unfold.

"The chief's son liked our shelter and brought his father back to the beach to see it. My dad was an architect, and the chief was impressed by the efficiency and overall design." Dax chuckles. "Our shelter was so impressive the chief thought my father was some sort of God, with great powers that allowed him to create such an elaborate home. He worried about the repercussions of killing a God, and he decided my dad could be a great asset to him. My dad caught on quickly and showed the chief some ideas to add to their meager homes. The people here live in crude houses very high up in the trees. Anyway, it was enough to make the chief decide to spare his life, and my dad agreed to help them if they spared Roxy and me too. They made us tear down the house on the beach because they didn't want anything visible from the shore, but we ended up building a massive tree house further inland, and my dad created many things to help the Anwai improve their way of life."

The realization hits me, and I'm more terrified than before. "So they don't know about me? Is that why you're keeping me hidden in this cave? Are they going to kill me?" My voice is full of panic.

"No, they don't know about you. And yes, that's partly why I'm keeping you in this cave. But I have a plan. Don't worry. I won't let them kill you," he says.

"But there's only one of you. What if you can't stop them?"

He smiles, and I'm not sure I trust his confidence.

"The Anwai tribe is a peaceful tribe for the most part," he tells me. "They eat outsiders unless they can find some use for them, like my dad. They also eat people from their own tribe if they believe they have turned into Khakhuas. That's sort of a witch or evil spirit they think takes over people's bodies. So they might be easier to convince. The Lambai tribe, on the other hand, is much worse. The size of their tribe has decreased significantly in the three years I've been here, and most haven't died from natural causes. I guess you could say they're human flesh-aholics."

I feel the fish start to come back up in my throat. "So why are you still here? Haven't you tried to escape?"

"The Anwai would never let us leave and the Lambai tribe guards the points of the inlet, making escape impossible. Both tribes migrated to this island as one long ago from New Guinea, so they could live peacefully and practice their tribal traditions. Then there was some disagreement concerning certain traditions... so they separated into two tribes. But they don't want to be discovered, and they hate outsiders who they see as a threat to their way of life. So chances are, if other people have ended up here, they've never been seen or heard from again. And trust me, I've seen evidence to support that theory."

"So let me get this straight," I say. "I ended up on an island full of cannibals, and I'm here in a cave with a wannabe cannibal, and no one will probably try to rescue me for fear of being eaten by cannibals, so I'm stuck here for the rest of my life with you and your village full of cannibals? Does that pretty much sum it up?"

This is beyond bad luck. It's absolutely insane and unbearable.

He gets up and comes to sit next to me, then hesitates before he puts his hand on my back. Part of me wants to brush it away, but a small part likes it there, and I hate myself for taking my frustration out on him again. Should I even trust him? He seems innocent and has been in the very same position as me before, except he wasn't alone. I put my head down on my knees. The reality of the entire situation hits me hard, and I can't hold back the tears.

"I know you're upset." His voice is smooth and comforting. I long for someone to comfort me, but I wish it were Preston. "Please try to believe me. I understand what you're feeling. But sooner or later, you have to deal with the situation," he tells me.

This is the problem. I don't want to deal with it.

"Why didn't you just leave me to die?" I say. "And let the sharks get me or the Lombini tribe?"

"Lambai," he corrects.

"Whatever! You would've done me a favor." My voice is weak and hoarse. But I can't stop myself from taking my misery out on him. "Everyone I care about is gone. Why did you have to save me?"

I lift my head and look at him. His eyes meet mine.

"I know this sounds selfish. But I'm glad I found you," he says. "It's hard to believe that you'd choose being eaten by sharks or a tribe of hungry cannibals over hanging out with me. Am I really that bad?" A small smile spreads across his lips and dimples appear at the sides of his mouth. "I mean—it could be worse. You could've been found by my stepsister."

He laughs and I manage to crack a smile, suddenly self-conscious of what I must look like with my swollen eyes and chapped lips. My skin feels sticky from the salt water, and I haven't brushed my teeth in two days. He doesn't seem to notice or even care.

"So why are we in this cave if you have a house?" I ask, my voice full of suspicion.

"Well, for one thing, my house is right next to the Anwai village. And don't take this the wrong way, but you were unconscious when I found you. I carried you into this cave, but I knew I wouldn't be able to make it up to my room. I'm not saying your fat or anything, I mean, 'cause you're not. You're perfect—actually. It's me. I just couldn't. You'll understand when you see the house. Okay. Anyway, I should just quit talking now."

His flustered comments make me smile, and I decide I don't hate him as much as I thought. Maybe he's right. If this is my destiny to be stuck in this horrible place without Preston, at least I'm not alone.

"So when can I see the house?"

"Let's not rush it. Maybe tomorrow. We still have to get you inducted into the tribe, and you need to be completely recovered first. I'm sure you got a massive concussion judging from the size of that lump. I can't risk you getting dizzy and passing out on me. Besides, if you think your head hurts now, wait until you've been around Roxy for five minutes." He laughs loudly at his own joke. "Speaking of your head, is it feeling better?"

"Yes. I found some aspirin in my purse. I guess I lucked out for once since my backpack followed me to shore." I notice him looking at me strangely, so I explain. "I'm sort of prone to bad luck."

"Well, you seem pretty lucky to me. I mean, you survived," he says with a grin.

"Yeah, and I ended up on an island full of cannibals. That's very *unlucky*, don't you think?"

"I guess if you put it that way." He laughs and points to my four-leaf clover bracelet. "Is that some sort of lucky charm?"

"Yes."

I glance at the clover bracelet Preston gave me, thankful I haven't lost it. Wrapping my hand around the locket and key on the chain around my neck, I squeeze tightly, pulling it to my chest. I should be happy I survived, but everyone I care about is gone. Nothing left of them but mementos on my wrist and neck. I blink back tears.

"So I'm curious," he says. "How did you really end up here? It wasn't a helicopter, was it?" He almost looks disappointed.

"No. We were on a Gulfstream, but I can't remember anything after getting on the plane. It must have crashed."

I struggle again to remember what happened but get nothing. He pauses for a moment as if debating on asking what I know will come next. I brace myself for his question.

"Who is *we?*"

He looks at me with gentle eyes.

"There were four of us—two pilots, a flight attendant, and myself. The chief pilot—is my boyfriend."

No matter how hard I try, I can't refer to him in past tense. For the sake of my sanity, I still cling to the smallest of hope that he's looking for me and will find me—if I can ever get out of this cave.

"Is your boyfriend's name Preston?"

My eyes flash to him. "Yes! Why? Do you know where he is?"

"Uhm, no." A look of shock crosses his face and then it's replaced by remorse, realizing he's given me a glimmer of false hope. "I was just guessing... you said the name earlier."

I did. As I look down at my hands in my lap, a single tear drips onto my leg. He starts to rub my back and instinct allows me to lean into him, putting my head on his shoulder before I start to weep uncontrollably. I feel him tense for a moment, and then he wraps his other arm around me. I sob until I'm too tired to cry any more.

"How long have you been on the island?" I finally ask, afraid to look up at him.

"We left California when I was sixteen and Roxy was fifteen," he says. "I don't know for sure, but I've tried to keep track of the days. If my calculations are correct, it's been a little over three years."

His embrace makes me feel better, but I sit up, and his arms fall awkwardly from my shoulders.

"Wow—three years. That's a long time."

"It is when you live with Roxy," he says, which makes me nervous about meeting her. "She's slightly bitter about her circumstances—completely miserable actually, and intent on making everyone else's life just as miserable. Well, not everyone—just me. I'm usually the only one around. So I try to find fun things to do to make time go by faster." He looks down at the sand. "I have to admit though, I was completely stoked when I found you and realized you were alive. It gets kind of lonely here, and I was so excited at the idea of having someone else to hang with."

I can relate to his blatant honesty. I know exactly how it feels to be lonely. "Speaking of Roxy," I say, "does she know about me?"

"No." He chuckles. "She won't even notice I'm gone until she gets really hungry. I have a place I go a lot for days at a time, mostly to get away from her. She probably just assumes I'm there. It's a secret place that not even she knows about. I'll take you there tomorrow, if you want."

"Okay. But what about the cannibals?"

"They don't go there. You'll be completely safe, and it's a much better hideout."

I'm sure his words are meant to be comforting, but they have the opposite effect. His plan conflicts with mine. My plan is to find Preston, and I can't do that if I'm hiding out.

A yawn escapes my mouth. I'm physically and mentally exhausted. Scooting down, I put my head on the backpack, determined to resolve the problem tomorrow. Something pokes me so I reach in and pull out my sketch-pad and pencils, setting them to the side, and then adjust my extra change of clothes so my makeshift pillow is more comfortable.

Dax is staring at me.

"What's wrong?" I ask.

"Nothing," he says. "Is that a drawing book?"

Now I regret pulling it out. I nod.

"May I?"

I hand it to him and then look away, not wanting to chance seeing the contents within. Maybe he'll accidentally drop it in the fire and do me a favor, because I never want to draw anything again. I hear him flip through the pages one at a time until the page turning stops. Opening one eye, I see him studying a page with a strange expression on his face.

"Is this your mother?"

I don't need to look at the drawing he's holding up to confirm his question with another nod. Flipping the page a couple of more times, he stops on another picture. He flips the notebook around for me to see.

"Preston?"

This time, I look and my eyes fill with tears. I nod slowly. I can't remember drawing it, and I stare at Preston's vibrant green eyes staring back at me from the paper. A vision of Preston sitting across from me on the plane flashes through my mind, but then it's gone just as quickly as it came.

"So where are all the portraits of your ex-boyfriends, or do they have a sketchpad of their own?"

I stare at my hands and twirl my fingers self-consciously in my lap. He smiles and waits for my response.

"There aren't any portraits, because I've never had a boyfriend. Until Preston."

The smile disappears from his face and he responds with an "Oh," before he quickly flips to the picture of my mother and studies the portrait again. His gaze jumps back and forth from me to the paper, but he doesn't ask any more questions. Instead, he closes the sketchpad and sets it down.

"You're a great artist," he says and then pauses, his voice gentle. "Go to sleep if you want. You don't have to worry. No one knows we're here, and I'll protect you. You can trust me."

He lies down by the fire and smiles, and I smile back at him before he closes his eyes. Part of me hopes when I wake up things will be different. *Maybe today will all be a bad dream,* I think, because the idea that I might never see Preston again is too upsetting to contemplate. If only I'd told him I loved him. Now I'm left with nothing but regret and a dying wish for a second chance, just like after the death of my parents. My life is beginning to seem like a vicious cycle. I blink back tears and let my memories of Preston take over my mind.

Dax

MIDNIGHT: DEJA VU

*I*T'S TAKING EVERY BIT OF SELF-CONTROL I CAN MUSter to lay here and pretend to go to sleep. My heart has been racing faster than a dragster at the end of a quarter mile ever since I saw the drawing and recognized Ava's mother.

It's her. It's her. It's her. It's her.

The words are echoing in synch with each thump inside my chest. I can't believe it's really her. My Ava. I wanted to tell her, but I worried she won't remember that day. She might not remember me.

I need to figure out some way to ask so if she doesn't remember, I can play it cool and not wind up looking like some stalker from her childhood. The last thing I need is ammunition for her to like me less than she already does.

Taking a peek at her, I watch the slow rise and fall of her chest. I knew she would fall asleep fast after her crying spell, but I need to be sure. I whisper her name, but it draws no response. The book slips out of my pocket with the ease of my hand, and I open it to the place I left off. Knowing she's *my* Ava brings the thrill of snooping to another level, like a covert mission to find classified information. I've been dying to know what she's been doing for the last ten years, and by nothing short of a miracle, the answers are sitting in the palm of my hand.

June 27

My prediction of Sergio being a pawn in fate's game against me has turned out to be accurate. He's beyond annoying.

Preston flew into Oceanview today. I almost stroked out with excitement when he asked me to go to dinner tonight, but now all I can think about is the first (and last) time I went on a date and got left in the backseat of a car while the driver walked his girlfriend to the door of her house and never came back—well, he did, but not for a really long time. When my date inched his way over to my side and asked me what I wanted to do, nerves took over and I challenged him to a game of rock-paper-scissors. Word traveled fast in my small high school, and that was the last time I got asked to a dance. I guess none of the other guys wanted to sit in the backseat of a car and play rock-paper-scissors. And lose.

Anyway, I rushed home after work to get ready, and then dug through my closet to find the only purse I own. I hate purses. In my opinion, they are a useless accessory and somewhat of a nuisance, an area where my mother and I always strongly disagreed. I threw lip gloss, my wallet, keys, and cell phone into the purse, just as the door-bell rang fifteen minutes early.

I hurried to the door, but my excitement immediately evaporated when I was greeted by Sergio, the king of ickiness. I hate the way he takes a long drag from his cigarette, and then blows a stream of smoke out of the side of his mouth. And the boy has no manners. He dropped the butt on my front step and extinguished it with his scuffed-up combat boot. Did I mention that he reeked of cheap aftershave? And his lame attempt to look like the bad-boy version of Colin Farrell is a major fail. I'm not sure which is worse—his hair that looks like it hasn't been washed in days or the ripped jeans that don't quite fit—a little too short and too baggy where it counts. The only part he got right was the tight, black V-neck, but that only drew attention to the industrial-sized silver chain around his neck and the skull earring in his left ear. Without his uniform on, I could clearly see his tattoo. The large snake slithered through the eye socket and mouth of a skull that covered his bicep and wound down his arm past his wrist to the head that covered the back of his hand. The serpent's mouth was open, bearing oversized fangs, and the long, forked tongue stretched up the middle finger of his right hand. Disturbing.

He whistled to let me know he approved of my appearance and then said, "Don't you look delicious?" His black T-top Trans Am, a collector's model with a large, gold eagle spread across the hood, was parked across the street, and a small worry formed in the back of my mind. How did he know my address? He proceeded to claim I owed him dinner and he came to collect, then he licked his lips with a wicked gleam in his eye. I felt like small prey staring into the eyes of a vicious wild animal and thought about slamming the door in his face, but then I pictured him kicking the door in. I'm positive he could.

I told him I already had plans and tried to shut the door, but it stopped three inches from the frame because the toe of his boot kept it from closing. I re-opened the door carefully and was freaking out, but I didn't want him to know it. Apparently, he wasn't used to rejection because his expression darkened and irritation was evident in his voice when he accused my mother of not teaching me any manners because I'd closed the door on him. I told him my mother had taught me not to talk to strangers or let them in the house. I think I was brave because I was counting on Preston to show up any minute and save me.

Then Sergio actually peeked inside my house and his wandering eyes fixed on my couch before he said, "If you let me in, we could eliminate the whole stranger issue in a matter of minutes." Dis-gus-ting! I swallowed back the bile rising in my throat and told him I had to hurry and get ready because Preston would be there any minute to pick me up. His brows lifted in shock at the mention of Preston's name and his sly smile vanished. In fact, he glanced down the street, looking a little flustered and angry, and then said, "So you'll go out with him, but not with me?" in an accusing tone and then said, "What's wrong? I'm not the right kind of stranger for you?" My plan backfired and I had no other, except to lie. I never lie. I told him, "Preston isn't a stranger." Liar. Liar. "I know a lot about him." Pants on fire. "And he knows a lot about me." Okay. Not a total lie. Preston does have a calendar that contains a brief description about Miss April.

I let that info sink in, and then I told Sergio I should hurry and finish getting ready. He eyed me with suspicion before huffing through his nose, telling me he'd take a rain check before he finally slid his foot off the threshold. I smiled timidly before closing the door and forced myself to shut it at a normal speed so he wouldn't know he terrified me, but I was too scared to look through the peephole to see if he was gone. Why did I feel like he could see me through the door? I turned the lock and hurried to the bathroom where I locked that door for double precaution.

So here I am, sitting on the edge of the tub, writing this entry and waiting for my pulse to slow and for Preston to get here. Despite a visit from the king of creepiness, this is still the best day ever because I get to spend the next few hours in the company of Preston.

I can only imagine what he

That's how the entry ends—right in the middle of the sentence. It doesn't take a rocket scientist to deduct two things. First, she tossed the journal aside to run to the door and greet Mr. Sizzling Hotness himself, and second, all the details of the big date are probably surrounded by Xs and Os on the next page. I don't know why, but a shot of jealousy works its way into my gut and warns me never to turn the page.

Jealousy and anger are two emotions I haven't felt in a while. That Sergio creep makes me want to rearrange his face, starting with ripping out his eyes for the way I imagine he sees Ava—like she's some economy car he's going to take for a test drive before he buys it and runs it into the ground instead of a one-of-a-kind luxury sports car in mint condition that should be cherished and treated with the utmost respect. He doesn't even deserve to be in the showroom.

Curiosity overrules caution, and I turn the page.

June 28

Okay Mom, this entry is for you because if you were alive, I know you'd want every little detail about my amazing date last night. Preston showed up in Mr. Caruso's private limo and looked like a GQ model standing in my doorway with his sunglasses on, his tan chest showing through the unbuttoned V of his dress shirt, and one hand in the pocket of his designer jeans. You would have been impressed and Dad would have been worried because Preston doesn't really look like a rock-scissor-paper kind of guy.

On the way to the restaurant, he asked me if I always went to dinner with strangers. I almost laughed. I wanted to tell him 'only the ones that don't make me want to bathe in hand sanitizer,' but I chickened out and told him we weren't really strangers. He agreed but pointed out that he knew a lot more about me than I knew about him when he said, "So, Ava Starr, who just moved here from Colorado on her own, who likes to play volleyball and soccer in her free time, who just graduated from high school with honors, and who loves rainy days and a really good book... do you want to know my last name?" He quoted the caption below my calendar picture, almost word for word. I let out a nervous laugh and asked him his last name. "Preston King," he said, holding out his hand in a gesture of a friendly handshake as the limo rolled to a stop. I shook his hand, and then he motioned toward the door, smiling in a way that made me want to melt into the seat.

He requested a table on the far side of the Mexican restaurant, in a quiet corner away from the bar. A waitress appeared out of nowhere with water, chips, and salsa. I picked up the menu and started looking it over, but Preston studied me instead. It makes me so nervous when he does that. He crossed his arms, tilted his head to one side, and then asked how my parents felt about their young daughter living alone in the golden state. A knot formed in my stomach, and I reminded myself to keep it together. I was positive crying might be at the top of the list of what not to do on a first date and could turn it into a last date even faster than rock-paper-scissors. The seconds ticked by until I decided saying the words would be easier if I didn't look him in the eye, then I spilled the news the same way you rip off a Band-Aid—fast to minimize the pain. I glanced up to see his reaction and wondered if I should ask for a to-go box, but then his playful smile returned and he leaned across the table to say, "Well, the good news for me then, is you don't have a curfew."

I was thankful he changed the subject and brought up the calendar. He told me he liked it better than the one last year, so I asked which month was his favorite, expecting him to choose one of the summer month beauties with their tan bodies sprawled across the aircraft, but he said "I'll give you a clue...it'll be April all year 'round in the cockpit of Hotel Charlie." I felt my face flush but recovered quickly and asked him if there was a misprinted calendar. "Not at all," he said. "I just like girls that are a little more natural—if you know what I mean." Then he winked and took a sip of his water. He must have been implying that there are body parts of my coworkers that aren't the originals they were born with. I hadn't noticed. I definitely needed to be more observant.

We talked about our favorite things during dinner. I told him I loved to write and draw, and there's nothing better than reading a good book. At least, I used to think so. Our date blew that theory right out of the water. Aside from PE, his favorite subject in school was speech and debate. He said he loved the competition, but there's a confidence about him that makes me think he was better than the average student. I imagine him rendering all the girls in debate class completely speechless—most likely even forgetting the topic—overwhelmed by his very presence. I'm also sure he was the guy in P.E that all the girls wanted desperately to have on their team, but the one the guys didn't want for fear he'd make them look bad.

I don't think he knows how heavenly he is. Every woman in the restaurant must have been dying to be in my shoes, including our waitress, who showed up with warm sopapillas and a tub of honey, gawking at Preston as he fed me the last bite of a taquito.

We were about to eat dessert when he pulled his phone from his pocket to glance at the screen. He apologized, explained that it was his boss, then he excused himself and headed for the bathroom.

My napkin slipped from my lap to the floor, so I bent down to retrieve it. When I sat up, Sergio was sitting in Preston's chair. He reached across the table to take a taquito from the platter, and I couldn't contain the horrified expression I knew was plastered to my face. I tried not to panic and asked him if he followed me there.

A sly smile crept over his thin lips, and I watched in shock as he helped himself to some chips and salsa. "Follow. Such a moot word," he said, and then told me he just happened to be driving in the same direction and decided the restaurant looked like a great place to stop and eat. Yeah, right. "The food and women are both mouthwatering," he said. Licking his lower lip, he then lowered his voice. "Well, not all the women, just one in particular." He winked.

I swallowed and looked around in horror, but no one besides me seemed to notice how repulsive he was. I asked him what he wanted and he laughed, delivering a healthy dose of mockery and condescension at the same time, and then his smile vanished before he said, "I wanted to have dinner, and you turned me down. But yet, here we are, having dinner together. See how that works? I always get what I want. Next time, maybe you'll accept my offer."

His dark eyes narrowed to emphasize his warning and I froze, entranced by his menacing stare, but then his sudden movement caused me to flinch. He leaned across the table to take my water glass and held it up. Spinning it around to find the pink print left by my lips, he licked it off before taking a swig of water. "Mmmmm. Cherry lip gloss. My favorite," he said, obviously relishing the fact he was causing me to squirm uncomfortably in my chair.

His boldness made it clear he'd had too much to drink, and he stunk of smoke and beer, mixed with his overpowering cheap aftershave. The smell made me nauseous. I glared and told him to leave before Preston came back and caught him bothering me, but he didn't act like he cared. He held a shrimp up to my mouth that he'd drenched in hot sauce, but I leaned away. "So you let Preston feed you but not me?

he asked accusingly, and I'm still creeped out because I have no idea how long he'd been watching us. I refused to comment, so he popped the shrimp in his mouth without losing eye contact and then licked his fingers, one at a time, with a soft smacking sound.

I stopped myself from gagging and held my breath as he leaned over the table to flash me a wicked grin. He told me to enjoy the rest of my evening with 'pilot boy,' but that he'd take pleasure in knowing he'd haunt my thoughts and maybe my dreams. "You'll definitely be starring in mine," he said, laughing in spite of himself. He glanced over his shoulder before getting up to leave and when he walked away, he dragged his serpent-tongue fingers up my arm, which caused me to cringe. Ugghh!

Preston came back a minute later and apologized again for leaving me. I shoved Sergio to the back of my mind but not before Preston noticed my distress and asked what was wrong. I just told him someone I didn't really like stopped by to say 'hi' and Preston said "Oh, no. What are the chances of that?" After I told him they were better than most because I'm a magnet for bad luck, he said, "Come on, how bad can it be? Give me some examples."

An endless list from my childhood flashed through my head, but then Preston drizzled his sopapilla with honey before taking a bite, and then licked the powdered sugar from his lips—lips I imagined myself kissing. Whoops! Sorry, Dad. Then I noticed he was staring at me—waiting for me to talk—and then I remembered he'd asked me a question so I snapped out of my daydream of kissing his sugared lips and filled him in on the history of my unlucky past.

Of course, I left out the obvious—that I've been orphaned at eighteen and am now being stalked by a psychotic coworker—because I didn't want to ruin the date. Instead, I told him about all the times the three of us went out to eat—how I'd be the one to find a fly in my hash browns or a hair in my soup. And remember when I broke my arm from tripping over that dog that ran into me at the park? I told him that, too, and how I sported a black eye in my ninth grade school picture from that softball that hit me as I ran to third base in PE. Then I told him the only pet I ever owned was Mr. Bubbles, the fish I spent hours picking out at the pet store—only to have it die on the way home. He laughed really hard and told me he considered it a miracle that he and Kirk arrived at the hotel in one piece with me behind the wheel, and he might be right!

The limo sat waiting out front when we left the restaurant, and Preston slid in beside me rather than across from me like before. The uncomfortable situation with Sergio in the restaurant left me too upset to be nervous about Preston's close proximity and his arm that draped over the seat behind me. He smelled so good. The combination of his cologne and freshly laundered shirt was incredible and the warmth of him beside me made me realize how lonely I'd been. I haven't sat that close to anyone since the plane ride to California. I was in heaven.

He told me his schedule was full the next couple of days but asked if we could hang out when he comes back next week. Of course, I said yes. He grabbed a loose curl resting by my neck, gently pulled it straight, then let go and watched it spring back into place. "So am I forgiven for my obnoxious behavior?" he asked, but the big smile on his face reflected his enjoyment of the memory. He examined my hair and then my face. I felt feverish. He is breathtakingly handsome, even when he's gloating. I told him I would if he promised not to do it again, but he said he wouldn't make promises he couldn't keep, adding that he'd just have to try harder next time to make me forgive him. (sigh)

The limo pulled up to my house, and the car door opened. I thanked the driver and then thanked Preston for dinner as he walked me to the door. He stepped ahead of me and stood in front of my door with his hands in his pockets as he leaned against the frame. I was searching for my keys. See, Mom. Another reason I hate purses. He asked if I wanted him to call and let me know when he was coming back in town, but I told him I wanted to be surprised. If I knew when, I'd spend all my time counting down the days, minutes, and seconds. Time seems to go torturously slow that way.

He placed his fingers under my chin and lifted it to look into my eyes. I waited for him to kiss me, but my heart dropped with his hand that he casually slid into his pocket. "Okay. Miss April. I'll see you soon," he said with a wink before brushing past me to stroll back to the limo. I'm sure you are both relieved to hear this and are somewhere in heaven elevating him to perfect gentleman status. As for me, even with the absence of a goodnight kiss and the unexpected appearance of Sergio, the date was incredible. Well, that's it for now, except that I must admit that for the entire next week, my every waking moment will be spent obsessing over my next encounter with Preston King.

I want nothing more than to turn the page and find out if when Preston came back, he hunted Sergio down to have a one-sided conversation using his fist, but I mark the page and tuck the book back into the safety of my pocket. Taking one more look at Ava, I close my eyes to drift off to sleep.

Ava

DAY TWO: THE PREDICAMENT

THE SMELL OF EGGS WAKES ME UP. THE ISLAND, THE cannibals, and the stranger named Dax, must have all been a dream—and now everything is as it should be. Preston must be preparing to bring me breakfast in bed. I smile before opening my eyes but my visionary bubble explodes, leaving me to see only the reality I'd hoped would vanish last night with the setting sun.

Dax sits by the fire, carefully scraping two eggs from a smooth stone that sits in the middle of glowing coals. He places the eggs on a palm leaf using a spatula-type tool made from what appears to be the bark of a tree. He looks over and sees me watching.

"Oh, good. You're awake. I made you some eggs," he says in a most cheerful voice, placing them in front of me before splitting two more eggs onto the rock. "Some mother bird isn't going to be very happy when she comes back and finds an empty nest, but I'm starving and you need some strength if we're going to venture outside today."

I sit up, and then I gingerly touch my forehead. The pain has improved from yesterday, and I wish I could say the same for my mood.

"Thanks," I say and then force a grin. "So you're a baby bird killer and a cannibal. I'm not sure you're the best company to keep."

He smiles but keeps his attention on the eggs. "Who says I'm a cannibal?"

"Well, are you?" I ask, studying his reaction.

He turns his head to look at me, his blue eyes vibrant even in the dim light of the cave. "That depends. What's your definition of a cannibal?"

I stop chewing and stare at him in disbelief. "Either you *are* or you *aren't*. The answer should be obvious. Have you ever—?"

"So if you pluck one grape and eat it in the grocery store, does that make you a thief—branding you for life?" he says, waiting for me to contemplate the comparison.

"I guess not, but—"

"Okay, so I don't consider myself a cannibal." He throws me a short smile before peeling the eggs from the rock with the spatula and dropping them onto the palm leaf in front of him. I watch him blow on them to cool them off, and then he starts to eat them with his fingers.

"So you have?" I ask, soft but with an accusing tone because I sense he really doesn't want to talk about it. My curiosity got the better of me.

He sighs. "I had to. When the Anwai allowed us to stay and live among them, they wanted to make sure they could trust us. So a few months after we arrived, they killed a member of the tribe they believed was a Khakhua and had a big feast. My dad, Roxy, and I all tried it because my dad said our survival depended on it. I haven't had to since."

I stare at him dumfounded. "What does it—?"

"It tastes like pork," he says with a hint of impatience, making it clear this isn't something he plans to discuss in depth. "Oh, I have something for you." He reaches in his pocket, and then extends his arm to hand me Preston's name tag.

I inhale sharply and practically snatch it from his fingers. "Where did you get this?" I say, and my voice is barely above a whisper.

"I found it on the beach this morning during low tide."

"So that's good, right?" I say frantically, and watch Dax's brow crease with concern—or confusion, but I'm too excited to care which one. "I mean, this means he's here on the island somewhere."

Dax stares at me for a second too long before he looks away and focuses on the fire. He shifts uneasily and runs his fingers through his hair before speaking.

"Ava, I don't think—" He stops and glances at me before continuing. "I guess it's possible."

I sense his reluctance in telling me what he really thinks. My irritation drowns out the voice in my head telling me to let it go. "But..?"

He clears his throat. "But I think it's more likely that it just washed up on the beach. I walked all around where I found it and didn't find anything else. No footprints. Nothing. And if he was here, don't you think he'd stay on the beach and look for you?"

I nod my head and blink back tears.

"Maybe he's hurt, or searching the entire island." I pause, knowing I sound absurd, but I refuse to give up and I'm determined to stick to my original plan. "So when we leave here, can we go look some more?"

"I told you—I already looked," he says gently. "Besides, wandering around isn't a good idea. There are boundaries, and yesterday, you crossed into Lambai territory when you *ran away*." His enunciation of the last two words suggests he is still irritated with me for doing it. "Besides, I still have to introduce you to Roxy and the Anwai tribe. But I want to take you somewhere else first until I'm confident my plan will work. And we need to leave here soon, before some of the men from the tribe come to the beach to check their nets."

"If you won't go with me, I'll look for him myself."

He laughs. "I thought I made it clear before. It's not a smart idea to wander off alone."

I cross my arms and stare him down, letting him know my intentions are serious. He appears to be assessing my stubbornness, and now a sly smile crosses his face.

"Okay. Fine." He stands up and throws his palm leaf in the fire. "We'll go look *after* I take you to my special place and *after* I convince Chief Anwai to let you live."

"No. We look first," I demand.

He smiles and shakes his head, then saunters over to sit on the ground in front of me. He holds up one hand, palm side up, then curls his other hand into a fist on top of his palm.

"Let's go. Rock, paper, scissors. Best two out of three wins," he says with a playful smile. "If you win, we go look first. If I win, we look later. Deal?"

I can't believe my ears and boast a real smile for the first time in days. I might be out of my league on this island with him, but he is definitely out of his league when it comes to challenging me at this game. I'm a master.

"Deal," I say and rest my fist in the palm of my other hand. "One, two, three."

My paper covers his rock.

"One, two, three," he says, and then lets out a quiet victory cheer when his scissors cut my paper. "Last chance," he warns, followed by a wink.

"One, two, three," we say in unison. He sighs and falls backwards in defeat, but I'm filled with pure satisfaction. My rock crushed his scissors.

"You win," he says. "Let's go."

I follow him out of the cave, but my contentment is replaced with sadness as we pass the surfboards with Preston's briefcase leaning against the wall. Next to them sits the life-raft case and an acoustic guitar. I rush outside to avoid looking at them but have to pause against a rock to wait for my eyes to adjust to the blinding sun.

"Now there's one condition," he warns. "You can't go yelling his name. We only look and we have to hurry. This is risky enough as it is. We'll walk along the beach to the borders of Lambai territory but if you yell his name, you will definitely attract some unwanted attention and... well, I didn't bring enough arrows. Let's just leave it at that."

I notice the bow and quiver slung over his shoulder and sculpted chest, and then I acknowledge his warning by nodding my head. I follow his every step as he climbs over some large rocks, jumping down off the last one onto the beach of white sand. We make our way to the water and I stay a few feet behind him, irritated that he doesn't seem to be looking, only walking in a path for me to follow. I turn my head from side to side as I walk, searching the water and the rocks on the opposite side, looking for any sign of Preston, Kirk, and Anna.

After a while, we reach the boundary line between the two tribes and walk back the way we came, passing the cave and continuing on until the beach runs into a high cliff. We've searched for what has to be over an hour when he stops walking and turns to look at me.

"Satisfied?" he asks, setting his foot on a rock and resting a forearm on his knee.

My heart sinks as the hope of finding Preston dwindles into a slim possibility. I fall to my knees and Dax comes over to kneel in front of me, dropping the bow and quiver and wrapping his arms around me, but I try to push him away. He holds on tight. I'm too weak to break away. A strange wailing sound escapes my throat and turns into a sob that echoes the hollowness I feel inside.

"I'm so sorry," he says, and his voice becomes soothing. "I know it's hard to accept. We can look again later if you want." He pauses. "But the truth is, if he did make it to the beach alive, there's really no place to go unless..."

He doesn't finish the sentence, but it's clear what he means. If Preston wandered into the tropical forest alone, into Lambai territory, his chance of survival isn't good. I stop crying and take some deep breaths, so he releases me and wipes away my tears before he rests his hands on either side of my shoulders. I look up to meet his worried face and muster a faint smile, more for his benefit than mine.

"Can I show you something now?" he asks. "I think it might cheer you up."

"Okay," I say, almost in a whisper, desperate to let him take my mind off Preston and escape what has become an unbearable reality.

He helps me up and says, "Follow me and stay close".

We walk back in the direction of the cave but after a few yards along the beach, we head into the forest bordering the beach. He holds some large palm leaves up for me to walk under and starts making his way through the dense trees and bushes. I can't tell if he follows a path, but he seems to know exactly where he's going. The forest is so thick and shaded that I don't dare let him out of my sight for fear I'll lose him in the sea of green.

Without any warning, he crouches down and grabs my arm to pull me down with him. "Lay down," he orders, and I obey, dropping to my stomach on the forest floor. He pulls out a knife and cuts three large palm leaves from a tree and carefully places them over me.

"Don't move," he hisses, stepping a few feet to my right. I can barely hear the men's voices over the loud pounding of my pulse. Dax calls out to them in a strange language and walks away from where I lay silent and frightened. They exchange a few words and then it's quiet. Too quiet. Where is Dax? How long should I stay here?

An insect makes its way up my leg in a slow, steady

path, and my imagination spins out of control. I picture the most horrifying spider my mind can conjure up—a centipede-type creature with millions of tiny legs and sharp fangs searching for the perfect spot to puncture my skin and inflict its poison or drink my blood. I stifle the scream wanting to burst out of my chest and fight every muscle in my body that wants to react to the overwhelming urge to swat it off. I want to jump up from this damp bed of decomposing leaves and dead flowers that house a swarm of other insects and creepy, crawly things, but I hold my breath, and now my heart races out of control at the sound of footsteps approaching. A leaf is lifted off my face, and Dax greets me with a smile before offering his hand to help me up. I brush the dirt, leaves, and insects from my arms and legs, but I can't brush away the jitters that I know will stay with me for the remainder of the day.

"Sorry about that. Are you okay?" He reaches up to brush the hair off my face and wipe off the dirt clinging to my cheek from the forest floor. "There were a couple of men from the Anwai tribe on their way to the beach to check nets. I told them I was hunting and steered them in another direction. You can relax; they won't come back this way for quite a while."

His words were obviously meant to comfort me, but they had the opposite effect.

"So how many of them are wandering around in the forest? How do you know there won't be more?"

"The tribe isn't that big, and they stay close to their village for the most part. They don't want to be discovered, remember? So they use the trees as cover. That's why I like hanging out at the beach. Only a couple of the men go to the beach every day to check their nets. And I'm familiar with where they go to hunt, so I hunt in different areas. I've had three years to get good at avoiding them."

He keeps talking, sharing all his insider info on his

carefully planned daily routines, but I'm not really listening. I'm too busy wondering if Preston could be walking around in the forest just like us, looking for me and managing to avoid a few wandering cannibals. Preston is smart, and unlike me, he seems to always have luck on his side. Dax made a weak effort to find Preston, like he's already given up on the idea that he could be alive. But I can't. Preston wouldn't give up on me. I have to ditch Dax and look some more, and this is my chance. I slow my pace, widening the gap between us, and my heart starts to beat in a nervous rhythm. I wait for him to peek back at me one more time before I start walking in place just in case he's listening. After a few seconds, I crouch down and wait.

He's still rambling on. "So when I get a large kill, I share it with the tribe to remind them how useful I am, but also to limit how often they have to go out wandering around because the truth is, most days, I like to pretend I'm living on the island by myself." He laughs. "That's funny because sometimes I daydream and wish it was just me and a really hot brunette... you know, spending the day doing fantastically fun things to pass the time." He laughs again. "Hey, you could audition for the role... and don't worry... your chances are pretty good since there's like... no other competition..."

His voice fades away and I sprint into the forest, dodging trees and bushes to make as little noise as possible. After a couple of minutes, I slow to a fast walk, searching the jungle of green for Preston, Kirk, and Anna. I know it won't take Dax long to discover I'm gone and I slow even more, hoping to hear him when he comes after me. There's a small break in the density of the trees, and I take the opportunity to stop and look behind me. I listen for footsteps, or my name, but all I hear are the call of birds and strange noises of unimaginable creepy, crawly things in the overgrowth around me. I take a couple of steps backwards and almost lose my balance when my foot sinks, so I turn around and take another step into soft, wet sand.

I hear a sound to my right and leap forward to run into the trees, but my legs are now knee deep in a muddy, sand mixture. Stifling a moan, I take another step, but it's as though the ground fell out from under me. I sink in up to my waist. Panic rising, I freeze and listen for any more sounds, but now it's unusually quiet. If I can just make it across this mud pit, I can continue looking for Preston, but when I try to move forward, I sink deeper into the abyss of sand.

Quicksand! The horrifying thought comes too late, and my panic spikes into sheer terror. I'm stuck, and the more I squirm to free myself, the worse it gets. There's a vine, but it's just out of reach. I lean toward it and stretch with all my might, but I only manage to worm my way deeper into the mud. It's almost to my armpits.

Crap! Crap! Crap! What was I thinking? I should have known an escape would end badly.

"Dax! Preston?" I whisper-yell, but then I worry I'll attract unwanted, cannibal-type company. I'm either going to starve to death or be eaten alive unless Dax or Preston find me first. I tip my head back and look up at the umbrella of trees that stand like giant, green ogres staring down at me, laughing at my foolish stupidity that will ultimately be my impending doom.

Dax

DAY TWO: THE PREDICAMENT

I WOKE UP IN A GREAT MOOD THIS MORNING AFTER reading about Ava's date with Preston that fell short in the romance department. And even her little disappearing act has added an element of humor to my day. I turned my head just in time to see her running off into the trees, so I snuck around to head her off.

She was easy to find—I heard her struggling in the quicksand before I actually saw her, and now I've made sure she can't see me while I wait to guarantee the success of my plan. And what better way to spend the time than read some more of her journal without the fear of getting caught? Everyone on the island is aware of this quicksand trap and avoids the area like the plague, which means as long as she doesn't scream, she's fairly safe from discovery. At least long enough for me to have some fun.

July 5

The strangest thing happened on Monday. After work, I checked my mailbox before going inside the house and discovered a curious envelope mixed in with the rest of my mail. I studied the typed return address, which matched the delivery address—and they were both mine. I opened the envelope and pulled out a folded piece of white paper with these typed words in the middle of the page.

HE KNOWS YOUR SECRET
BE CAREFUL

I stared at the note in my hand, trying to get over the initial shock, and panic tugged at my insides until I realize it was probably one of Preston's tricks. I fell for his last two pranks easily but this time, I won't be so gullible. Next time I see him, I plan on congratulating him on his efforts, which should be soon because last Saturday he promised we'd do something again this weekend.

Every time I think about him, butterflies fill my stomach. I waited all day to hear his voice on the radio and was so disappointed by the end of my shift that I dreaded going home, knowing I'd spend another evening alone. That's why I gladly accepted when my supervisor asked if I wanted to stay and wait for a late arrival, but I cringed when Sergio also agreed to stay. The plane was a quick turn, and Sergio left as soon as they were finished fueling the plane. The last line guy waited for me to finish at the front desk, and then we exited the building. He locked the door and said goodnight as he headed for his car.

My keys were playing hide and seek in the bottom of my purse and when I finally found them, I looked up to see Sergio leaning against the trunk of his Trans Am with his legs crossed casually at the ankles and both hands in the pockets of his pants. His car was parked conveniently next to mine and while he'd been waiting for me, he'd removed his work shirt to expose a white tank. The large chain around his neck glistened in the bright glare of the overhead street light. "W'sup, Ava," he said, through lips that held his cigarette.

I tried to sound calm when I said, "Not much," but my heart pounded against my ribs as the other line guy pulled out of the parking lot. I hurried to get in my car, and he remained standing against his to finish his cigarette. Putting the key in the ignition, I gave it a turn. Nothing happened. I felt a wave of panic and then the heat rising in my cheeks, cursing my bad luck. It was foolish to leave the top down because I was so exposed—eliminating any hope of him leaving and not noticing my predicament. I could feel him staring at me. Pleeeease start, I begged the car and turned the key again. Nothing. I know, un-freaking-believable.

I saw him in my rearview mirror. He extinguished his cigarette and walked around the car to lean down and rest his arms on my door. "Bummer," he said, but his voice lacked sincerity. Then he said, "Looks like you need a ride," and jerked his head in the direction of his car with the utmost of cockiness. I told him I'd call a taxi and pulled my phone from my purse to look up the number, but he snatched the phone from my hand and made it clear he'd offered to drive me home for free. I had my doubts about him not expecting some sort of payment in return, so I folded my arms firmly across my chest and watched him taunt me by twirling my phone between his serpent fingers. I asked for the phone back. He flashed a short smile that immediately disappeared, and then said, "Sure, after you get in my car."

My mother's familiar 'be safe' warning echoed in my head and walking home at night or hitchhiking definitely wouldn't fall under her definition of safe—especially without a phone. Getting in a car with Sergio wasn't much better, but I hadn't forgotten what happened last time I rejected his offer, so I ignored my conscience and spastic heartbeat telling me it was a bad idea. I stormed to his car and got in while he casually walked around to the driver's side. He started the muscle car, backed out of the parking spot, and then his eyes slid down the length of my legs.

Instinct and regret kicked in. I reached for the handle to get out but he stepped on the gas, squealing the tires and forcing my head back in the seat. It was too late to change my mind. He drove like he had a death wish. My seat belt was on, but I refrained from grabbing onto the dash or the door because I didn't want to give him the satisfaction of knowing I was worried. I stared at the serpent on top of his hand as he shifted gears and saw him glancing at me as he darted through traffic, but I avoided his gaze. "If you're waiting for me to apologize for last Friday, it ain't gonna happen, baby," he said while waiting at a red light. In a not-so-nice tone, I assured him I wasn't his baby.

A hint of impatience flickered across his face before he regained control, brushing my comment off with a "whatever" and then said I owed him an apology for going to dinner with Preston instead of him because he'd asked first. There were still two more traffic lights to go, but in my best brave voice I told him I didn't recall him asking. He contemplated my words, and then his expression softened into a cheesy politician grin, full of arrogance. He actually agreed and admitted asking wasn't really his style because he'd never had to work so hard to get a girl to go out with him, laughing as if he could hardly fathom the idea. "I know you're fascinated with Preston because he's like a shiny, new toy," he said, "but the shine will wear off, and then you'll realize your mistake."

Despite my irritation and refusal to look at him, he offered to fix my car and bring it to my house tomorrow after his shift. "Then you'll owe me dinner," he said, but I turned my head away from him and contemplated ways to make myself sick. Are heebie-jeebies a legitimate illness?

I hurried out of the car when he pulled up to my curb; amazed he actually brought me to my house and not a dark alley somewhere.

I thanked him for the ride and forced myself to walk at a normal pace to my front door because I felt his eyes on me the entire way. I sighed with relief when he peeled away like a big show off. Now I'm hoping my nerves will settle enough to let me succumb to sleep, but more than that, I'm hoping Preston will show up tomorrow before the end of Sergio's shift.

July 6

There was another blank envelope mixed in with my mail today, and the note inside said...

YOU'RE BEING WATCHED

The paper had a faint, musty smoke smell that immediately made me think of Sergio and wonder if this might be some evil plot of his—to scare me so he can pretend to rescue me from danger that doesn't really exist. But then I decided he doesn't seem capable of pulling off such an elaborate scheme. There's a certain pilot though who is definitely capable and who also seems to be motivated by my naïve nature, so I've decided to see how far he will actually take it.

And speaking of the devil (an extremely handsome one), Preston showed up unannounced at my house this afternoon and said he was worried when he saw my car at Oceanview and I wasn't there. I told him it wouldn't start last night, so Sergio drove me home and offered to fix my car sometime today. I didn't miss the quick rise of Preston's brow at the mention of Sergio's name, and he insisted we drive straight to Oceanview so he could look at it himself. After looking under the hood briefly, he found one of the battery cables had come loose. Go figure. My car started right up and I drove it home, trying not to dwell on the disturbing fact that Sergio must have tampered with it on purpose so he could 'fix' it and pretend to be some kind of hero. Ugh!

We dropped my car off and then went to a quaint Italian restaurant where it seemed like we spent the entire time talking about me. He asked a bunch of questions about my parents, their occupations, and my friends and every time I tried to find out anything about him, he somehow managed to turn the conversation back to me.

After dinner, he drove to the beach and parked the car on the street in front of some posh-looking houses. He made me think he was breaking into one and waited until I was completely and totally freaked out before he told me it was Mr. Caruso's. Ha. Ha. Ha. It's a good thing he's so heart-stoppingly handsome, which makes it impossible not to forgive him.

So I'm happy to report that we aren't going to jail and Preston isn't a criminal—at least not in the literal sense of the word. There should be a law against taking advantage of gullible people.

We shared a circle-shaped lounge chair for two and ate strawberries in front of a spectacular sunset. We lay there for a long time, enjoying the backdrop of the sky and ocean, intertwined in a perfect combination, until the sun disappeared completely behind the horizon and was replaced by the night sky. Away from the glow of the city lights, a few stars sprinkled the darkness above the ocean.

The conversation turned to his trick earlier, and he bragged that it was so good he wished he'd gotten it on film. I told him he may have succeeded in royally freaking me out that time, but at least I didn't fall for his little mystery notes. It was a lame attempt to redeem myself.

He rolled towards me and propped his head in his hand. His eyebrows furled slightly but even in the dark, his smile remained dazzling. "What notes?" he said. Does he seriously think I'm that gullible? Whatever. He even sounded convincing when he told me he didn't know what I was talking about, but I will not be fooled. Apparently he's still trying to salvage the stupid prank. Weird.

But the evening got even weirder when he drove me home and walked me to my door. I stepped inside, and then he stepped closer until we were sharing the same air. When his eyes dropped to my lips, my heart literally—stopped—beating. His head tipped and he froze, lips hovering over mine, and I closed my eyes, breathing in his unbelievable scent—waiting, exploding with anticipation, but he left only a whisper of a kiss on my lips and then he was gone. Not all of him, just his lips, the only part that mattered at the moment.

He was about to kiss me—I'm sure of it, but something made him change his mind. He held my hand on the beach... told me he thinks I'm beautiful while watching the sunset... and last weekend, he even mentioned whisking me away with him on his new sailboat. I didn't imagine those things, so the sudden change is a mystery to me. Maybe that's why I made a complete fool of myself when he started to step away.

He was staring at a spot on the door behind me when he tried to distance himself, so I clung to his T-shirt and held him there. With my heart feeling like it would explode from my chest, I wrapped my arms around his neck and pulled him close for a hug, but I felt him stiffen in my arms.

"What's wrong?" I whispered into his shirt so quietly I wasn't sure if he heard me—then for a second, I hoped he hadn't. I sounded desperate—clingy, like a hormone-crazed teenager. His quiet laugh fueled my worries, and I wanted to die of embarrassment, but then he relaxed and his hands slid around my waist to return my hug. "Not a single thing," he said, and then his laughter was lost in the quiet night air around us. The seconds ticked by, and neither of us spoke. A police siren in the distance faded away into nothing, and then a car passed by on my street, turning the corner and leaving us again with the silence. He seemed torn between wanting to be with me, and wanting to keep a certain distance. His lips were right there, so close but so far away. Any normal guy would make a move, right? At least, that's the way it happens in the movies and in EVERY romance book I've ever read.

He released his grip around my waist to run his finger along the curve of my jaw. I was staring into his green eyes as he studied mine, and then my gaze dropped to his lips in anticipation. His smile weakened, and he suddenly took a step back to put some distance between us. My hands that were resting on his chest fell awkwardly to my sides, and I felt a twinge of rejection mixed with embarrassment.

The words, "Why won't you kiss me?" slipped out of my mouth before I could stop them, and I focused on his chest while I waited in misery for him to say something. Anything. After a few agonizing seconds, he told me he's wanted to kiss me since he stepped off Hotel Charlie and saw me for the first time, but then he paused before he said, "I just don't think... I should." All I could do was stare—blink—breathe—blush. I'm still horrified and wonder if I misjudged his feelings and he thinks of me more like the younger sister he never had. Or worse. Maybe he already has a girlfriend in another town and his conscience is getting the better of him. Whatever the reason, he didn't want to tell me because his arms slid away and he started towards his car. He turned back to tell me he'd see me Friday and gave me a warm smile to cushion the blow. "Okay," was all I could say, and then I stood there stunned before I shut the door. I went to the window to watch him drive away and then my seven-day countdown began.

Ava seems bothered by the fact that their relationship started out abnormally slow in the romance department, but I couldn't be happier. I can tell she's new to the whole dating routine thanks to the fact she was homeschooled until her freshman year and a little shy. But she must have heard girls around her talk about their dates and weekend flings to give her a pretty good idea of how things usually work, which was quite opposite of their relationship. And considering Preston's age and supposed eye-popping good looks, I'm confident he's no beginner when it comes to romance. Either Preston is the most-chaste twenty-three-year-old guy on the planet or he's hiding something, and I'd bet on the latter.

I'm dying to read more and find out if I'm right, but Ava is stuck up to her chest and on the verge of crying. With a satisfied grin, I drop the book in my pocket and step out from behind the tree.

"Well, well, well. What a predicament. Gives new meaning to the phrase 'sticky situation' doesn't it?" My voice startles her and causes a sharp intake of breath as she opens her eyes.

"Dax," she says with a relieved exhale.

"Hey princess." I give her my best Cheshire smile. "Looks like your little escape plan didn't work out so well, huh? Well, I hope you have better luck escaping from that pit of quicksand."

I turn to walk away.

"Wait! Where are you going?" she asks, and desperation oozes from her voice.

I pause to get control of the amusement cracking away at my serious expression before turning around. "I don't know. I think I'll head back to the beach and wait for a hot blonde to wash up on shore." Her mouth falls open right on cue. "Oh, and sorry to break it to ya', but you didn't get the part. Since it's my fantasy, I was looking for someone friendlier, a little more trusting, a little less sassy, and what was the last thing? Oh, yeah. Someone who actually likes me. But don't feel bad—you nailed the physical profile," I say with a wink.

"Stop being a jerk and help me," she says, and then

softens her tone. "Please?"

I uncross my arms and rest my hands on my hips. I'm pretty sure she already regrets that last comment, but I can't stop now. "Look, princess. I'm a lot of things, but a jerk isn't one of them. And don't worry; I'm sure someone else will find you soon. A hungry cannibal—or Roxy. And I'm starting to think you and her might make a good team. The pity-party duo. She's hateful, complains constantly, and she's also a member of the 'I hate Dax club', just like you."

I turn my back on her again and take a step.

"Wait! I *don't* hate you. Please don't leave me. I'm sorry."

I'm a sucker for apologies but when I turn to face her, I can't resist putting one hand behind my ear and tilting my head.

"I'm really sorry," she says again. "For running away and being so grumpy." I wait for more, and she grits her teeth. "And for not listening to you."

This is the part where I know she expects me to jump to her rescue, but I lean against a tree with a cocky grin and pull a banana from my pocket. She stares while I peel it, take a bite, and chew slowly. I'm savoring the fruit but also my triumph in having the upper hand.

"Aren't you going to help me?" she finally asks with a hint of worry.

"I'm still debating. If I leave you here, at least I'll know where you are and won't have to worry about you running off. I could even build a little hut around you and toss you food and water now and then. You'd be a lot less trouble that way."

"Very funny," she says, but I think it is and I can't keep from laughing.

I pop the last bite of banana into my mouth. Tossing the peel over my shoulder, I set the bow and quiver on the ground beside me. After strategically placing some palm leaves at the edge of the quicksand, I lie on my stomach and extend an arm so she can take my hand.

"Okay, now instead of trying to walk out, you have to get horizontal and sort of swim across the surface," I tell her.

"I can't move my legs," she says, but I know she can. I don't want to tell her I've been stuck here before and had to get out on my own. I know it feels like cement that's started to set up, and I hope she has enough strength to put forth the effort required to get out.

"Yes, you can," I tell her. "Don't make me come in there because I will grope around for your legs and pull them out myself. Grope being the key word."

"That won't be necessary," she assures me with a roll of her eyes.

I have her concentrate on one leg at a time and after a few minutes of struggling, she manages to work her legs close to the surface. I pull until she makes it to the edge and then I help her stand, but when she tries to drop my hand, I don't let go.

"Uh-uh. No more running off to look for Preston. We can look as we go. And if it makes you feel better, I can snoop around the tribe later and see if anyone's talking about an upcoming feast, but for now, I need to get you somewhere safe. This way," I say. "We've wasted a lot of time."

I tug impatiently on her arm and cut swiftly through the lush green plants surrounding us. She's not talking because I told her not to, but I wish I knew what was going through her head. She seems to be a magnet for trouble—unaware of how best to stay safe and instead gravitates toward danger like people in scary movies who always go wandering in the dark instead of staying put.

This island is full of dangers she can't even imagine, and yet she still doesn't realize she needs my protection.

Her taking off could have ended badly just like her attempt to escape yesterday. Escape. That's something people do to get away from harm, and all I want to do is help her. If the quicksand scare wasn't enough to convince her to want to stay with me, this next plan should do the trick. That is, if she remembers.

One of the many things I've learned so far from reading her journal is that she likes to be surprised, and mine will be the whopper of all surprises. Even Preston had picked up on that little tidbit of info and showed up in a convertible red Ferrari Spider at eight in the morning the weekend after their first date to surprise her. The last journal entry I read this morning before she woke up included all the boring details of that day, enough to make me cringe at the extreme effort he went through to impress her and sweep her off her feet. I mean, the guy obviously had an overabundance of appeal and the money to match, but apparently, he didn't think that was enough because he couldn't resist buying a freaking sixty-foot sailboat so when he wanted to whisk her away in the future, he wouldn't have to use his boss' multi-million dollar plane.

Must be nice having a dilemma like that. The startling info was almost depressing until I read Ava's account of the night ending without so much as a hug. Preston talks like a professional Casanova, but then he fails miserably at following through. But hey, I'm not complaining, I just think it's weird. What guy could resist a goodnight kiss from a willing participant like her?

I stop at the wall of moss-covered rock in front of us that spreads out in both directions as far as I can see. Helping Ava climb to the top, I lift the lush greenery to pull her through the opening, and she gasps at the unexpected sight. We are looking at an island within an island. I'd never seen anything like it until I discovered this spot over a year ago. Below us is a nature-made pool of water and in the very center, a huge rock formation juts up towards the sky, resting on its own private beach. The sound of falling water can be heard in the distance.

"This is so cool," she says. "Is there a waterfall?"

I nod. "It's on the other side. Come on, I'll show you."

We make our way down the pile of rocks that surrounds this magical place like a protective wall, hiding it completely from view. We reach the bottom, and I wait for her to marvel at the massive formation across the water. I pull my canoe out of its hiding place in the thick foliage and drag the boat across the sand to the water, holding out my hand to help her climb in. Then I surprise her again by pulling a quarter from my pocket.

"Heads or tails?" I say, and she looks at me with a suspicious glare.

"What are we flipping for?"

"Whoever loses the coin toss has to row. Call it while it's in the air. Ready?"

I flip the coin.

"Heads," she says.

I catch the quarter and slap it down on the back of my hand, and then slowly uncover it. She laughs because I lost, but I would gladly lose every time just to hear her laugh again. Leering playfully, I slip the coin back into my pocket.

I row toward the mountain of rock and she sits silently as we glide through the water, taking in the majestic beauty around us. The canoe slides onto the sandy beach and after I help her out, I pull it ashore and tuck it between two rocks covered with greenery to disguise the canoe completely.

She stands near the water like she's waiting for something, so I hold out my hand. Hesitating, she finally puts her hand in mine and follows me around the massive rock to walk along the narrow beach that is the small island.

The sound of falling water gets louder and after a couple of minutes, we reach the far side. Above us is the waterfall that starts from the top of the mountain of rock and cascades down into the cove of water below.

I lead her under the falls where we stand in waist-deep water and let the falls wash off the caked-on mud and sand from our clothes and hair. She's right next to me, close enough to touch, and if she were mine, I would pull her into my arms and kiss her, but her heart still belongs to someone else. I take a step back and watch her lift her head to welcome the spray of water on her face while she drags her hands down her hair. She looks good enough to be on a postcard, centered in a cloud of mist and droplets that dance around her before resting on her velvet skin.

I stare. I wait. When she's finished washing, I lead her out of the water, let go of her hand, and turn to face her.

"Welcome to Daxwood Castle," I say. "What do you think?"

11

Ava

MID-MORNING: THE REVEAL

*D*AX IS FACING ME. *I* WATCH THE WATER DROPS FALL from his wavy hair and roll down his chest, slowing across abs that act like speed bumps. The drops lead to a small trail of hair below his belly button, trailing down to his shorts hung low on his hips. I look away before he can think I'm staring, but not fast enough, and now a crooked smile has formed on his lips. He's asked me what I think of his castle but every time I try to look at the natural rock formation, my eyes are drawn back to him.

"I've never seen anything so amazing," I say respectfully. "I can't take my eyes off it."

"I was talking about the castle," he says, and his lips twitch as he tries to keep from laughing.

My face flushes, and I hate him a little more. "So was I," I tell him. "It's the only thing in front of me worth looking at."

I meant to punish him, but now he looks even more amused.

"Would you like to go inside?" he asks.

"What do you mean?" Confusion shows on my face. "We can go inside?"

"Of course," he says confidently. "There's a secret entrance. You can go inside any castle if it's allowed. Or in this case, if you know the password." A sly grin crosses his

94

lips. "So... do you know the password?"

I cross my arms in protest. He's so annoying. Why does everything with him have to be a game? I sigh a deep breath and sarcastically blurt the only thing that comes to mind. The password whispered into my ear by a boy on the beach many years ago.

"Palomino."

I expect him to burst out laughing and allow me at least two more chances to get it right. But he doesn't laugh at all. In fact, all traces of a smile vanish from his face and for half a second, I think he's upset by my lack of effort. He takes a step toward me and just as quickly as his expression disappeared moments ago, his face now explodes into one of pure happiness.

"You remembered," he says with a satisfied grin, his voice full of awe and reverence. "It really is you."

I blink, and then his words register, conjuring up a pleasant recollection in the back of my mind. Happiness pours over me, and I smile back at him. Dax takes another step forward, studying my face as though he's seeing it for the first time. Our eyes meet with mutual recognition, sharing the same treasured memory, and all my hate and irritation vanishes. He was my *first* friend. And as incredible as it seems, my one wish of seeing him again has come true, like I finally managed to twist luck and alter it to go my way. Suddenly, a happily ever after seems less like an unachievable dream, and more like a realistic possibility.

I was never one for make-believe. It seemed so irrational and silly. Even as a child, my imagination led me to only dream of realistic goals in my future and the destiny I was determined to choose for myself. With one exception. This had been the one time I'd gotten caught up in an imaginary world, a fairy tale so magical I'd wanted it to really exist. And the person responsible for breaking down my wall of serious practicality, the star of the fairy tale, is standing before me now.

Maybe I'm in a coma—or worse, maybe I really am dead. Dax takes both of my hands in his, anxiously waiting for me to respond, but words escape me.

I was eight years old the first time I went to the beach. The sound of the water rolling onto the shore, the squawking of seagulls, and the screams of delight mixed with the laughter of other children are etched into my brain like it was yesterday. I can recall the smell of the air—damp and salty, the scent of fish and seaweed the water left on my skin, and how I crunched my toes as the receding waves pulled away at the sand beneath my feet. I was humbled by the vastness of the ocean and intimidated by the power and strength of the waves crashing around me. But what I remember most about that day was not the sight, smell, and feel of my surroundings.

My father and I were walking along the water's edge to look for shells and came across a marvelous sand castle built by a young boy and his father. Judging from the size and complexity, the work of art must have taken them all day. They were working on the finishing touches, adding intricate details using small sticks.

The boy was about my age, copying his father's every move, and my father and I joined a small group of bystanders to marvel at the castle. When the pair finished, they stepped back to admire their masterpiece as the onlookers dispersed. My father struck up a conversation with the boy's father. He was fascinated by his artistic design.

The boy walked up to where I stood holding my father's hand.

"Do you wanna come see our castle?" he asked me.

Being home-schooled meant I didn't have much interaction with other kids my age, and this left me lacking in the conversation department. I looked up at my father rather than answer him myself.

"Can she talk?" he asked my father.

"Yes, she's just a little shy," he told him with a smile, and then he bent down to look me in the eye. "Go on, honey, he wants to show you his beautiful castle."

He held out his hand and waited for me to take it. His friendly eyes matched his warm smile, so I hesitantly let go of my father's hand to take his. Then he turned and ran towards the castle, pulling me behind him.

"What's your name?" he asked, after telling me his.

"Ava."

"Ava? That's a weird name," he said, and then he laughed.

We sat down in front of the entrance to his castle. I craned my neck and squinted into the blazing sun to see the top. The enormous fortress stood as tall as my father with multiple towers of different sizes, notched walls, and winding staircases. A drawbridge led to the gatehouse in front, and a moat of water completely surrounded the citadel of sand. I listened attentively as he showed me the different parts and their purpose.

"That's the keep," he said, pointing to the main tower in the center with pride. "My dad says it's the heart of the castle. It's the most important part because it's where my dad and I would live. He's the king and I'm the prince, of course.

He lowered his finger to some vertical sticks that blocked the main entrance inside the gatehouse. "This is the portcullis. That's to keep out enemies and princesses," he told me, and then hurried to clarify. "Well, you know, enemies and *sister* princesses that get on my nerves. Princesses from other kingdoms would probably be okay... if they knew the password."

I remember looking at him strangely.

He ran out of patience waiting for me to ask the question he expected me to ask. "Well? Don't you want to know what the password is?" he asked, looking at me intently with eyes as blue as the hotel pool I'd swam in earlier that morning.

I nodded my head shyly.

"It's Palomino," he whispered in my ear, even though there was no one around to hear but me. "But don't tell anyone, because it's a secret."

My parents talked with his dad for hours, which meant I spent the majority of the day with him. He became my first friend. I didn't say much after telling him my name, but he didn't seem to mind. He did enough talking for the both of us. I followed him around in the sand to search for treasure and then, before I was ready, it was time to go. I cried, not wanting to leave my new friend and his castle behind.

The next year when my parents asked where I wanted to spend summer vacation, I requested the same beach in San Diego, California, and told them I loved the town. And I did. After that, an annual trip to San Diego became a family tradition. But my parents never knew that the real reason I wanted to visit was the hope of running into *him* again.

Like all other eight- and nine-year-olds, we created our own fairy tale. He was the prince, and I was his princess. We rode our sand shovel horses across the kingdom in search of treasure, bringing special rocks and shells we collected back to the sand castle for safekeeping. He'd been my brave knight, promising to protect me from the imaginary, fire-breathing dragons that ambushed us on our way back through the forest. He assured me they'd been sent to destroy us by his wicked stepsister, as he fought them bravely with his stick sword and Frisbee shield.

I'd followed his every command, ducking when he ordered and shooting my pretend bow and arrow to assist him in exterminating the dragons. And finally, we retreated to the castle and made it across the moat just in time before the drawbridge was raised and the portcullis lowered, cheering in unison for our victory. We celebrated by sitting down at a feast fit for a prince and his princess, the finest food in all the land, created from sand of course.

"It's me," he says now. "Dax. I showed you my sand castle on the beach when I was nine and—"

"I know," I reply with reverence, remembering everything about that day, especially the part of me not wanting to leave. "How did you know it was me?"

He smiles a big smile. "When you told me your name, I thought of that day and then decided it was just coincidence. But when I saw the pictures you drew of your parents, I recognized them and knew it had to be you. I just didn't expect you to remember." He glances down at his feet. "I've thought about you a lot. Even though it was ten years ago, I remember that day like it was yesterday."

My face is suddenly hot. I'm feeling awkward and a little embarrassed by the fact that the one day we spent together as children meant as much to him as it did to me.

"Do you want to see inside?" he asks again.

I smile at Dax and nod, feeling childlike, as if we're back on that beach again. We walk under the falls to a wall covered in winding, green overgrowth. He lets go of my hand and grabs a rope made of woven vine that hangs to the side, and pulls downward using a pulley he's carved out of wood. Instantly, a portcullis begins to rise, made from small branches beneath the green, exposing an opening into the small mountain he calls Daxwood Castle.

I peer inside while he finishes tying off the rope, and then he motions for me to enter. The tunnel opening extends for a few feet before opening up into a massive room. This cave is four times the size of the one we came from on the beach, and this ceiling is extremely tall—giving it a castle-like feel. High up on either side of the walls, small crevices allow bits of sunlight to peek through the cracks, enough to dimly illuminate the inside of the cave. Small trickles of water run down the walls in various spots and seep into the floor. I look around in awe.

The entire room is filled with furniture, and I step towards a massive, rectangular table in the center of the room, large enough to hold a feast for a king. Made from long planks of wood, it's held together by some long strips of vine. The base of the table is formed from two massive sections of tree trunks, cut at the point where the branches fan out like fingers, seeming to balance the table top like a gigantic hand.

"Did you make this?" I ask in shock.

"Yeah. It gives me something to do. Here, sit down."

He pulls out a chair at one end of the table. He has carved the back from a solid piece of wood in an ornate pattern like the one I saw on the canoe. Across the table on the opposite end sits another identical chair.

"This is unbelievable. How did you carve this?" I run my hand across the intricate design before sitting down.

"My father had a knife strapped to his belt." He pulls the knife from a discreet spot in the hollow wood quiver that contains his arrows and holds it up. "This knife has saved my life many times, as well as my sanity. Without it, I might have gone crazy by now." He removes the bow and arrows from around his chest and sits down in the other chair. "Come to think of it, that may be what's wrong with Roxy." His laughter echoes around the room.

"So no one knows about this place?" I ask in a quiet voice, afraid of exposing us even though I know there's no one around.

"Roxy doesn't. She has her own special place. I followed her there once. It's near a waterfall too, but definitely not as cool as this." He grins. "She never follows me though. In fact, she makes an effort to keep her distance."

I feel empathy for her situation. "Isn't she lonely?"

He leans back and puts his feet up on the table, crossing them at the ankles. "She has her multiple personalities to keep her company," he says with a wink, his dimples prominent.

"What about the tribes?" I ask. "Don't they know about it?"

"The Lambai Tribe knows, but they won't come onto Anwai territory unless they're provoked or are visiting Chief Anwai on official business. And the Anwai don't come here because they think it's the sacred house of the spirits. I asked the chief about it once and he told me I should stay away, warning me of making the spirits angry." His laugh lacks concern. "So I guess it's just Prince Daxton and Princess Ava like the old days, except the castle isn't made of sand and the fire-breathing dragons have been replaced by flesh-eating cannibals. Unfortunately, the wicked stepsister still exists."

He looks away from the knife he twirls in his fingers to smile at me, and for some reason, his look makes me blush. Without warning, he flings the knife at a wooden bull's-eye across the room. The knife lands in the center with a thud, causing me to jump.

I smile at him before quickly looking away at the other furniture around the room. There is a couch carved out of a large tree trunk and on either side are matching chairs. The set surrounds a small fire pit in the floor. Behind Dax, I notice a counter-like table protruding out from the wall, supported by small tree trunks. In front, there are three intricately carved bar stools made from tree trunks as well.

"You're so talented," I say, admiring his handiwork.

"Thanks." He stands up. "You haven't seen the rest of the castle. Come on."

I follow him to a small opening. Ducking to walk through another tunnel, we step into a smaller room with an enormous bed in the center. And like the last room, the sun peers in through a tiny opening in the rock wall. I walk to the hammock-like bed floating above the floor, secured to tree stumps at all four corners, and drag my hand across the weave, made from tiny, braided vines, and then hesitantly sit on one side. The pillow is made from the skin of some unfortunate marsupial and stitched around the edges with fine strips of bark. I squeeze it with curiosity to figure out what's inside.

"Bird feathers," he says, answering my thoughts. "Go ahead. Try it out."

I tuck the pillow behind my head and stretch out across the bed. It's surprisingly comfortable. "Wow, I'm impressed," I tell him, and then notice the expression on his face.

He's blinking and fidgeting and staring at me, as if he's not sure if he's imagining a real girl lying across his bed.

Embarrassed, I get up and walk to what looks like a sink against the wall. An inverted turtle shell rests on top of a hollowed-out, waist-high log, and the humble vanity is placed strategically under the opening in the rock.

"When it rains, the bowl fills up," he says before I can ask.

He's still standing near the doorway of the room with his hands hung low on his hips, like he's afraid to step inside his own room with me here.

"Anyway, I have to go hunting before Roxy gets so hungry she comes looking for me. Make yourself at home, relax, and I'll be back in a while," he says.

I follow him back into the main room where he hurries to retrieve his knife, and then he hastily slings the bow and arrow over his shoulder before heading for the main entrance to leave. Worry starts to sets in and I tag along, half walking and half running to keep up with him. He grabs a spear he left stuck in the sand and goes around to the other side where the canoe is hiding in wait.

"Dax?" I say in a panic, and he turns around. "Can I come with you?" The question comes out sounding a little more desperate than I intended, and I don't know which one of us is more surprised. Hours ago, I would have given anything to be rid of him, and now I want to beg him to stay.

He shakes his head. "Next time, I promise. No offense, but you'll slow me down. Plus, your fluorescent shirt might scare off the animals and draw the attention of some hungry cannibals. Don't worry though, you're completely safe."

He retrieves the canoe, and then turns like he'd just had another thought.

"And please don't do anything stupid. Just stay here. After I'm done hunting, I'll snoop around a little and see if I can learn anything about Preston and your friends. I promise."

I nod, watching him climb into the boat and start rowing across. The distance is short enough to swim, but would be a difficult task while holding a bow and arrow, not to mention a spear. He stashes the canoe on the other side and climbs the small wall of rocks. He dips under the green foliage, and then he's gone.

I head back to the castle, feeling a little disheartened. The wooden couch in the main room welcomes me and after sitting, I glance around. Behind the counter that juts out from the wall is a small door made from sticks woven together at the top and the bottom. Another door is underneath that one, and both are attached to the wall with vine that is strung through small loopholes in the lava rock. I walk over and open the top one to see inside. There's a pocket in the rock, almost like a recessed cupboard, and sitting inside are dishes carved from wood. I have to squat down to peek in the other cupboard. I expect to find more wooden dishes but instead, I find a small passageway, so tiny that I'll have to crawl to see where it leads.

The tunnel is dark because my body blocks the light from the room behind me. I crawl a few feet and debate backing out the way I've come, but then some light appears ahead of me. In a matter of seconds, my head pokes through the opening, into what looks like a room full of pirate treasure. I stand up to brush myself off and then spin around slowly, gawking at the endless trinkets and miscellaneous items.

This room is smaller than the other two but considerably brighter. The large gap above me lets in a lot of sunlight, highlighting the glimmering gold and silver on some of the objects. They are sorted into piles with similiar things grouped together. There are some books, random shoes and clothes, and lots of dishes—mismatched but unbroken, set together with jewelry and a few tools. Scattered all around them are various coins, and not all of them are American.

A violin is propped against the wall next to a collection of empty glass bottles. Behind them, an empty champagne bottle tips to the right against a worn and faded buoy from a ship. The combination of the two items causes a lump to creep up in my throat as I remember the magical night Preston and I spent on his sailboat. The night we shared our first kiss. The memory is too painful. How did we spend our last moments together? I struggle to recall the events right before waking up on this island, but I still can't remember what happened after I got on the plane. What if Preston is really gone? The ache in my chest is unbearable. I rush out of the treasure room and into Dax's room where I collapse on his hammock bed and cry.

Dax and his castle managed to take my mind off Preston until my stupid curiosity dragged it back up. And Dax isn't here to make me forget that Preston is missing, even though I cling to a sliver of hope that he survived and will come looking for me. A slim possibility, but better than the alternative—accepting the fact that Preston, Kirk, and Anna are all dead and have left me to survive on my own.

Preston

Day Two: MINOR SETBACK

INDING THE CLIFF WHERE WE FIRST ENDED UP WHEN we washed up on shore was easy, the hard part is convincing myself I don't deserve to be pushed off the edge for my betrayal.

I sit close to the edge and dangle my feet over the side. My shirt clings to my skin from perspiration, so I remove it and start to lay it next to me when my name tag catches my eye.

Preston King
Chief Pilot
HC Enterprises

What a joke. I chuck it out over the edge as far as I can and watch to see where it lands. Halfway to the bottom, it vanishes from sight. I feel better now that I've disposed of it.

The beach below makes me think of Ava again and the time I took her to the beach and didn't tell her we were standing in front of Mr. C's beachfront Tuscany-style mansion. It is four stories tall with floor-to-ceiling windows. Three rounded balconies are staggered on each floor, and each one boasts elaborate, wrought-iron railings with hanging boxes filled with greenery that spill out over the edges and look like they might drip onto the beach below. In the middle of the first-level balcony are two huge French doors and a small stairway leading to the beach.

I saw her admiring it so I asked her if the houses in front of her were all for sale and she was buying, which one she'd want to see first. She chose Mr. C's of course.

I suggested we check it out. Following me until we were really close, she then pulled back on my hand. She had no intention of going further, so I slipped my sunglasses down to look at her and in my best alluring voice, I explained that if we got caught, we could claim a case of mistaken identity. "You know, 'I thought this was my uncle's house' kind of thing," I told her.

She was determined to hold her ground, so I quickly ascended the stairs two at a time to the first-level balcony and leaned toward the glass to look in the windows. Afterwards, I leaned over the railing to tell her she was making us look guilty. "Just act natural—pretend you live here," I said with a wink and watched her hurry up the stairs to peek in the windows.

The entire house is elegantly decorated and looks like the setting for MTV Cribs. She was taking it all in when she noticed my reflection and turned to stare at me in shock. I pretended to snoop around the patio, casually lifting up furniture and flower-filled planters one at a time. Walking to the large French doors, I lifted the mat. "Bingo," I said, holding up the shiny, gold key for her to see, and then said, "They should put this someplace a little less obvious, don't you think?"

She told me to put it back but instead, I put the key in the lock and turned it. Ava actually sprinted for the steps, but I caught her arm and convinced her to stay in my best enticing voice. She was too scared to speak but followed me inside and rushed to the huge couch. Sitting on the very edge, she watched me wander around the room to look at the art on the walls.

She almost fell off the edge of the couch when I sat down next to her, took her hand in mine, and whispered in her ear, "Seriously, you can relax. This is Mr. Caruso's house." I couldn't stop the low chuckle that bubbled up from my throat, and it took only three seconds for the words to sink in. Her mouth fell open. I told her Mr. Caruso was out of town, and I was staying there. She tried to punch me, but I managed to dodge the hit and wrap my arms around her in a tight hug to diffuse her anger.

How can something that amused me then make me feel so guilty now?

I pick up the shirt and head back the way I came, but when I come to the place I should veer right, I go left instead. My exploring has turned out well so far and besides, I'm done following orders.

I'm careful to count my steps and study my surroundings to guarantee I'll find my way back. Just when the thought pops into my head that I should probably turn back, something in the trees ahead catches my eye. I move forward with caution to see what it is.

A large structure floats in the trees a few yards ahead, and two more massive tree houses float in giant trees close by. I've discovered a cannibal village. Kirk is going to freak. I told him the cannibals weren't real.

A rustle in the bushes nearby startles me, and I crouch down under a bush. Someone is coming. I know I'll regret ditching my shirt but in a sea of green, the white will surely give me away. I stuff it under a bush and back away from the approaching predator on my hands and knees until I can't hear anything but the wild calls of birds.

I run all the way back to the fork on the path and veer right. In a matter of seconds, the hangout comes into sight where I know Kirk and Anna are waiting impatiently for me to return. It's a miracle I didn't get lost, but I need one more miracle right now. I have to convince Kirk to come with me. I'll be exploring again tomorrow, but this time, I won't be doing it alone.

13

Dax

MIDDAY: THE KISS

THE BOW FEELS NORMAL IN MY HANDS, BUT MY AIM IS anything but. I can't believe I missed a perfect shot. I never miss. But I can't seem to focus on hunting. The image of Ava sprawled out on my hammock bed like a Victoria Secret's Angel in her hot pink tank and white shorts that show too much of her long legs is now stuck in my head. Normally, I wouldn't complain, but the vision is making concentration virtually impossible—like putting a crack addict in a room full of crack and asking them to pass a math test.

At least my plan worked and she doesn't seem to hate me anymore. She even asked to come with me, and the desperation in her voice made me think it wasn't to try and pull off another escape. I just want her to give me a chance to be her friend again, and then maybe that friendship will lead to something more.

I know she's not really mean to the core like Roxy; she's just upset about the unfortunate circumstances she's had to deal with recently. And who wouldn't be? I can only hope she learns to deal with her loss better than Roxy did. Roxy let the anger overtake her soul until there was nothing left but an overabundance of bitterness she feels inclined to pass around on a daily basis. Ava is softer, quiet and shy like I remember, but I can tell by her journal entries she's also sensitive and caring, stubborn and loyal, naïve but smart, and if I can win her trust, maybe I can convince her to release some of her guilt and pain by talking to me.

I settle further into my hiding spot, scooting along the thick branch of the tree to lean against the trunk and wait for something else to wander into my sight. Hopefully, it will be something other than a bird this time since apparently, I need a gigantic target in order to be successful today. Stillness settles in around me, and I resort to passing the time by pulling out the little book that's become my favorite hobby.

July 12

Today finally came, and a million tiny birds took flight in my stomach at the sound of Preston's voice calling over the radio for permission to land. Parking Hotel Charlie, placing the welcome mat, getting instructions from Kirk, and assisting Anna went by in a blur until Preston stepped off the plane and made time come to screeching halt. It seems like he's become my reason for everything—eating, breathing, sleeping, waking up, and going to work are now just ways to pass the time until I can see him again. I wish he felt the same way about me.

His eyes met mine and then he flashed my favorite smile. The words I was supposed to say pertaining to my job floated away like I'd written them on a helium balloon and let go of the string. He lowered his glasses to wink and asked, "Miss me?"

I told him "a little" and didn't realize I was biting my lower lip until his eyes pointed it out. Then I thought my heart would stop beating when he said he could hardly wait to take me to dinner tonight.

He picked me up in the same red Ferrari he rented before and drove to the marina in San Diego. Making me close my eyes, he took both of my hands to lead me to his surprise. The air smelled of fish, and I could hear the seagull's high-pitched screams and flapping wings mixed with random voices that got louder and then faded as we passed by.

He squeezed my hand and slowed to a stop, then stepped behind me and placed both hands on my waist. The tips of his fingers brushed my neck to sweep my hair behind my shoulders, and then he tucked his chin next to my neck. My heart stuttered. This was an obvious change from the Preston I knew. Today, he seemed more relaxed, like the strange formality of our first dates had dissipated and now he didn't seem to mind being close to me. In fact, it almost seemed like he was making up for lost time. "Open your eyes," he whispered, and a pleasant shiver ran through me from his warm breath next to my ear.

I peered through the boats in front of us, over the water to his sailboat, and saw immediately what he intended me to see. Miss April was now sprawled neatly across the back of his boat. The vibrant gold and black letters sparkled in the sunlight against the polished, glossy red background. The boat looked like new and I couldn't believe the transformation, but it was nothing compared to what waited for me inside the cabin. My mouth literally fell open when I saw the candlelight dinner for two.

Modern shades replaced the flowery curtains and the faded pillows on the couch were gone too. A few deep red and gray satin pillows were displayed elegantly on the black leather couch that surrounded the table. The shades were drawn, letting in only a small amount of light, and scattered around the room were red and white glowing candles of various shapes and sizes. The setting was beyond anything I could ever imagine.

After dinner, we walked above deck and slipped off our shoes. I followed him out to the bow of the boat. On a silver tray sat a very expensive bottle of champagne and an opener. I remember him telling me that changing the name of a boat was considered bad luck and not only did he change the name, but he also named it after me—someone luck tends to avoid.

He claimed he did some research and discovered that to avoid the bad luck, a name-changing ceremony must take place. I wasn't convinced he didn't make the whole thing up, but I decided to play along. He opened the bottle of champagne and moved closer, stunning me with his alluring smile, and I giggled as he shared the legend.

According to mythology, gods of the air and the sea keep logbooks with the name of each vessel from the high seas. Whenever a new ship is built, it's commissioned to the gods for entry into their logs. So, of course, it wouldn't be good for any sailors on board if Poseidon, the god of the sea, looked up one day and found a ship sailing in his domain that wasn't logged in his book. So if you wish to change a ship's name, you must petition him to strike the old name from his rosters to avoid incurring any wrath from the gods. AKA—bad luck. Crazy, huh?

Preston had already taken care of the first step and removed everything aboard the ship bearing the old name, then replaced the name on the ship and made sure everything else bore the new name. The next step was the ceremony.

He poured some champagne off the bow into the water, and then held up the bottle in the air with one hand. His other arm draped over my shoulder. Then he said, "Great Poseidon, ruler of the sea, thank you for allowing this ship safe passage in the past. We humbly ask you now to strike 'Little Red Hen' from your rosters." He finished the ceremony speaking in a silly pirate accent that made me laugh. Afterwards, he poured the remaining champagne into the water, and then sat the bottle back on the tray.

I asked him if that was all we had to do, and he told me he'd added one last step. Before I knew what was happening, he took my face in his hands and leaned in to kiss me.

Oh my gosh!

My first kiss! It lasted for only a few seconds, but when he pulled away, I was more than satisfied. On a scale of one to ten, I'd definitely give it a ten. It was perfect—just as I imagined our first kiss to be.

Then like an idiot, I asked, "Are you sure you should be kissing me?" and regretted it immediately. Leave it to me to ruin the moment—the one I've been waiting for FOREVER! He blinked at me, his lips curving into a mischievous grin before he said, "No. But I don't care anymore. This is what I want—I want to be with you," and he kissed me again. And I didn't want to know his reason for holding back before because all I cared about was being in his arms.

Great. The big first kiss. So that's what girls do when you kiss them for the first time. They write about it in their stupid journal and rate it on a generic scale. A ten. Pl-ease. How can she rate it when she has nothing to compare it to? It couldn't have been *that* good. Perfect? Completely satisfied? I mean, really? A kiss isn't perfect if it leaves you satisfied. A kiss should blow your mind—leave you unsatisfied and secretly begging for more. Pathetic. I guess that's what happens when first kisses are left up to pretty boys. Geez. If a girl doesn't rate the kiss a twenty, then a guy isn't doing his job.

I will kiss Ava. And it will blow Preston's kiss away. The thought makes me smile and disintegrates the jealousy. I take a quick look around the forest below me and then turn the page.

July 13

I think those mysterious notes are making me paranoid. Last night after the big kiss, Preston invited me to be the first overnight guest on Miss April. I dreamt Preston and I were sailing on the ocean, floating peacefully in the calm water while the moon reflected off the gentle waves. Preston went down into the cabin to get something and that's when I noticed another boat—a big pirate ship, old and ominous, heading straight for the sailboat. We weren't moving at all. Our sails were up, but an eerie stillness settled around us, leaving the air completely void of any breeze. I called for Preston, but he didn't answer. I ran into the cabin to look for him, but he'd vanished.

The huge, dark ship was approaching rapidly. A pirate stood at the bow, with a black beard and long, black hair, dressed completely in black from his boots to his large hat that hid his face. He faced me, but there was no place to hide and nowhere to run. I felt so helpless

I wanted to cry, so I yelled out for Preston again, louder, my voice filled with panic. The pirate ship floated to a stop, the sailboat so small in comparison to the ship's giant shadow.

An unexpected blanket of fog crept across the water and surrounded Miss April. A small rowboat broke through and came to a stop at the stern of the sailboat. I ran to the bow, but turned to see the pirate in black step off the rowboat onto the stern. He came towards me, past the helm and onto the bow. The sound of his boots got louder—he was getting closer, and I was trapped. I cried out, one last plea for Preston, then turned and jumped into the dark, menacing ocean below.

I screamed out loud and sat up in the bed, my heart feeling like it might jump out of my chest. The cabin door flung open. Preston rushed to my side with an alarmed look on his face and asked if I was okay. I flung my arms around him. Instantly, he wrapped one arm around me and put the other behind my head as I buried my face in his neck. We sat there for a minute and he said nothing, waiting for me to get control of my emotions and my breathing to return to normal. I told him I had a nightmare. He tucked my hair behind my ear and then said, "So my kissing gave you nightmares? That can't be good." He laughed, but I was mortified and assured him the kissing was not the cause.

He lay down on his side next to me, and I rolled over to face him. After promising to stay with me, he kissed my forehead and then ran his fingers through my hair until I fell back asleep.

I told myself it was just a stupid dream but this morning before Preston brought me home, I noticed a familiar car in the parking lot at the marina. It looked like the same black Mercedes that's normally parked across the street from my house that I've always assumed is a neighbor, but about fifteen minutes after Preston dropped me off at my house, the black car pulled up in its usual spot. I watched out my window for someone to get out, but no one ever did.

Since Preston had some errands to run, I decided to make a quick trip to the library. Reading is a successful way to kill time when Preston isn't around and that means I need at least five books to cover me for the next week.

On my way to the checkout, I stopped at the Newspaper Archives and typed my aunt's full name on the search line. A page full of articles popped up, so I opened the notebook I'd brought with me and began scribbling down some notes. One article included a picture of her at a charity ball, and at her side was the man from the photo in the cigar box. They were dressed in formal attire for the black-tie event, posing alongside other guests for the newspaper photographer. There were other articles with pictures similar to this one, at other formal events, my aunt always on his arm or at his side. Clearly, he was well known, someone worthy of attending all the events and also someone the public seemed to care about.

I scribbled down the names of all the places where the events were held, hoping I could visit them and find out more info about this man. I couldn't ignore the possibility that he may be my biological father, and if not, he might have information about my aunt. There was even a picture of them at a ribbon-cutting ceremony outside a building in L.A., which I thought might be useful for showing to people since I hadn't brought the one from home. I wrote down the address of the building, then pushed print and walked to the counter to pick up the photo.

A feeling of uneasiness made me look over my shoulder, but no one appeared to be paying any attention to me. I paid for the copy and slipped the printed picture into my notebook. Returning to the desk, I typed the man's name into the search line. The page exploded with articles, but the name was common. Without a middle name, I'd be there forever. Forever was not an option when Mr. Gulfstream himself would be returning to my house in less than an hour, so I grabbed my notebook and library books and headed for the exit.

While waiting on the sidewalk, I opened the inside jacket of one of the books to skim through the description. The crosswalk sign changed and I started to step off the curb, but someone yelled, "Look out!" A firm hand grabbed my arm and yanked me backwards as a car whizzed by only inches away. The pull to safety caused me to lose my balance and fall backwards onto the hard concrete. The books in my arms went flying through the air. So embarrassing! I was momentarily stunned, and a group of passersby gathered around me.

The man in a baseball cap who had jerked me back immediately took to looking me over and asking me a million times if I was okay. Besides being embarrassed, I had no visible damage so he helped me up and then joined the strangers to pick up my items strewn all over the sidewalk. They handed me my books, and a nice woman put my wallet and other contents back into my purse. The man called the driver an idiot and someone else asked if I needed an ambulance. All the while, I'm brushing myself off with trembling hands and reassuring everyone I'm fine.

I thanked the man for saving me and took a quick inventory of the books in my arms. He made a comment about how bizarre the whole thing was. I wanted to tell him not really since I was the person standing on the corner, but I was too preoccupied with finding my missing notebook.

I scanned the ground while he picked up his backpack from where he'd dropped it and looked me over one more time. Someone asked if anyone got the license plate and a lot of 'no's' shot through the crowd before my rescuer pointed out it was a black Mercedes. Such a weird coincidence. But even weirder was the fact that my notebook was missing, which meant someone in the small crowd of strangers must have taken it. I searched the faces looking for the traitor, but all of them looked suspicious.

Three teenagers stood huddled together carrying backpacks, with earbuds stretching from their ears to the iPods in their pocket, and they were whispering in hushed voices. The woman with the glasses that helped put the items in my purse had a huge bag over her shoulder, large enough to fit a notebook. Even the man in the shirt and tie could have easily slipped the notebook into his laptop bag. I searched the others in the crowd with stacks of books in their arms and figured my notebook could be wedged in any one of those piles. It was a lost cause.

They were eyeing me as I scrutinized each one of them. I thanked the man again and darted across the street to my car. If he hadn't jerked me out of the way. I'd be dead or lying in a hospital somewhere with serious injuries, and dead won't do because I plan to spend a long lifetime of dates with Preston. So for now, I'll count my one lucky star that I'm still in one piece and chalk the whole thing up to coincidence and bad luck. (And there are a million black Mercedes crawling around town, right?

What the hell was that about?

Movement in the bushes below grabs my attention before I have time to analyze Ava's bizarre near-death experience. I carefully slip the journal back in my pocket and load an arrow into my bow before lifting it to take aim.

The boar steps out. It's a small one, but it will do. Just one step closer. That's right. Keep turning... keep turning... right...there. Perfect. My left eye closes in preparation, and I slowly exhale.

A bloodcurdling scream that can only be Ava's pierces the air.

14

Ava

MIDDAY: THE GAMBLE

*M*Y INSIDES ARE HOLLOW, AND I WISH MORE THAN anything Dax had let me go with him. I struggle with the idea of needing him, when only hours ago, I wanted nothing more than to be as far away as possible. He has no idea that leaving me here alone has allowed the sorrow to sneak up in his absence and take over my soul.

Only I know that even in his most annoying moments, Dax erases my pain and wipes away reality to wrap me up in his fairy-tale dream, and this one is real enough to touch. How could I let him out of my sight? What if he never comes back? I wipe the tears away and run outside to stare at the spot where he vanished just minutes ago. He couldn't have gone far.

The water separating me from the forest is warm like a fresh-drawn bath and soothes my skin as I swim across. I push past my exhaustion and climb to the top of the natural rock wall. Ducking under the leaves, I peer into the dense forest before climbing down to the bottom.

"Dax?" I yell in a hushed whisper and take a few steps into the forest.

Nothing.

"Dax?" I say again, a little louder.

A branch snaps in the distance to my left. My heart pounds and I run a few feet, pushing back the branches in my path and then stop.

"Dax? Is that you?" I hear nothing but birds.

The thick forest blocks out so much sunlight that I strain to see something white moving through the trees in the distance. It looks like a shirt—one white enough to be a pilot's shirt like Preston, Kirk, or Anna's. My breath catches and I stumble forward, catching a glimpse of dark hair before the figure disappears into the trees.

Preston!

I take off running and keep my eyes fixed on the place where I saw him.

"Preston!" I yell, then listen for a response and pray I'll hear it over the thrashing as I make my way through the trees and bushes. I pick up speed, frantic to catch another glimpse of him to assure I'm headed in the right direction.

"Preston!" I yell again and then pause.

A cracking sound comes from the same direction. I sprint towards it, repeating his name in a desperate plea—afraid he'll move too far out of range to hear my voice. The noise gets louder, and I know I'm getting closer. I'm moving as fast as I can in the thick underbrush, trying not to trip on small tree roots and vines. A glimpse of white fabric confirms I'm heading in the right direction.

"Preston!" I whisper-yell just as my foot catches a large root and sends me plunging forward onto my stomach. When I lift my head, I'm face to face with a skull, laying in a crude graveyard full of bones scattered among crawling vines speckled with small flowers. Judging from the size and shape—they're human. Stifling a scream, I scramble to my feet, unintentionally kicking and displacing another skull that rolls to a stop inches from my left toe. I lunge forward through a bush of dense green leaves in front of me to escape the nightmarish scene. In my haste, I trip and fall again.

I've fallen into a clearing filled with huts and stick

houses built high up in the trees. I search the open space and my hope of not being discovered dissipates when I make eye contact with a man only a few feet away. He's holding a broken branch in both hands and is staring at me with wild eyes. My stomach rolls into a tight ball.

He lets the wood fall to the ground and starts sprinting toward me, so I push myself to my feet and turn to run back the way I came, kicking and tossing the bones astray with my feet as I sprint to get away. At first, all I can hear is the squishing of wet moss under my shoes combined with my rapid breaths as I tear through the wall of green with absolutely no sense of direction.

I have to get as far away as possible, but now I can hear him behind me, his steps softer than mine but deafening in my head as the realization hits that he's gaining on me. And I'm a hot pink moving target. I'm panting and gasping for air while I contemplate removing the tank top and ditching it in the trees, but I know that will only slow me down. If I can just make it to the beach. *Where is the beach!?*

His body smashes into me like a freight train, hurling us both to the ground. I scream out and struggle to break free from his grasp, but he's too strong. He sits on top of me and pins me down while staring at me with wide eyes, the whites of them prominent against his dark face covered in bright-colored paint.

He's holding my wrists. An evil smile spreads across his face before he goes for my throat with a mouth full of jagged, yellow teeth. I flinch and whimper as he drags his tongue across my skin like a wild animal, from my neck to the top of my cheek, and then he licks his lips slowly with a crazed look in his eye.

Both of my hands are held together with one of his, and he yanks a vine from the forest floor to wrap securely around my wrists. Grabbing another vine, he manages to wrap it around my ankles while he holds down my legs and fastens them tightly.

I'm still screaming and calling out Dax's name. The mostly naked man stands above me with a satisfied grin, and then bends down to pick me up. I try to squirm away, but he throws me over one shoulder and makes his way back to the clearing. My screams are lost in my sobs, and I beg him to let me go. I know he can't even understand me, but I beg anyway.

Hanging upside down is disorienting, but the ground become less green and the branches dragging across my sides become absent. He stops walking and speaks in a language I don't recognize. There are other men talking, but I can't see through my hair that hangs over my face.

He puts me on my feet and shoves me to the ground. I'm completely enclosed in a wall of scantily clothed cannibals, adorned with necklaces made of human finger bones and teeth. A few women stand behind the men with bones embellishing their hair and stare at me in a demented sort of way, as if summing up my size to determine how long I'll need to cook.

And then I see her.

A woman from the tribe holding a basket of fruit, wearing a white shirt unbuttoned—and I recognize it. Preston's shirt is the only thing covering her besides a short skirt of leaves. I inhale a sharp breath and mumble Preston's name between sobs, wishing now that Dax hadn't swam out to save me. Drowning had to be less painful than the fate I was doomed for next.

Two men slide a large stick of bamboo between my wrists and ankles to pick me up. I dangle there helplessly while my captor speaks with a man wearing a crown of feathers.

"Please," I plead in a pathetic whimper. "I'm with Dax." Maybe the mention of his name will somehow help my dire situation.

The men carry me to a crude animal pen and put me inside. They shut the cage door and walk away to gather broken branches like the ones my captor first had in his hands before discovering me, and then they toss them into the large pit.

I put my head down on my knees, hating myself for leaving Dax's castle to begin with. That was the stupidest thing I could have done—maybe I deserve to die. I hope the end will come quickly, sparing me from a torturous death of suffering in agony, but that hope dwindles with each stick they throw on the fire shooting up from the hole in the ground.

I fumble with the vine around my ankles, but my hands are bound so tightly I can barely move the tips of my fingers—not enough to allow me to undo any knots. There's no hope of escaping. I watch helplessly as the entire village prepares to make a meal out of me. My captor and the man with the feather crown are still arguing. Two men approach the pen, and my heart rate picks up.

This is it. I'm going to die.

Using the stick of bamboo, they carry me towards a human-size spit over the large pit of flames in the center of the village, but my captor's voice stops them. They pause for him to bark a command, and then they take me to a small hut on the ground at the far end of the village. With no regard for my spine, they drop me on the dirt floor and laugh as they exit. I'm alone. The only exit is the small doorway they carried me through with an animal skin flap covering the opening. Underneath the flap, I can see their feet standing guard outside the doorway.

Determined to free my legs, I pick at the knotted vine holding my ankles, but my hands are shaking so bad I don't make much leeway before my captor pushes aside the flap and enters the hut. He's a solid mass of muscle, dwarfing the already tiny room, and he steps closer to tower over me. This is not good. My breath hitches in my throat, but I refuse to cry.

Don't show weakness. Don't show weakness. Don't show weakness.

He pulls a bone knife from his hip, and I flinch when he stoops down with it in his hand. I close my eyes and pray for a painless death. I'm going to die! *He's going to kill me!* My heart is pounding so hard I wonder if it will explode in my chest and kill me before he has the chance. *Nothing is happening... nothing is happening... when is it going to happen? Do it now—do it—do it!* I picture Preston's angelic face and assure myself I will be with him soon. DO IT!

The touch of a hand on my head startles me, and I let out a cry—then hold my breath—repeat Preston's name a hundred times in my head—but I'm still alive. He smoothes his hand over my hair, and I want to look—I can't look—but I want to. *What is he doing?*

My lids flutter open, and I stop breathing. He's leaning over me with the knife in one hand and my hair in the other. He's studying the strands and pinching them in between his rough fingers, rubbing them together before bringing the tuft to his nose. He smells it, and then a sly smile creeps across his face. I'm trying not to breathe, but I can't hold the air anymore and let out a jagged breath.

Only a second passes before he slices the vines holding my ankles with unexpected swiftness, and I stare up at him in shock. With a less-than-gentle touch, he yanks me to my feet. A tinge of hope flickers inside me. Is he going to let me go? I start to thank him but before I can even form the words, he shoves me back against the wall of the hut. The sound of ripping fabric snaps me back to reality.

No, no, no!

My hands fight him as he tears at my tank top and then before I know what's happening, his massive hand clamps down on my jaw, pressing my head against the bamboo to hold me in place. I grope for the knife I know is at his waist, but his other hand snatches my bound wrists and squeeze them so tight I think he'll snap them in half. I want to scream, but I can't get enough air into my lungs. I jerk my knee up, but he deflects my jab with a twist of his hips and moves closer. The struggle loosens the vine and one of my wrists springs free. Instinct tells me to claw at his face, but he releases my jaw to secure both of my wrists again above my head and holds them easily with one hand. His other hand wraps around the hair at the base of my neck, and pain splinters my scalp. He forces his lips down on mine, and I'm gagging and choking and suffocating.

No, no, no!

Why can't he just kill me? I muster every bit of courage I have to fight and do the only thing I can—bite down hard. He jerks back with a growl and a trickle of blood springs from his lip. I can taste his blood in my mouth and I should run, but I'll never make it—not more than a foot. He wipes his mouth with the back of his hand and looks at the blood. Anger spreads across his face and without warning, the back of his hand slams into the side of my face.

The dirt floor is hard and all I see for a moment is black, then swirling stars as the thatch ceiling comes into view. Maybe I should pretend I'm knocked out, and then run when he least expects it.

Then he's on top of me, pinning my arms and legs down like he did in the forest. My attempts to fight my way free are nothing more than wiggles with his massive weight presses down on me, so I scream with everything I have left.

Through the blur of my tears, I see the door flap open. One of the guards sticks his head inside to speak, and there is a frantic edge to his voice. My captor grabs the vine from the floor and reties my wrists together, then yanks the knife from his side and grabs my hair. I whimper, waiting for him to slice my throat, but the slicing sound next to my ear brings no pain. He holds a severed wisp of my hair and wipes his mouth again with the back of his hand. Standing up, he follows the guard outside.

Over my sobbing, I hear someone yelling from the opposite side of the clearing. I scoot to the doorway and peer underneath the flap. The men have stopped gathering wood and are facing the intruder, blocking him from my view. The man with the feather crown must be the chief, because he stands with his arms folded across his chest and the others wait, prepared to defend him. The mysterious, stern voice talks in the same language and the men listen.

The chief finally speaks, and the two argue back and forth. The chief points to my captor on his left, and more words are exchanged between the three. Then, after a moment of silence, the chief gives a command and the men step aside, one by one. And as they separate, I exhale with relief to see Dax standing before them holding his bow—with an arrow aimed at the chief's head.

I let out a hoarse cry. "Dax!"

His eyes dart in my direction. One of the guards outside the door reaches through the flap and grabs me by the hair. The pain is too much. I cry out as he drags me outside, and then lifts his hand to silence me. I brace for the blow, but the man lets out a painful yelp and lets go. He's staring at the arrow through the lower part of his arm, and the threat of vomiting forces me to look away. Faster than I even think possible, Dax has a new arrow aimed at the chief's head.

For a second, all I can hear are my short, panicked breaths before the chief barks an order. The second guard yanks me off the ground, frees my wrists, and drags me to where Dax stands waiting. His expression is unreadable.

The man shoves me forward and I think Dax will catch me before I fall, but he keeps his eyes and bow on target. I pull myself up and stand as close to Dax as possible.

My captor and Dax exchange a few angry words, and then Dax groans.

"Give him your bracelet," he says without a glance in my direction.

Surely, he's not talking to me. "What?"

He lets out an irritated sigh and repeats the sentence through his teeth. "He wants your bracelet. Give it to him."

I glance around at all the faces peering back at me, waiting for me to obey. But I can't seem to do it.

"Now!" Dax yells, and I jump.

Why the bracelet? It's the only gift Preston ever gave me, and the only piece of him I have left. Fighting back tears, I reach up with a shaky hand to unhook the clasp. I start to step forward, but Dax stops me.

"Stay where you are and toss it to him."

I do as he says. He spouts off a few more words before telling me to follow him, and then he slowly backs out of the clearing.

When we are safely hidden from view behind the bushes, Dax lowers his bow and grabs my hand. He starts running into the forest, pulling me behind him. I start to thank him, but he shushes me and orders me not to talk. We are moving fast and he seems to know exactly where he's going, but then he stops so abruptly to look behind us that I can't stop in time and plow right into him.

I don't even have a chance to apologize because he grabs what's left of my tank top and yanks it over my head before I can protest. He picks me up, running to a large tree where he shoves me in between the enormous root system that extends from the ground up along the trunk. Wedging himself inside the small space with me, he presses his body up against mine. I'm pinned between him and the inside of the trunk. We're completely hidden from view. One of his hands is pressed so hard over my mouth that I think I might smother.

The thick roots block out most of the light, but I can still see his face, so close to mine that only his hand separates our lips. He looks into my frightened eyes and holds one finger of his other hand to his lips, signaling me to not make a sound. Next, he reaches down and with precision, he pulls out his knife without a sound and grips the handle inches from my face.

I peel my eyes away from the six-inch blade to look into his blue eyes, but they aren't scared, just serious and intense, as if he's looking at me but concentrating on something else. And then I hear what he's been waiting for and must have heard before. Someone's approaching a few feet away, slowly and precisely, the sound barely audible over the loud beating of my heart as it pounds against him.

The heat and humidity is almost suffocating. I'm not sure if it's my sweat or his that drips onto my chest and trickles down on a slow course, torturing me as it rolls across my exposed skin. I should be horrified that I'm standing pressed against his smooth, bare chest in my bra, but all I care about is not being discovered by whatever hunts us a few feet away.

I can hear feet treading in circles around us, and I imagine the hunter studying broken branches and freshly pressed earth, looking for clues to our whereabouts. We stand motionless, staring at each other and listening intently. Finally, the sound of footsteps in the forest begins to fade away until I can't hear it at all.

I sigh in relief, but Dax shakes his head and remains perfectly still with his hand over my mouth. Wanting to protest, I feel my brow crease with concern, but his stern look holds me there.

After what seems like an excruciatingly long minute, I

hear the footsteps approach again in a casual run. I hold my breath as the sound gets closer than before, but instead of stopping, the footsteps continue on past us in the opposite direction from where they had come.

His body relaxes and his forehead rests against mine. After he's sure the hunter's gone, he removes his hand from my mouth, but not before he motions again for me to not speak by putting his finger to his lips. I nod in response, and he steps out from behind the root system. Grabbing my hand, he runs, still pulling me behind him.

For a few minutes I think we're heading back to the castle, but then we break through the trees onto the beach where he found me. I'm afraid to talk and he doesn't speak to me at all, so I follow him in silence until we reach the rocks and climb to the cave that's waiting at the top. Once inside, he turns to face me with his hands on his hips. His expression is unmistakably angry. A fine line separates his lips, his jaw is clenched tight, and I can't help but notice the sharp rise and fall of his tan, muscular chest. Air's rushing in and out of his lungs, and it's not because he's out of breath. His narrowed eyes make me feel like a small child about to be scolded for misbehaving badly.

MIDDAY: SERENDIPITY

"*Can I have my shirt?" she asks in a timid voice.*
"Damn it! What were you thinking?" My voice is harsher and louder than either one of us expects. I pull the tank top from my pocket and fling it at her.

"I'm sorry, I just didn't want to be alone," she says, pulling the tank top over her head. "I got scared that I might never see you again, so I went to find you. And then I thought I saw Preston and ran after him—but it wasn't him."

The fabric is torn down the front of her tank, exposing part of her chest. She fidgets nervously with both sides to cover herself. As she glances up at me, my anger melts into one of regret before I step forward to wrap my arms around her. The tears she'd been holding back stream down my chest.

"I'm sorry," I tell her and hope she'll only hear genuine kindness and not the fear in my voice. The jealousy I felt after reading about her first kiss pales in comparison to the jealous rage and possessiveness that tore through me after seeing her held captive by those men. I'm still amazed I was able to keep my composure because second to getting Ava back, I wanted to kill them all.

"I was just so angry," I say in a weak attempt to explain taking my anger out on her. "I told you it was dangerous.

They could have killed you. Are you alright?"

"Yes. I thought he was going to let me go, but then he attacked me and ripped my shirt so—I bit him. And he cut off a piece of my hair."

I suppress my anger and lean back to look at her with an amused grin. "So that's why his lip was bleeding?" I ask, and she nods. "Good. I hope it leaves a scar."

I brush the hair behind her ear the way I imagine Preston used to do. My fingers move to the spot under her chin, and I tilt her head to the side to confirm my eyes aren't deceiving me. There's a bright red mark on the side of her face that is starting to swell.

"What happened to your face? Did he *hit* you?" I try to keep the morbid shock and disdain out of my voice but fail miserably. She nods again, and I feel a muscle pop in my jaw. "Sit down. I'm going to get something to put on it. I'll be back in a minute."

She slides down the wall to wait and touches the tender spot on her cheek and jaw. I'm surprised her teeth aren't jarred loose. I storm out of the cave and rush to the rocks near the shore to grab a handful of cool kelp. Returning to sit down beside her, I gently press it to her cheek.

"I'm glad you're okay," I say, fighting the urge to kiss the angry red spot the way my stepmother used to do when I got hurt, but Ava's mind is far from noticing.

Her eyes meet mine and she quietly says, "That woman had on Preston's shirt. I followed her because I thought she was Preston. Why is she wearing his shirt?"

"I don't know," I tell her, but the shocking and realistic possibility I'm afraid to say creeps into my mind.

"They killed him, didn't they? He's really dead. Noooo..."

I pull her into my arms again and when she stops crying, I try to comfort her as I carefully wipe the tears from her face. "You don't know that. Maybe he took it off and they just found the shirt somewhere like I found the name tag."

I'm not sure if she really believes what I'm saying or if she knows I'm saying it for the sake of her sanity, but she clings to my words with every ounce of hope she has left and nods her head.

I wait for her to look up at me. "I shouldn't have yelled at you."

"No, I deserved it. That was really stupid," she says. "I started missing Preston because you were gone... then I started missing you too... so I panicked and decided to go look for you."

A flicker of happiness flashes inside my chest, but she looks down, ashamed, and I don't know if it's from her foolish behavior or her admitting to missing me. I laugh to distract her from her worried thoughts.

"I forgive you. Just promise me you won't go wandering off like that anymore. It's suicide. If you cross into their territory again, I assure you that we won't be so lucky."

She's quiet for a minute before she asks, "So how did you convince them to let me go?"

I could lie and get away with it, but what would be the point? Besides, Preston's forwardness worked well for him and I have a lot of catching up to do. I choose my words carefully and try to control the laugh tugging at my lips.

"Well... the arrow pointed at Chief Lambais' head definitely helped. And I told them in so many words... that you were my wife," I say hesitantly. "And that the entire Anwai tribe was out searching for you."

She pulls away and glares at me with her arms crossed. Her mouth falls open for double measure.

"Hey—it worked, didn't it?" I smile and pull her back towards me to hold the kelp on her cheek. "The other alternative was for me to tell them you were the main course for my next meal. And that would have ended in a case of finders keepers, losers weepers—you know what I mean?"

"Then why were they chasing us?" she says, and her tone suggests she's confident I'm holding back part of the story. And I am.

"Well, I ordered them to release you and told them you were my wife—"

"And?"

"Then the chief informed me that you had trespassed onto their land and so you were—fair game, so to speak." I sense her impatience and talk faster. "So I told him you were special, that I'd made a sacrifice to the spirits and they'd rewarded me by sending you. I told them you fell right out of the sky."

I explode into a fit of laughter, but she doesn't join me. How can she not laugh? That's hilarious.

"Seriously?" she says with one eyebrow raised. "That's what you told them?"

"Come on. You don't like that? I personally thought you falling from the sky was a nice touch. And it's probably not a lie." I laugh again and then stop. My attempt to make her laugh has made her think I'm insensitive. I clear my throat. "Sorry, I realize now that's not as funny as I initially thought it was."

Is it my imagination or is she trying to keep from smiling?

"So... who followed us?" she asks me.

"That was Zoron. Chief Lambai claimed that Zoron, his eldest son, had been making sacrifices to the spirits too. So in his and Zoron's opinions, the spirits had delivered you to *him*."

Her eyes widen in horror. "He was planning to make me his wife?"

"Don't flatter yourself. He would've had his fun with you and then when you refused to cooperate, they'd have killed you and served you as the main course. Why do you think they were starting a big fire in that pit? I'll tell you why. Because one of two things was going to get cooked, a pig for the wedding feast—or you."

I can tell she's shocked by my blatant honesty, and she takes the kelp from my hand to hold herself. I want to take it back because I love the way my hand feels against her cheek. Briefly, I entertain the thought of kissing her lower lip she's so intent on chewing, but the only thing that would accomplish is that I'd have a matching red cheek to go along with hers, compliments of the palm of her hand.

"Look, I told him I would personally be responsible for you and make sure you didn't trespass again, but that if he didn't release you, it would bring war to his tribe. He was contemplating my threat when you yelled my name."

I pause, remembering the chill her desperate scream left in my gut, and swipe a lock of wavy hair from my forehead before continuing.

"I could have gotten us both killed by taking my eyes off the chief, but when that loser raised his hand to hit you, I lost it. He's lucky I aimed for his arm or he would have been a goner. And Zoron may suffer a mysterious untimely death now that I know he laid his grubby fingers on you too." I peek up at her from under my lashes and force the hard line of my jaw to relax into a smile. "Anyway, Chief Lambai knows they're slightly outnumbered by the Anwai tribe, and he knows Chief Anwai thinks highly of me, so he didn't want to risk it. That's why he went with Zoron's suggestion to trade. I'm sorry about the bracelet. I know it means a lot to you, but it was that or my bow, and unless you tell me that bracelet could have summoned a ninja leprechaun, I clearly made the right choice. Zoron followed us, hoping to kill me and recapture you before we could make it back to Anwai territory. He sort of has a reputation for disobeying orders. As do you, apparently."

She exhales loudly. "Well, the entire ordeal was horrible," she says and looks down at her hands. "But thank you for rescuing me. Again."

"No problem."

An awkward pause falls between us, and I run my fingers through my hair while she fidgets with her torn shirt. Like an idiot, I feel the need to extinguish the silence.

"So which part was the worst for you?" I lean back against the rock wall with my arms resting on my knees. "Being strung up like a roasting pig on a stick, getting a taste of Zoron's rotten breath, or our half-naked bodies pressed up against each other inside the trunk of a tree? Cause I have to admit, the last part wasn't that bad for me."

I love the color and expression in her eyes. Just as predicted, they widen and then narrow to thin slits.

"You did that on purpose!"

"Did what on purpose?" I ask with complete sincerity because I'm appalled by her accusation. "I did what I had to in order to save our lives. You might prefer to be the wife of a savage over me, but I don't care to be an appetizer at the wedding."

"Well, was it really necessary to yank off my shirt?" she asks, apparently reminded of the embarrassing situation she'd been too upset to be mad about until now.

"Yes," I tell her. "That florescent pink shirt was like a beacon in the forest, flashing *meal of the day*. If your white shorts weren't camouflaged by dirt, I would have ripped them off too. I mean, maybe you didn't notice—but a vicious cannibal was pursuing us. Besides, you should be happy I removed your shirt without damaging it further. Although one could argue that the alterations are an improvement. I'm definitely not complaining. Maybe Zoron should go into fashion design."

The heat shows on her cheeks and she slugs me, but the small upturn of her lips makes taking a punch in the shoulder well worth it.

"Relax," I tell her. "I have an idea."

I reach for her foot, pull it into my lap, then untie the lace and remove it from her shoe. After doing the same with her other foot, I grab my knife and reach for her shirt.

"Do you trust me?" I say, asking permission with my eyes.

"With my life? Yes. With my clothes? No," she says with sly grin.

I laugh and scoot closer. Taking one side of the torn fabric in my hand, I use the knife to carefully puncture a row of tiny holes near the edge of the tear on both sides.

"So how did you find me?" she asks, and I wonder if she's trying to distract both of us from my fingers and gaze hovering so close to her exposed chest.

I glance up before answering and wish I could read her nervous thoughts. "I was perched on a branch with my bow aimed at a wild pig and the second I released the arrow, I heard you scream and almost fell out of the tree. The arrow got him in the leg instead of the chest and he took off into the trees, but I ran back to the castle as fast as I could. When I saw you weren't there, I went looking for you. I saw the tracks from your Vans and followed them straight to the Lamarai border."

She listens to my account and then understanding registers on her face. "So that's why you picked me up when Zoron was chasing us. You knew he was following my footprints." She studies me with her amazing eyes. "Wow. What would I do without you?"

"Uhm—drown. Get eaten by cannibals. Starve. Something along those lines." A wide smile that I'm sure looks arrogant pulls up at my lips. I thread the lace through the holes starting at the bottom and pull the sides together, finishing with a neat bow at the top.

She looks down at my patch job. "Thanks. You're awesome. Looks like Zoron might have a *Project Runway* competitor."

"Ha. Ha. Ha," I say, offering my hand to help her up. She follows me to the entrance of the cave.

"So what now?" she asks. Her stomach growls for the second time in the last five minutes.

"Now I—or *we*—have to go hunting and hope we don't run into any more cannibals. It's midafternoon, so the men from the tribe are probably done hunting, which will be to our benefit. But I'm not taking you in *that*. We need to find you something else to wear that's a little less neon. Maybe if we ask nicely, Roxy will loan you her only spare shirt." I cringe just thinking about it.

"Actually, I have another shirt in my backpack," she says, and the thought instantly cheers me up. I'd forgotten about the clothes that were at the bottom—right on top of her journal. My heart leaps into my chest.

"I'll go get them," she says, and I follow her back inside the cave. I'm so busted. I hold my breath while she pulls black board shorts and a gray T-shirt from her backpack. Standing up, she pauses to stare at me. *She knows!* What can I possibly say that will make this situation better?

My mouth jumps ahead of my brain and the word "What?" slips through my lips. *Brilliant, Dax.* I just gave the typical response every guy on the planet uses when caught red-handed, and I probably have the stupid dumbfounded look on my face to go along with it. My heart picks up pace while I wait for the accusations to go flying.

But she's looking at me like I'm the one missing something. It's the same look I get from Roxy sometimes, and she usually accompanies it with the word 'duh'. What does she want me to do? Is she waiting for me to admit what I've done?

"I need to change," she finally says, and relief spreads over me like a warm blanket.

"Go ahead, no one will see you." I wave my arm in

the direction of the beach. "I promise there isn't anybody around."

"But you're around."

The realization hits me and catches me off guard like an unexpected ocean wave from behind. "Right. Well, I just remembered something I have to take care of down by the beach, so you can change and I'll be back in a few."

I turn to leave. Whatever. Has she forgotten I've already seen her half naked? If she cares so much about privacy, maybe she should have stayed put in my secluded castle. Wait, did I just say that out loud? I glance over my shoulder before exiting the cave and judging by the grin on her face, my mumbling complaints didn't go unheard.

I find the same hiding spot on the beach as before, behind a rock that will provide me some cover but allow a good view of the cave so I can feed my new addiction without being discovered.

July 14

Preston picked me up this afternoon, and then we grabbed Chinese food before heading to Mr. C's house. Mr. Caruso has been in L.A. all weekend, so Preston and Kirk are staying there like they always do when he's away on business. We sat together in my favorite oversized lounge chair on the deck and ate the food straight from the box while watching the sunset in the sky.

I complained about having to work tomorrow and was cherishing every minute I had left with him. He acted surprised and said he thought I liked working for George. Then he fed me some noodles with his chopsticks and flashed a smug grin. I couldn't stop myself from telling him the job was great, but that Sergio was responsible for making me dread going to work. It felt good to get that off my chest.

He laughed and said, "Don't worry about him; he's harmless. And unfortunately, he won't be leaving Oceanview Aviation anytime soon. The perks of being Mr. C's nephew."

Can you believe it? I had no idea. So just like his uncle, I guess Sergio has money. That doesn't make him any more appealing to me, but it certainly explains why he's used to getting what he wants. Preston said he's Mr. C's personal mechanic, but George hired him no questions asked when he needed something else to do while Hotel Charlie was gone. Preston laughed when I told him I thought Sergio was creepy and that his staring makes me uncomfortable. "Of course he stares: he can't help himself." Preston said. "Maybe I should warn Georgie your good looks are a menace to the workplace."

He took the Chinese box from my hand, sat our food on the table beside him, and leaned in to kiss me... and we couldn't stop kissing! It's like Preston is making up for all the time lost when he thought he shouldn't be kissing me. When our lips finally parted, I melted into the chair and laid my head on his chest.

He laced his fingers through mine. We sat quietly for a minute before he offered to take me home, but I begged him to let me stay a little longer. I wasn't worried about the late hour—only that our time was running out. He kissed me on the forehead and told me to meet him on the top floor in five minutes. "And that swimsuit I told you to bring might come in handy." he said with a wink before he turned to stroll inside.

I escaped to the bathroom to change and then started up the stairs to the third floor. Turning at the landing, I spotted Preston's jacket hanging on the end of the railing and then halfway up the stairs lay his vest. I gripped the towel and stepped over it, but I stopped dead in my tracks when I noticed his shirt and bow tie puddled at the top of the stairs. I reached the fourth floor and looked down the hallway to the double doors at the end. One was cracked open, beckoning me, so I walked silently in my bare feet and entered the lavish master suite that consumed the entire floor.

The lights were dim and I could hear the gurgling of a Jacuzzi from the balcony just beyond the open French doors, so I took a step forward, but paused when I noticed Preston's pants sprawled sloppily in the middle of the floor next to his shoes and socks. My eyes followed the path leading from the pants to the gently waving curtains.

and my breathing stopped entirely. Right in front of the open door laid a pair of boxers and a hastily strewn undershirt. Of course, I could only assume one thing. Preston was waiting for me on the balcony—wearing absolutely nothing.

My chest filled with panic. I was totally unprepared for the situation and way out of my element, so I just hoped the hot tub was very, very large, and that Preston enjoyed a good game of rock-paper-scissors. I stepped outside and just as I expected, Preston was awaiting my arrival.

He looked up and invited me to join him in the enormous Jacuzzi. I couldn't take my eyes off his smooth, buff chest—chiseled to perfection and better than I'd imagined numerous times. I tossed the towel over the back of the chair and turned to step in. Pausing, I realized my previous worries about him seeing me in a bikini were nothing compared to the worries flying through my brain at that moment.

He started to stand up so my eyes clamped shut and one hand flew over them for double measure. Then he asked what was wrong and coaxed me to open my eyes in his gentle voice. My heart pounded like it might explode, but I peeked with one eye and then both flew open. He was wearing board shorts. I exhaled, let out a nervous laugh, and then reached for his outstretched hand. A big grin spread across his face at my misunderstanding. He burst out laughing, and I thought he'd never stop. When he finally did, he slid around next to me to drape an arm around my shoulders. He stared at me with a mischievous grin while the fingers of his other hand slid to the end of a dangling curl, and then continued to glide down my arm all the way to my wrist. His touch made goose bumps rise on my skin.

All my stress evaporated away with the steam that rose in the air, and I was on the verge of drifting off to sleep when he said my name. The bubbles had just shut off so the only sound was the low hum of the jets. I lifted my head to look at him, and that's when he said he'd been thinking about quitting his job with Mr. C to sail away somewhere. I literally stopped breathing. He was sitting so close that he must have noticed because then he asked me if I would come with him.

Of course I told him 'yes' without even thinking about it, and then asked him where we would go? He played with my hair as he talked and suggested we could start in France and then tour all around Europe, even mentioning that we could go to school there. I love the idea and know there's no way I can afford to go to school in Europe, but the offer made me ecstatic so I'm determined to find a way. Now I have something to look forward to in my future even if the dream is a distant one.

Ava is ready and waiting when I return to the cave. I look her over and nod my approval of her shorts and shirt. "That will work. Now stay close and try to be quiet."

16

MIDAFTERNOON: HEADS OR TAILS

*W*E DRINK WHAT'S LEFT OF THE WATER DAX BROUGHT this morning before I follow him along the beach and into the forest. Dark clouds have formed in the sky, and I hope the rain will cool me off. I braid my hair while we walk, plucking off a tiny vine to tie in a knot around the end of my braid.

Dax stops suddenly and squats down to look at some tracks in the mud. He points to some blood drops. "We can follow this trail and hope he didn't wander too far."

"What exactly are we looking for?" I ask in a whisper, trying to be quiet like he said.

"A wild boar," he says, "and I don't know about you, but I'm starving."

He walks with careful steps and keeps his eyes on the ground. I stay close so we won't get separated. Soon, we come to a small clearing where the trees and bushes are less dense. He holds up his hand to tell me to wait, so I lean against a tree to watch him.

He kneels down on one knee before pulling an arrow from his quiver to place against his bowstring. Then, in one fluid motion, he raises the bow and draws back the string without making a sound. He holds the bow steady, and I strain to see what he's aiming for in the sea of green.

A small, wild boar springs from the bushes a few feet in front of him and causes me to jump. Dax's arrow hits its intended target. After the second arrow pierces its chest, the boar falls to the ground, snarling and squealing.

Dax rushes to the pig and plunges his knife into its neck at the base of its skull. I watch, fascinated, as he slits its throat and then digs a hole with his hands in the soft earth next to the bleeding pig. He slices the belly open, starting just below the neck, then cuts all the organs and guts free, tossing them into the hole. I cringe, squeeze my eyes shut, and turn my head to lean further into the base of the tree.

When I'm sure the worst is over, I open my eyes. Dax turns to me, but the victory grin drops from his face. Without any warning, he throws the knife. The blade strikes the tree just inches above my head, and my hands fly over my mouth to muffle a startled scream.

"What was that for?" I hiss at him, mortified and staring at him in shock.

"That was me rescuing you for a third time," he says, stepping forward to pull me away from the tree.

Dax's knife impaled the head of an enormous snake only inches above where my head was moments ago. The body continues to twitch and writhe on the branch. I shudder and take another step back.

"I guess you weren't kidding about having bad luck. I mean, that's only the third one of those I've seen in the three years I've been here, and you just managed to cozy up next to one. Unbelievable."

"Thanks," I say, my voice barely audible. Talking about my bad luck reminds me of the bracelet and the thought puts a damper on my mood.

"You're welcome," he tells me. "But I'm keeping a tally so you can repay me at a later date."

He must sense my saddened disposition because his

smirk vanishes. Using some vine, he ties the wild boar's feet together and slings the pig over his shoulder. He strolls to the tree and pulls his knife from the bark to let the dead snake fall to the ground.

"Time to meet the tribe." I'm surprised when he hands me his bow and arrows along with his spear and starts walking. He drags the snake behind him. "Let's hope my idea works. Just stay close," he says.

"Wait," I say.

Dax stops and turns around.

"What if it doesn't work?"

He laughs. "Then our teeth will make a nice necklace on some cannibal's neck."

I'm shocked by his words and also his nonchalant attitude. "You mean they'll kill both of us? Why would they kill you?"

"Because I'll probably die trying to save you like your knight in shining armor," he says with an amused grin. "Any more questions? This pig isn't getting any lighter,"

"Yeah. You said you had a plan. What is it?"

He blinks. "Well... since you don't speak Lamarai, all you need to do is stand there and leave all the talking to me. I don't know how good your acting skills are, but if you could look like a goddess who might strike everyone with lightning or catch something on fire with your mind—that would help a lot." He laughs in response to the widening of my eyes. "Okay, scratch that. Just try not to look scared."

"That's it?"

"That's it. Now let's go."

I follow him through the trees and wonder how I will force myself not to look terrified. I'm careful not to step on the snake or the trail of blood dripping from the neck of the slaughtered boar, catching myself studying the perfect lines of Dax's tan, muscular back as he walks in front of me.

He's so strong. The image of bravery and confidence all rolled into one—with a wild boar slumped over his left shoulder and a huge, venomous snake at his side. The colors seem unrealistic—the stark contrast of the forest greens, the bright red blood of the boar, Dax's corn silk golden hair, even the striking vibrant orange pattern running down the snake's body looks like someone painted it on. The combination is visually appealing like a piece of art, one that I could almost imagine hanging in a collection in a gallery.

I'm struggling to keep up with him, which is pathetic considering he's carrying a wild pig and a snake, but I'm so tired—the stress of this seemingly endless day is taking its toll. The air is hot and muggy, and I wipe my forehead on the sleeve of my shirt. Maybe I'm foolish to have so much confidence in Dax keeping me alive.

The trees grow thin, and floating houses come into view in the distance like the ones I saw at the Lambai village. The clearing is filled with villagers hanging out and working on various tasks, but my smile is greeted by blank stares. A few children stand near women adorned with long skirts made of feathered palm leaves and coconut shells worn in a bikini-type fashion. I'm fascinated by the geometric designs tattooed all over their arms, necks, and faces.

The spear feels awkward in my hand. My heart pounds as the tribe people gather around us and eye me with what I hope is curiosity and not a morbid desire to chew on my arm. I look to Dax for some type of moral support, but he pays no attention. He's stopped in front of a ladder that extends sixty feet in the air to a large house at the top of a tall tree. I pry my gaze away from the two skulls standing guard on top of bamboo sticks on either side of the ladder, and focus on the man climbing down to meet us. Two men grab me from behind and take Dax's spear along with his bow and quiver from my shoulder. Two more men appear with bows drawn and their arrows aimed at my chest.

"Dax!"

He drops the boar and snake, hurling words at the men with the arrows and the ones holding my wrists, and then turns his attention to the man climbing down the ladder. The man jumps the last few feet to the ground and faces us with his arms folded across his chest. Various bones and tusks adorn his face as piercings, and the necklace of teeth that hangs around his neck makes my pulse skyrocket. On top of his head is a large headdress made of black and blue feathers, and just like the other men in the village, a short skirt of small palm leaves hangs from his waist—the only thing that keeps him from being naked.

I assume this is the chief. He stands silent and stares at me while Dax talks. I'm trying not to panic and force myself to stay calm when all I want to do is fight them off and run. Dax is doing all the talking. He picks up the snake and drops it at the chief's feet. The chief barks an order, and a man hurries forward and drags the snake away. There's an uncomfortable silence. The chief's eyes dart from Dax to me and now the tribe people stare at him, waiting for what I assume will be some sort of decision that involves my fate.

The chief says something to Dax, and Dax nods in reply before they lock hands in what looks like some sort of handshake. I exhale as the men lower their arrows.

Dax hoists the boar onto his shoulder and grabs my hand to lead me towards a group of trees on the far side of the clearing. My paranoia won't let me stop looking over my shoulder every five seconds, and I almost miss the large structure in the trees. The house was built to blend in with the treetops rather than tower above them.

Dax steps through the trees, and the whole house

comes into view. It's an intricate web of different structures all connected by hanging bridges and walkways—not as high up as the other tree houses in the village, but still sits a good fifty feet from the ground. I notice the narrow and very steep ladder leading to the main part of the house, and I smile. It would have been impossible for Dax to carry me up the ladder-type stairs.

"Roxy?" he calls out, but he's answered with silence.

A group of curious children gawk at us from the edge of their village, and one of the older ones runs over to say something to Dax.

"It seems she got impatient and went to find some fruit."

Part of me is disappointed but mostly, I'm relieved.

"Well, here it is. Would you like a full tour now or would you rather wait until after we eat?" he asks, his dimples showing through the dirt on his face.

I'm extremely curious but worried I won't make it to the top without eating first, and my legs are so tired they feel like they could give out at the least bit of strain. "It's very fascinating, but I'm pretty hungry," I say, hoping I won't offend him.

"Me too," he agrees. He sees me looking around nervously at the children who have gathered to stare at me. "Do you want to go back to the beach? It's a little more private."

I nod, so he waves to the children and takes me back to the small cave that waits above the rocks on the beach. He gathers various things along the way, which he hands me to carry since he still carries the boar. I have a bunch of greens in my arms and some fruit I've never seen before. Near the beach, he picks up a coconut.

"So was that the chief?"

He smiles. "If you're talking about the guy that looks like he fell face-first into a pile of sharp bones before a peacock landed on his head, then yes."

"What did you tell him?"

"You don't want to know," he says, and I don't miss the amusement creeping across his lips.

"Actually, I do."

He picks up the pace because it's starting to rain, and I hurry to keep up.

"I told him I found you on the beach, and you were alone." His guilty grin tells me there's more.

"And?" I prompt.

"I told him you used special powers to lure that snake out of the tree so you could kill it."

"Very funny. What did you really tell him?"

He laughs. "Funny? That was brilliant. I painted you as a goddess who will offer protection to the people of the tribe."

"Why would you tell them a ridiculous lie like that?"

"Trust me; it's better than my original plan. Until the snake came along, I was contemplating telling them you were a mermaid." He laughs. "But to pull that one off, you'd have to play the part, and something tells me you wouldn't be willing to cooperate. Maybe you should consider yourself lucky the snake showed up because plan A involved you walking into the Anwai village not wearing any clothes."

My mouth falls open in shock. "Both ideas are absurd."

"Maybe to you, but not to them. They don't have books and resources like we do. They rely on legends of spirits and gods with powers that have been passed down from generations. Besides, two things make women valuable on this island—bearing children and helping gather food and prepare it. I just used a different approach to make you a valuable contributor so that he'd allow you to stay on the island with me and not kill you for dinner. The special powers and protection bit was just an added bonus."

"Oh," I say, stunned that I was so quick to put my life in Dax's hands with complete trust as we stood among the Anwai. "Then thanks."

He pauses for a moment. "And I might have also mentioned something about making you my wife."

I punch him in the arm and drop the coconut and some of the fruit on the ground in the process. "What is wrong with you?" I ask. I gather all the food I dropped and hurry to catch up with him.

It's hard to tell over the sound of the rain, but I think he's laughing. By the time we reach the cave, we're both drenched from the steady drizzle. I stagger inside. After sitting the items down on a large palm leaf, I collapse onto my backpack to watch Dax make quick work of starting a fire. There's a stack of firewood I hadn't noticed before. Since I've been on this island, I've forgotten about my commitment to being observant. But it seems being observant here is more important than ever, and I make it my new top priority, right next to finding Preston.

Dax pulls some vine from his pocket. In a matter of minutes, he's built a spit over the fire. He sits the empty pitcher outside in the rain, and then walks outside with his knife and the pig, promising to return shortly. I stare at the flames, lost in thought, as the day's adventures race through my head.

Things would have turned out very differently if it weren't for Dax. At least he knows I'm a magnet for danger. Every time trouble found me in California, Preston was never around to witness it. Like when Sergio decided to grace me with his presence or when I began noticing the constant appearance of a black car everywhere I went. Even the mysterious notes I started receiving always showed up a day or two after he left. Funny how my old worries have just been replaced by new ones.

Dax is still gone, and the fire is dwindling. Before he

left, he asked me to add small pieces of wood to keep it going. I got so wrapped up in my thoughts, I forgot. I grab some small pieces and toss them into the fire. However, the flames are smothered and now only a few red coals glow below them.

In a panic, I look around the cave and grab my backpack so I can tear paper from my sketchpad, but the envelope containing my paycheck catches my eye first. I sigh with relief. Tossing the paycheck to the side, I tear the envelope into small pieces, tucking them under the wood next to the coals and watching them catch fire. The paper burns, but it's not enough. The flames start to drop. I need more paper. Reaching for the piece of folded paper, I start to toss it on top of the fire but notice large, typed words in the middle of the page.

DON'T GET ON THE PLANE

I re-read the words at least ten times and am no less shocked the last time. Why didn't I listen? And when did I first read this warning? I toss the letter on top of the wood in frustration and watch it ignite. The flames get higher and I replay the hours before takeoff over in my mind, but the memory always stops in the same place.

Dax returns and sits the pitcher in front of me, filled to the brim with fresh rainwater. I thank him and give him a weak smile, hoping he mistakes my distress for exhaustion. The rain has washed the dirt and blood off his hands, chest, and back, and now only water droplets remain. After studying my face for a brief moment, he seems to notice my mood change and busies himself with preparing dinner.

He positions the skinned pig on the spit over the fire, cutting off a few pieces to skewer on small sticks. Tearing up the greens and fruit, he uses the juice of the fruit as a dressing, and slides some to me on a large palm leaf.

We eat in silence while we wait for the skewered pieces

of meat to be done. The discovery earlier consumes my thoughts. The note was wrapped around my paycheck. My mind races with multiple possibilities but reaches only one conclusion. All the notes must have been from George.

Dax

JUST AFTER DARK: SECRETS

THE FIRE HAS GAINED AVA'S UNDIVIDED ATTENTION. Every time I glance up at her, she's staring at the flames like she's waiting for Preston to jump out of the center and yell, *'Surprise!'*. Whatever thoughts have taken over her mind won't be leaving without some coaxing from me.

"Great job on the fire," I say, "I'm impressed. Maybe you really do possess magical powers. I'll tell Chief Anwai you are *Ava*—goddess of fire and snakes." I laugh, but she barely manages a smile.

Her pleasant mood disappeared when I left to go out in the rain, and now I'm cursing myself for leaving her alone. What happened in those few short minutes? She's not talking at all. Maybe she discovered her journal is missing and is angry about my betrayal. I mentally prepare to apologize and give the journal back along with a lame excuse of uncontrollable curiosity, but then I see a tear trickle down her cheek that she tries to quickly wipe away unnoticed. Of course. How ridiculous of me to think I might be the source of her worried thoughts.

"So, what was he like?"

"Preston was perfect," she says quietly.

I was right. "No one's perfect."

She frowns, but then her expression softens. "Well, almost perfect. Except for his annoying habit of tricking me and taking advantage of my gullibility."

Her fire-staring trance has been broken, but now she looks down at her hands.

"Where were you headed?" I ask with caution, trying to avoid the wrath she inflicted on me yesterday.

"We were flying to Australia, to pick up Preston's boss." Her own words trigger another thought and she looks up at me, her expression full of hope. "So if the plane crashed and we never arrived... Mr. Caruso would have sent out a search party to look for us. How stupid of me. I should have stayed on the beach today," she says in hurried sentences.

I pause before answering, knowing I'll probably regret what I'm about to say. "We would've heard a plane. Besides, they search the water looking for survivors, and like I told you, I'm sure this island tends to be avoided. Mostly because they figure if you ended up here, you wouldn't have survived for long."

"Well, if that's true, a search team could have found Preston, Kirk, and Anna already. Then Preston will come looking for me for sure. Maybe he just took his shirt off in the water, and it washed up on shore along with his name tag."

She's beaming with happiness from her conclusion but as hard as I try, my voice doesn't match her enthusiasm when I tell her, "Maybe." After an awkward pause, I say, "So you still don't remember anything?"

She shakes her head.

"Well, I'm not surprised you can't remember. You must have had a concussion. You'll remember eventually, but it might take a while. But I think it's a safe bet to assume the plane crashed. Everything I found was on the plane, right? And you were wearing an aviation life vest, so at some point, you must have known you might crash."

"Yeah, and now I think it may have been intentional."

"Intentional? Are you serious? Like someone wanted you to crash?" I catch myself scooting closer to her. "No way. Why would you think that?"

"It's a long story."

"Oh, right. And I'm super busy. Let me check my schedule and see if I have time to hear it." She peeks up at me. "Wait, that's right. I don't have a schedule." I beg with my dimples. "Come on. It's the least you can do to repay me for saving you from certain death four times—actually five, if you count the fire-breathing dragons ten years ago." Her contagious laughter echoes through the cave, and then she takes the cooked meat I offer her with puppy-dog eyes. "Please?"

She sighs, starting with her moving to California after her parents died and then moving on to tell me about getting the job at Oceanview Aviation while I pretend the info is something I don't already know.

"So that's where I met Preston," she says.

Here we go. I brace myself and hope the verbal version is less gushy than the written one so I won't end up gagging on my food. But she's not gushing. In fact, she's stopped talking and is glancing around the cave and at me like she's debating on telling me anymore. My thoughts slip out of my mouth.

"That's it?"

"No. It's just that I've never talked about Preston to anyone." She pauses to take a deep breath before exhaling slowly. "Shortly after we started... you know, dating... I started getting anonymous notes, like warnings."

Acting is not something I'm good at. Neither is lying.

"What did the notes say?" I ask, with a sudden interest in the coconut I hold in my hands.

"The first one said, '*Be careful—he knows your secret*', the second one said, '*You're being watched*', and then the third

153

said, '*Don't push your luck*', and—"

My laughter interrupts her. "Don't push your luck. That's funny." I'm laughing alone, so I stop and clear my throat. "Sorry, please continue."

"Anyway, the last note said, '*Don't get on the plane*'."

What? Is she messing with me? Because that's not cool. Man, and I got sucked right in like a Boy Scout waiting on the edge of his log to hear a ghost story around the campfire.

"Right. I see how it is," I tell her. "If you want to mess with me, that's fine. But next time a fire-breathing dragon shows up, you're on your own."

"I'm not kidding. I wish I was," she says, watching me thrust the coconut onto a rock and then wedge the blade of my knife in the crack to pry it open.

I hand her a piece. "If that's really what the last note said, then why'd you get on the plane?"

"I just found the last note in my backpack while you were outside earlier. I don't remember reading it, so I must have opened the envelope after we were already flying. Unless you opened it."

"What? No. I didn't—open any envelope." *Just your personal journal that I've been studying like a weekly churchgoer studies a bible.*

"Well then, I must have opened it too late."

"Wow." I crack a smile to lighten the mood. "That is some wicked luck. Did you tell Preston about the other notes?"

"I tried, but he laughed them off and blamed it on a secret admirer. At first, I thought the notes were from him, but he denied sending them. I didn't want him to worry, so I went along with his theory even though they didn't have an admirer type of feel. I never told him exactly what they said."

"So who do you think sent them?"

"I know who sent them now. I just don't know why."

"Well, obviously they knew someone wanted you dead."

She flashes a look that makes me glance away. My blatant honesty must be irritating her. Preston would probably say nothing of the sort. He'd tell her I'm wrong before assuring her not to worry about it, then promise to make it all better and take care of her. But the truth is, he failed to take care of her, and now here she is.

"So why would someone want you dead? Besides the fact that you would make an excellent meal," I say, adding more wood to the fire.

"I'm not sure, but it could have something to do with a trust my parents left me."

"So there are benefits to being poor. I didn't think so until now. So is that the secret?" I wait for her to answer, but she stubbornly refuses. "What? Are you're afraid I'll tell someone? Relax. Roxy and I don't have slumber parties. We don't sit around the fire sharing girly gossip while we braid each other's hair. Spill it already."

Her eyes narrow. "Why do you want to know?"

"I'm just curious," I say. "And maybe I'm wondering if I should sleep with one eye open."

"So if I was a wanted fugitive, would you think twice about rescuing me next time?"

"No. Because judging by your reaction when I slaughtered this pig, I don't think you killed anyone, at least not intentionally." I lie down on my side to face her and prop my head up with one hand. "But I've been wrong before, and I'm all alone with you in this cave. So if you do decide to kill me in my sleep, do me a favor and grant my dying wish first. I want a kiss, and make sure to make it a good one." The comment elicits a piece of coconut shell being thrown at my head. "Come on. Don't hold out on me. Everyone has a secret."

"Do you?" she asks.

"Of course. I have a few. One of them I already shared with you—the castle. Now it's *our* secret."

"What's another one?"

"I asked you first."

"Fine. I found out my parents adopted me. They weren't really my parents."

"Whatever. I don't believe that for a second. You look exactly like your mom."

"That's because she has a twin sister, who's my birth mom. But she died right after I was born, and her death is still a mystery. Some think she committed suicide, but witnesses claim she was murdered. My parents never told me the truth, and I think they were trying to protect me from something or someone. Maybe from the person I was being warned about. I discovered the secret after my parents died. I just think it's strange, you know, that they didn't tell me. And her obituary doesn't say anything about me. It's like I didn't exist, to her at least."

"That's kinda weird, but it doesn't seem like something worth killing over," I tell her, but then I can't help saying, "And speaking of killing, I guess this means I won't be getting my dying wish since you're not secretly planning to kill me in my sleep."

She shakes her head. I see the hint of a smile before she crisscrosses her legs and takes another bite of coconut.

"So tell me another one of your secrets," she asks, waiting patiently for a response.

"Okay." I make a dramatic pause. "My name is Dax, and I'm a coconut-aholic. I've been this way for three years, and some days are harder than others." I give her a sideways glance, and then burst out laughing at her taken-off-guard expression. She laughs too and chucks another small piece of coconut at my chest.

"So where were *you* going before you ended up here?" she asks.

"We were running away to Australia. My stepmother was convinced that someone was trying to kill her, but I think she was just crazy. That's hereditary, you know—keep that in mind when you meet Roxy tomorrow. Anyway, she had a lot of money so she bought a boat and made my dad take boating classes. Then she convinced him to take us away. I was mad about it for a long time. I resented her for taking me away from my friends and my perfect life, until I figured out that anger just eats away at you, little by little, until it consumes you and you can't enjoy anything. So I let it go, but Roxy refuses to."

I sit up to rotate the pig, and then continue. "Roxy had a boyfriend in California, and like you, she thought the world revolved around him. I tried to console her on our trip by telling her there were plenty of other guys, and she'd find some hot Australian guy. Of course, she makes me eat those words now until I choke on them, almost on a daily basis."

After a minute of silence, I tell her, "Well, I'm beat," and grab the life vest by the wall to tuck under my head. "Being your knight in shining armor and rescuing you two times in one day is a taxing job."

I close my eyes and picture her rolling hers before curling up a few feet away. It takes her a long time to fall asleep and when she finally does, I silently flip to the page in her journal bookmarked with a small piece of vine.

July 19

I'm still super irritated about my notebook. The whole incident might have ruined my week if Preston hadn't picked me up at noon today and drove to a scenic spot overlooking the beach. He brought a picnic lunch and we sat on a blanket, eating sandwiches and enjoying the view. He fed me a grape and then said, "So, Miss April. Tell me something I don't know about you. What's your biggest fear?"

Losing you and being alone again is what I thought, but I couldn't say it out loud so I decided to go with my second biggest fear. I told him I thought I was being followed.

His mouth twitched on one side, and then he shot me a narrowed glance. "By who? Your secret admirer?" he said, trying to lighten the mood. I told him about the black car and the second note that said I was being watched. The concern on his face lasted for only a moment before his expression relaxed. His thoughts led him to some conclusion that erased his own worry, but not mine.

He glanced over his shoulder and then back to me. "Do you see the black car now?" he asked. I looked in every direction and started to feel relieved, but then I caught a glimpse of a black car below us, parked on the side of the road. It was a Mercedes, but from that distance, I couldn't tell if it was the same one. I wanted to tell him about the library but I'm sure my paranoia is just getting the best of me, so I struggled to think of something else to say. Before I could answer, he said, "My biggest fear is that you worry too much," and turned my face to his.

His eyes dropped to my lips at the same time mine fell to his, and my heart swelled in my chest, pounding harder and faster as he leaned closer. My worries about the car were immediately forgotten as his hand slid across my stomach to rest at my waist. He kissed me tenderly, but when he pulled away, I caught sight of that stupid, black car. "What if someone is watching us right now?" I said, regretting it immediately.

He blinked at me and then his lips curved into a mischievous grin. "Then let them watch," he told me. He casually reached for a grape to put it in my mouth. "Now that you have a secret admirer, that means I have competition," he told me with a playful smirk before he mumbled that whoever it was couldn't be much of a looker if he was resorting to secret notes. Then, out of the blue, he asked, "Do you want to go to a party tomorrow night?"

I hesitated, wondering if it was some sort of trick question, but then he explained that Kirk's mom owns an art gallery in L.A. and she's having a private exhibit next Friday, an opening party for an up-and-coming artist. It's invitation only—an exclusive reception with food, music, art, and an auction. After I agreed to go, he gathered everything up and said we had to go downtown to pick up his tux.

When we arrived at the formal boutique, a curvy, platinum-blonde came rushing toward us. She greeted Preston with a peck on the cheek and a, "Hello, darling," then turned to look at me. She was tall and slim, making the stiletto heels seem unnecessary. I felt simple and plain standing next to her and hoped Preston wouldn't notice. He gave my hand a squeeze before asking her to find me a formal gown to wear to the party. I must say she definitely knows what she's doing because the elegant, white gown fits like a satin glove. Eloquent scrolls of black rhinestones mixed with a trail of glitter run down one side, and the back drapes to the floor and pools behind me. I can hardly wait for tomorrow.

I purposely skip the next entry and bookmark the entry after. The last thing I want to read about is how Preston looked like a GQ model in his designer tux, or how they danced all night until the clock struck midnight and Ava ran down the stairs and left her glass slipper behind.

Yeah. I'm jealous.

I close my eyes and try to imagine her in that dress, the smooth satin hugging her skin and making her look curvy in all the right places. Now I'm picturing myself in a tux, my hands gliding over her waist, the thin, silky layer of fabric separating my hands from her soft skin. I'd pull her close on the dance floor and keep her pressed against me, and then I'd kiss her until she forgot there was anyone else around.

18

Preston

JUST BEFORE MIDNIGHT: THE LOTTERY

KIRK ALMOST HAD A NERVOUS BREAKDOWN WHEN I told him about the cannibal village and not only is he refusing to come exploring with me tomorrow, he's demanding I stay put. He even ratted me out. I wish that guy would man up. He has to know the only reason Anna is giving him the time of day is because he's the only available guy on the freaking planet considering the circumstances.

I'm so irritated. Even his snoring is grating on my nerves. Nothing like being stranded somewhere with your best friend to shed light on all the annoying habits you never noticed or cared about before.

I need to calm down.

But I'm so pissed that he ratted me out. What happened to loyalty? He claims he did it because he doesn't want anything to happen to me. Whatever. I think that knock on the head during the crash turned him into a freaking girl.

Loyalty.

That's funny. I guess I'm not the person to judge anyone when it comes to loyalty. If Sergio were here, he'd be the first one to point that out. I should have put him in the hospital when I had the chance, and maybe things would be different. I wanted to kill him for the way he stalked Ava, but who could blame him? She was amazing.

I remember how exquisitely beautiful she looked the night of the art reception. When I went to pick her up, she opened the door. I took off my sunglasses and examined her from top to bottom. It was a risk to take her out in public looking so good because she'd attract attention and that was the last thing I needed, but at that moment, nothing was going to change my mind.

On the way to L.A., I glanced in the side mirror and saw the black Mercedes three cars back. Ava saw it too so I took her hand and told her not to worry. I then talked about what still needed to be done to the sailboat to distract her and get her to relax.

The art gallery is an exquisite model of modern architecture, and I know Ava was impressed. People dressed in formal attire were scattered everywhere in various groups, engaged in casual conversation, and a live band played on one side of the room. In front of the stage, a few people were dancing, and servers walked around with trays of gourmet finger food and goblets of champagne. All along the walls were fine pieces of art.

I spied Kirk standing on a loft balcony from across the room. He waved cheerfully before stepping behind a wall and reappearing on the main level to make his way through the crowd. He gave Ava a big hug and gave me a cheap shot to the gut. Kirk told Ava to make sure I bought something, and then gave me the two fingers at the eyes 'I'm watching you' point before he walked away.

We walked around to look at the art pieces and paused by a picture of a large, purple cobra, emerging from piles of money and looking as though it might strike and jump right off the canvas. Just below the head, the snake morphed into the muscular upper torso of a man. Ava and I looked at each other and snickered at the couple in front of us debating the hidden meaning.

"Interesting," I said in a hushed voice, and she nodded in agreement. That was when I saw it. "That's it."

She followed my gaze to a smaller painting with a bright red elephant holding a four-leaf clover in its trunk on a completely black background. We stood in front of the painting, humored by the artist's interpretation of good luck and fortune.

I winked and said it would be a perfect addition to Miss April. She agreed until she glanced at the price displayed underneath the title. Her eyes widened in perfect synch with her mouth, but then Kirk came bouncing up behind us to slap a sold sign on it.

"Excellent choice, buddy," he said.

I sarcastically thanked him before lowering my voice to ask, "Did you make the arrangement we talked about?"

Kirk smiled. "Of course, who's the man?" and then told me to give him the 'signal' after the auction that would be starting in a few minutes. He thanked Ava over his shoulder for helping out and then headed for a group summoning him on the other side of the room. That was an idiot move on his part but, luckily, she didn't catch on to his comment.

I led her to the middle of the dance floor and wrapped my arms around her waist to pull her close. Flashing a smile at her, I lowered my lips to her ear. "I feel sorry for the artist," I whispered. She looked at me in confusion. I told her the pieces weren't getting the attention they deserved with her in the room because "no one can take their eyes off you long enough to look at the art."

It was definitely a cheesy line, but the distraction worked. When the song ended, Kirk took the stage. After a quiet round of applause, he thanked everyone for coming, and then he announced it was time to proceed with the event everyone had been waiting for. He held up a bowl and explained that it contained the names of ten eligible bachelorettes attending the party that night, and one lucky girl would be chosen to be auctioned off to the highest bidder. The proceeds of each and every bid go to charity, but only the highest bid is the lucky winner of a romantic dinner with the chosen bachelorette.

Kirk said, "Drum roll, please."

It was fascinating to watch her mind put the pieces together. I knew she assumed the auction was for the art, but after his speech, she must have realized the beautiful women that filled the room were the eligible bachelorettes. Men gathered in front of the stage, and the live band obliged with a drum roll as Kirk swirled his hand around in the bowl. He pulled out a white slip of paper and examined it before leaning into the microphone.

"And the lucky bachelorette is... Miss Ava Starr!"

It was a perfectly orchestrated masterpiece.

Men were clapping and cheering, glancing in every direction to spot the girl they were waiting to bid on. She glanced around too, and then noticed Kirk motioning her to join him. Over the calm applause of the men, he mouthed the words, "Come on, Ava," and her face flushed.

Yeah. That's what he'd meant when he thanked her for helping. She turned to glare at me with my guilty grin, but then I could see her anger dissipate and be replaced with a wave of panic.

"Don't worry, Miss April," I told her, "I don't like to lose."

I winked and nudged my head in Kirk's direction. The applause died down, and Kirk spoke into the microphone again, telling her not to be shy and to "come on up." Horrified, she made her way to the front and took her place on the stage next to Kirk.

Kirk read from his cue card using information he acquired from her calendar blurb—that she was a recent high school graduate who moved from colorful Colorado to sunny California to try her luck in an exciting career of aviation and modeling, making sure to point out that she was currently featured in Oceanview Aviation's upcoming calendar.

Kirk continued with, "An outdoor enthusiast and an all-star athlete, accompanied by her 4.0 GPA, make her a true all-American girl. There will be no shortage of conversation over dinner with Ava; just don't arm wrestle her unless you want to lose." Snickers ran through the crowd. Kirk started the bid at one-hundred dollars, and an offer shot up near the back of the room. Then a hand popped up near the front with a bid of two hundred. She watched me stand there with my hands in my pockets.

Then she did something that surprised me. She started across the stage, got to the end, and posed. Releasing the clip holding her hair in a twist, she shook her head so the long, brown waves fell down her back. She flipped her hair and spun around, finishing in another pose, lips in a slight pout, then tilted her head and looked the audience over through her hair that covered one eye.

It was so hot.

Whistles and hoots emerged from the men, and hands shot up followed by shouts of multiple bids. For a second, I wondered if I'd have to jump on stage and become her personal bodyguard. Kirk's mouth popped open for a second, but then a satisfied grin shot across his excited face. He was thrilled.

The bids came pouring in, and she made her way across the stage again. Now the bids were up to eight hundred. Her hips swayed back and forth with the gracefulness of a pro. I could tell she was so nervous that she probably thought she might puke, but she held her chin high, placed one hand on her hip, and blew me a long, exaggerated kiss off the other.

The crowd of sophisticated men went wild. Hands flew up and the bidding skyrocketed. Nine hundred. Twelve hundred. Fifteen. I decided to have a little fun and wait until the last second to bid. She was horrified.

She walked to the center and stood next to Kirk, forcing a big smile even though I knew she was wondering if I would really let her to go to dinner with one of the strange bachelors.

"Five thousand!" someone yelled from the back of the room, and I recognized the voice immediately. Irritation boiled to the surface but as usual, I kept my cool.

The curious stares of the other men led Ava right to the one who threw out such a ridiculously high bid. Sergio stood near the back in a black tux the same color as his hair.

"Five thousand going once..." Kirk said. Her eyes darted back and forth between Sergio and me. "Five thousand going twice..." Her eyes closed in preparation for what must have seemed like a death sentence. Then, at the last second, I shouted, "Ten thousand!" and she exhaled as shocked whispers flew through the crowd before it fell silent.

Kirk beamed from ear to ear. I wanted to look over my shoulder, past the bewildered faces of the other women, to see Sergio's lips that I knew were pressed in a hard line as his eyes pierced into the back of my head with a vengeance. Kirk was saying, "Ten thousand going once... ten thousand going twice... Congratulations to bidder number twenty-three." Afterwards, he thanked all the bidders for their generous donations and gave instructions for payment.

Sergio's icy-cold stare followed me to the counter to settle up. He was crazy if he thought I would actually share her with anyone, especially someone like him.

I paid and turned to find Ava face to face with him. My irritation boiled into rage. He thinks replacing that skull earring with a diamond makes him look respectable, but he's nothing more than a wolf in sheep's clothing. I couldn't make my way through the crowd fast enough. He slid one hand around her waist, grabbed her hand with the other to dance, and whispered something in her ear. She tried to push him away subtly, but he tightened his grip and pulled her closer. I was going to kill him right there in front of that crowd of very sophisticated people.

She glanced around, and relief swept across her face when she saw me approaching. I was one dancing couple away when a hand caught my arm.

"Preston." Kirk's mom offered me a kiss on the cheek. Her timing was terrible. "I'm so glad you could make it. Kirk tells me that beautiful girl has caught your eye, and it must be true for you to bid such a ridiculous amount. Please, you have to introduce me."

"Later, I promise," I said, swallowing back my impatience. "I promised her this dance, and someone else has beat me to it." I winked and forced a smile. She laughed and started to say something, but I quickly turned and snuck up behind Sergio.

"I'm sure you're thrilled that pilot boy just paid an insane amount of money to take you to dinner," I'd overheard him say to Ava. "Kind of unnecessary if you ask me. Unless it's part of his master plan." She saw me standing behind him, but she played it cool and asked what plan he was referring to. "The plan to keep your head in the clouds so you won't figure out he's too good to be true. May I suggest you save yourself the heartache and go to dinner with me instead?"

"And may I suggest you take your hands off my girlfriend unless you want to be permanently disabled," I said, stepping into view.

Sergio hesitated before he dropped Ava's hand and took a step back. He slid his hands in his pockets and cocked his head to the side.

"Girlfriend?" he asked with an evil grin. "Is that what you're calling her?" he taunted. "Because I can think of some better words to describe what she is to you."

I wanted to punch him in the face. "Careful. No one likes a sore loser." I draped an arm over Ava's shoulder and started to lead her into the crowd, but Sergio laughed and called out to me over the music, "You're the one who should be careful and decide where your loyalty lies. Switching sides always comes with a cost."

I distracted Ava with my lips and dance moves just long enough to get Kirk's attention. He snuck us out a back door where his white Hummer was waiting outside with the engine running. I'd arranged to switch cars with Kirk to ditch Ava's shadow.

"Now I have you all to myself," I said with a flirtatious smile, hoping the words were actually true, and then I cut through alleys and back streets to the main highway that would lead us home.

Ava

DAY THREE: DOUBLE VISION

I SIT UP AND SEE THE FIRE STILL SMOLDERING. Look-ing over where Dax should be, I discover he isn't there. The pitch black hovering at the opening of the cave tells me it's the middle of the night, and I'm filled with panic at the sight of him being gone. I crawl to the entrance and stare out into the dark night, lit only by a crescent moon.

The steady tide washes up on shore, and a flash of movement catches my eye. I squint to see the shape of a person at the edge of the trees disappear behind the dense leaves. I run out of the cave and down the rocks, convinced it is Dax, and race through the sand to try and catch up with him before he gets too far into the forest. Why would he leave me alone again?

I cut through the trees and call his name, pausing every few feet to search for him in the dark, and then I start moving faster, darting around the bushes and calling his name louder. He couldn't have gotten far because I ran to catch up to him, but now I feel uneasy about finding him because the more I venture away from the beach, the dark-er it gets.

Flames flicker through the trees in front of me, but wide leaves separate me from the light. I push them aside and walk into a small clearing. In the middle sits a short table with no chairs, made with tree stumps for legs and large planks of smooth wood on top. All around the table are torches atop tall sticks that are staked in the ground, forming a large semi-circle that beckons me to come closer.

I call for Dax again, positive that he's nearby, hoping to ask him where we are and what this place is as I walk to the table and search the surrounding trees for any sign of him. A shadow becomes the shape of a person against the trunk of a tree, but when I blink, it's gone.

My eyes drop to the table and now that I'm close, I lean down to stare at the wet puddle of water that reflects the shimmering image of the fire-lit torches. The puddle leaks over the edge of the wood and drips onto my foot on its way to the ground. I instinctively wipe the spot with my fingers and find the liquid is dark—not clear as I expected. It's a deep shade of red like the color of—

Blood!

I stumble backwards away from the table that just revealed itself to be some sort of alter and bump into something solid. My startled scream pierces the silence and I swing around to stare at the large trunk of a tree, with a diameter five times my size. I exhale and prepare to run around the tree, but then something near the bark makes me hesitate.

A triangle, like a giant, pointing arrow, is noticeable by the off-white color that stands out against the dark bark. It's inside the large root system that wraps up the tree, much like the one Dax hid me in. I lean my head closer to focus while my pupils adjust from the blinding light of the torch flames I'd been looking at moments ago. I blink twice and then stop breathing. It's a large tusk below a set of nostrils. And without warning, a set of wild eyes belonging to Zoron flick open a few inches from mine.

I jerk awake with a gasp. I'm drenched with sweat and my heart is pounding but I'm relieved to see Dax is actually asleep a few feet away, across from the dwindling fire that dimly illuminates the cave.

My racing heart skips another beat when I think I see something move beyond the mouth of the cave, and I squint to peer into the darkness. Is that a person crouched near one side of the opening? I open my mouth to warn Dax but when I blink, the shadow is gone. *No one is there*, I tell myself. My mind must be playing tricks but I'm still scared so I silently scoot next to Dax, being careful not to touch him. I watch him sleep until my heart rate slows, and I can't keep my eyelids open anymore.

***

It's morning, and Dax's explosive cursing startles me awake before the sun ever has a chance. He bolts upright and jerks backwards because my close proximity caught him off guard.

"You scared the hell out of me!" He runs his hands through his hair and then slowly down his face.

"I'm sorry." I can feel my face flush. "I had a really bad dream, and I was scared. It made me feel better to lie next to you. It won't happen again."

"No—no." He's quick to backtrack. "It's fine. I mean you can lie next to me—if you want. I just—well, next time, a little warning might be nice." He sounds flustered but shoots me a quick smile. "Trust me, I don't mind at all. I'm just used to sleeping alone and you—were just—right there. Okay. Never mind." He sighs, and then hurries to change the subject. "Speaking of scaring people, are you ready to meet Roxy?"

"I guess." He's made me so nervous about meeting her that part of me wants to stay in the cave and go back to sleep. "She has to be less terrifying than Zoron."

He narrows his eyes and scratches his chin playfully as if pondering the comparison. "Well, it's a close tie, but she won't want to eat you, so you'll be fine," he says with a laugh and offers his hand. "Come on."

Dax carries the cooked pig on the spit with one hand and still manages to hold my hand with the other, giving it an occasional squeeze to calm my nerves as we cut through the forest to the tree house. We are walking in silence and I wonder if he's nervous too, trying to figure out the best way to break the news to Roxy. When the tree house comes into view, he gives my hand one last reassuring squeeze and then steps into the clearing. He sits the meat in the kitchen hut and then points to a slim girl who stands with her back to us, hanging a shirt to dry over a laundry line made of vine. She must hear us approaching, but she doesn't bother to turn around until Dax clears his throat.

Roxy stares at me with wide eyes, and I stare back. I expected her to be unfriendly, but her expression far surpasses that. It is one of disbelief, looking me over as if I'm a figment of her imagination.

Her hair is invisible, tucked up into a wide-brimmed hat made from woven strips of palm leaves. She wears a faded black bikini top with jean shorts cut off just above her thighs. Boar tusks occupy both lobes of her ears and what looks like a very small rodent bone pokes through her left brow. The piercings surprise me, but not nearly as much as what hangs from her neck.

"Roxy, this is Ava," Dax says cautiously. "I found her three days ago near the beach. She doesn't remember how she got here, but we think the plane she was on may have crashed."

I smile weakly, still self-conscious of her relentless scrutiny. Suddenly, her brow creases and she tears up.

"Impossible," she hisses, almost in a whisper. Glancing at Dax, she whips her gaze right back to me. She takes a sudden step towards me, causing me to step back and position myself partway behind Dax. Something about her makes me feel threatened.

"Roxy, don't freak out, okay? I'm sure there's a logical explanation," Dax says in a soothing voice.

Logical explanation? I feel like I'm an outsider to an inside joke. Before I can ask anything, she ambushes me with questions.

"What's your last name?"

"Starr... Ava Starr." My voice surprises me—it's quieter than I intended.

"Where are you from, Ava Starr?" Her lips are pursed together and her hands are on her hips in an authoritative manner.

"I'm originally from Colorado, but I moved to California four months ago."

She takes another step forward, and I'm glad to be standing behind Dax. Then she walks in a slow circle around us to study me intently. As soon as she completes the circle, she stops in front of me and then reaches for my necklace. I stop myself from flinching.

"Where did you get this?" she demands, holding the locket and key in her hand for examination. An identical key hangs on a chain around her neck. She's making me feel like a criminal—interrogating me like I'm guilty of a crime.

"My parents gave it to me."

She looks at the necklace for a second longer before she lets it fall back to my neck. I look at Dax for support, but his eyes are fixed on her.

"It's her," he tells Roxy. "The one from the beach when I was nine. The one I told you about." A sly smile crosses his face. "See? I told you she was real. If you had any gum, I'd make you pay up. We both know you lost the bet."

She stops staring at me to glare at him.

"I don't understand," I say. Now I'm irritated, but they don't notice because they're staring each other down. Roxy sighs, and then her expression softens. She slowly reaches up, and with one fluid motion, she removes her sunglasses and hat.

It's as if I'm staring into a mirror. She looks so much like me that we could almost pass for twins, but she's younger and her hair is a light shade of strawberry blonde. My mind spins with possibilities.

She surprises me by holding out her hand in a friendly manner to shake mine. "My name's Roxy Miller. Nice to meet you, I guess."

She drops my hand as quickly as she grabbed it to twist her hair back up into her hat.

"Nice jewelry," I say as a friendly gesture, and then I feel awkward in the moment I created. She returns my smile, but it is short and immediately disappears from her face.

I want to say more, but her body language stops me.

"I'm going to show her around," Dax says. He takes my hand to lead me around Roxy, who doesn't move from where she stands with her arms folded across her chest.

I want to see the tree house and I don't want to offend Dax, but mostly, I just want to get it over with. I'm dying to ask Roxy more questions, to figure out how someone could exist that looks so much like me. A glimmer of hope stirs inside me, and I'm positive that together we can solve this mystery. Maybe I can finally get some closure to my past.

Dax lets me go first and I ascend the steep ladder, trying my best to not look down. The large hut is simple but very impressive for a tree house. There's furniture made from lightweight branches tied together with fine strips of bark. I explore everything in the room while Dax watches me from the doorway with his hands on his hips.

"So doesn't that weird you out a little?" he asks.

I glance at him over my shoulder. "The tusk gauges I can handle but yeah, the stick in the eyebrow is a little freaky."

"It's a bat bone. And that's not what I meant. You guys look like you could be sisters."

I'm still trying to make sense of it myself, and there's only one explanation I've come up with. "Maybe we are," I say. "I was adopted. My birth mom died right after I was born, but I don't know who my birth dad was. Maybe Roxy and I have the same father."

I turn around to face Dax and giggle at his creeped-out expression.

"Where's your room?" I'm anxious to finish the tour before Roxy disappears like yesterday.

"Follow me."

Dax walks out to the walkway and around the hut to a bridge that extends out to one side. I hold the railing tightly and try not to look down again as we cross to a smaller hut. Inside is a bed centered in the room, smaller but similar to the one in the castle. The frame is an open box made from solid planks of wood. Stretched firmly across the top is the hammock-style woven pieces of vine. A large animal skin pillow rests at the top.

There's a small table pushed against one wall with a turtle shell sitting on top for a sink. On the opposite wall is an extensive assortment of weapons—a large stone axe and a collection of bone knives, numerous spears, and an extra bow. A hollowed-out log filled with different types of arrows sits in one corner.

Dax drops his bow and quiver on the floor and walks to a doorway opposite from the one we entered.

"Come check this out," he says with an eager wave of his hand.

The doorway leads to a small deck. At one end is a closet-size space, blocked off except for a small opening. I peek inside and at first I'm baffled, not sure what he intends for me to see. Unlike his room, this part of the floor is made of sticks of bamboo lying side by side, with small gaps between them, allowing me to see the ground far below.

"Look up." He points above me.

A few feet above my head is a funnel-shaped tube made from overlapping palm leaves, hanging from the tree because there's no ceiling. At the smaller end, a wooden cork plugs the water from the inside. He reaches over and pulls a piece of vine that dangles near the wall, and the cork lifts upward inside the funnel, allowing water to flow out around it. It's a shower.

"Dax, that's brilliant."

"My dad and I came up with it," he tells me, and a hint of sadness crosses his face. "Let's go; I'll show you the other rooms."

We walk across another bridge to Roxy's room. I remain outside to look in and as crude and plain as the room is, she has warmed it up by draping various garlands of brightly colored dried flowers along the walls. Everything else looks the same as Dax's room, minus the weapons.

The last room he shows me is larger than the other two bedrooms and the bed in the center is more like a king-sized.

"This was my dad's room so you can stay here," he says. "Make yourself at home. I'll be in the kitchen hut if you need me."

I thank him and wait all of one minute before stripping off my clothes on the way to the private deck, anxious to try out the shower and enjoy the one piece of normality since waking up on Lamarai Island. I've never been so thankful for a shower in all my eighteen years of living, even though it's nothing more than warm water dribbling from some palm leaves above my head.

I find Dax in the kitchen hut behind a large counter where the wild boar lays on the spit he carried from the cave this morning. He's just finished cutting a large section of meat and places it on a wooden tray covered in palm leaves for the three of us. We carry the rest of the meat to the Anwai village. Chief Anwai thanks Dax, and then we head to the cave on the beach to get his guitar. The walk is only about ten minutes but by the time we climb up the rocks to the cave, I have to sit and rest.

Dax picks up Preston's board and looks it over. "So since we're here, I say we surf for a while. I'm dying to get on a board even if it means surfing waves as weak and lame as those. Which one's yours?"

"Neither," I tell him. "That's Preston's and the other board is Kirk's, the co-pilot. I don't surf."

"How did you live in California and not surf?" Dax seems appalled. "Didn't Preston teach you?"

"No. He didn't think it was a good idea for me to go surfing." I don't know why, but I'm annoyed by his shock and confusion. "Sharks? Bad luck?" I say, waiting for him to catch on. He raises one eyebrow and starts to make what I assume is a snide comment, but he closes his mouth and pauses before speaking.

"Well, I can teach you. I'm not afraid of sharks. I used to be until I found there are much scarier things than sharks on this island... and worse ways to die." He winks and waits precisely one second before he gives up on a response. "Come on, you know you want to."

His dimples are making it hard to refuse, and I do want to learn. I just always thought it would be Preston who would show me. I reluctantly agree, and his smile doubles in size. He carries the boards to the water while I change back into my tank top. When I get to the beach, he's traced both boards in the sand with his finger and drawn a line down the middle of each. We lay on our stomachs on the surfboard outlines and Dax shows me where I should be positioned on the board, but I find myself a little distracted as he demonstrates how to push to a standing position.

His movements are so fluid and graceful that I worry about looking clumsy and awkward in comparison. I copy him and try it a few times, then we wade out in the water with the longer board. He holds the board for me in the shallow surf so I can practice getting up in the water. After what I feel is a lot of un-earned praise and encouragement from him, we head out together on Kirk's board.

We paddle out far enough to catch a wave, and my stomach fills with butterflies the minute we stop paddling. The sun is high in the sky, reflecting off the water like diamonds as we wait for the next set of decent waves. Dax is straddling the board behind me and when his hand brushes my lower back, it gives me a start.

"Sorry," he says, and I know he's only apologizing for startling me, not for his happy hands that have now nestled their way around my waist. He's explaining what will happen next and I should be listening but I'm so distracted by his touch that when he tells me to start paddling, a surge of panic hits and I scramble to pick his last few words of caution out of memory. What did he just tell me to do? Or not do? Am I standing first or is he? But now it's too late because we are paddling fast, and he's standing and gently guiding me up in front of him. My stubbornness doesn't want his help, and I pull my arm free. I hit the water and before I can open my eyes and look around, I feel him beside me. He laughs and offers encouragement.

"You almost had it," he says, climbing back on the board and pulling me up in front of him. We paddle into position, and he must have scooted forward because I'm suddenly aware of how close he is. I can feel the heat radiating from his chest against my back. "Don't fight me this time," he says, and I'm about to say something but he beats me to it. "You need to relax. When we stand up, lean into me and let me guide you."

This will be hard for me. It reminds of the stupid trust

game my coach had us do where you close your eyes, fall backwards, and trust your team to catch you, but I'd agonize over which teammates should be checked off as trustworthy while waiting for my turn. That first year of public school had been a rude awakening of just how mean some girls could be to each other. I'd glance across the circle and decide where my fate would lie. *I loaned that girl a pencil one day—that should count for something, right? And I told that one I liked her hair, only after she'd glared at me because she caught her boyfriend leaning over to ask me the answer to number three. Does a compliment cancel that out?*

And my worries weren't unnecessary because I'd seen betrayal first hand at a pep rally my sophomore year. The cheerleaders were performing a routine and after tossing a girl in the air, their arms suddenly became Jell-O on the way down. She fell to the floor with a flat sound, body against wood. They all claimed it was a fluke accident as some students pointed and laughed while others stared horrified at the injured girl who laid there and cried. But the rumor quickly circulated that the fallen girl had gone out on a date with a recent ex of one of the other girls, and speculation grew that the accident wasn't really an accident at all.

I push these thoughts aside when Dax lines up the surfboard for an oncoming swell.

"Get ready... okay now!" he says, and we start paddling to catch the wave.

He's up and I start to stand, but my foot slips. I think I'm going to fall, but his hand catches my arm and steadies me before he pulls me against him. He tells me to trust him and his left arm circles my torso while his other hand takes mine to hold it out to the side. I relax a little but not enough because his arm tightens around me. We're actually doing it. I'm surfing and it's such a rush that I want it to last forever, so I do my best not to ruin it and melt into his body for the last few seconds before he pulls me into the water with him.

Dax never lets go of me except to help me onto the board, and I beg him to go again each time we fall just like I remember doing as a child. I begged my father for one more airplane ride until he'd grab my arm and leg to spin me through the air until we were both dizzy. Dax laughs at my enthusiasm and doesn't admit being tired even though he must be, because he's doing all the work.

We tandem surf over and over with a high rate of success except for the few times I move too quickly and send us toppling ungracefully into the water. This is the most fun I've had in weeks, maybe months, and my stomach hurts from laughing so hard. Surfing is such an adrenaline rush and I've become a junkie, craving the excitement of facing my fear of the ocean while gliding gracefully through the water in Dax's arms. And I try not to think too hard about the last part, because a little voice in my head tells me it might be part of what I crave.

Dax helps me onto the board first this time and climbs on in front of me. He straddles the board knee to knee with me and I know we can't surf like this, so he must need a break. He lies on his back and lets his arms float out to his sides, then closes his eyes. I'm tired too and the idea of lying down seems nice, but since he's hogging the board, my only option would be to lie down on top of him. So I sit, wait, and hope he doesn't fall asleep from sheer exhaustion. Studying the beach is only interesting for so long before my eyes are drawn back to him, to his sculpted arms and chest, his bronze skin beaded with drops of salt water. He looks perfect and royal lying there, with his wavy, golden hair, and I can almost picture him with a trident in hand and a crown on his head. Prince Daxton.

"What are you thinking about?" His voice startles me and my eyes dart to his, expecting him to be peeking up at me, but they're still closed. My face floods red with guilt, and now he really is looking at me with one squinted eye because I haven't answered.

"Uhm, nothing really," I say, but the hint of a smirk on his lips tells me he's already filling in the blanks with his hormone-fueled imagination. I better set him straight. "I was just thinking about mermaids... you know, like mermaid people in general... mermen... princes and castles underwater." He quirks an eyebrow, and I still haven't succeeded in wiping away that smirk. "It's no wonder sailors imagined them after seeing places as beautiful as this." The exaggeration of my thoughts spilled out of my lips with little effort, but now it is requiring a great deal of effort to keep a straight face.

He sits up and now he's studying me with curiosity and probably trying to decide if my answer's acceptable or nothing remotely close to the truth.

"That's funny, because a mermaid is what I thought about the first time I saw you." He reaches up to slide a lock of my wet hair through his fingers. "You have amazing eyes, long, wavy hair, and looks I'd definitely consider enchanting."

His hand drops from my hair to my knee, and I want to glance down to see it resting there, but I can't break away from his gaze. I'm not thinking about mermaids now, or surfing, or sharks, because all I can think about is what it would be like to kiss him, and that's weird and crazy because I know there's something else I should be thinking about instead—something important that I'm forgetting.

He leans closer, and I don't think I'm imagining the slight tremble in his fingers that leave a burning trail as they move away from my knee to skim the outside of my thigh on their way to my hip. I don't know where to look because his eyes are full of want and his lips are too close and he's moving so slow he's barely moving and now I'm sure he's really going to kiss me. Our foreheads almost touch. His gaze drops to my lips and I wish he would kiss me already—I wish I was brave enough to close the gap—I wish the movement out of the corner of my eye would stop fighting for my attention. But then it succeeds with a blast of reality, and I gasp.

Dax straightens and jerks around to follow my gaze to the beach where two men from the Anwai tribe have come to check their nets. And the moment is gone, because that flash of movement jogged my memory and now I know what it is I almost forgot.

Those men could have been Preston, Kirk, and Anna, breaking through the trees to find me at last, only to catch me about to lock lips with a beautiful boy from my past. What was I thinking? I'm wracked with guilt, and the pained look of disappointment on Dax's face is only making me feel worse. He's so patient and kind, and now he's giving me control to take this moment whichever direction I choose. He's watching me, waiting for me to say something, and his eyes beg to know what I really want. I can't tell him that I wanted to kiss him just moments ago, but now I want to find Preston more.

Dax

DAY THREE: PUSHING LUCK

"MAYBE WE SHOULD HEAD BACK," AVA SAYS, AND HER comment rocks me to my core. "I think I've had too much sun because I'm not feeling very well."

The last part might be true but my spidey senses tell me it has nothing to do with the sun.

I nod my head before falling into the water and swimming around to climb on the board behind her. I'm not as close as before, and the cold gap between us feels like a mile. She lies on her stomach, and I lay on top of her legs to paddle toward shore. When we reach the surf, I pick up the board and head to the cave without giving her a second glance. When she catches up to me, I've just placed both boards against the back wall.

***

"We should leave the boards here so they're close to the water. I guess we can leave this, too," I say, kicking the life raft. "Nothing screams 'I'm trying to escape' like a fluorescent orange inflatable boat."

I laugh, but she is drawing in the sand with her toes and making the situation even more awkward than it already is.

"What about the briefcase?" I ask. She must be thinking about what happened in the water because my question seems to catch her off guard. She glances at the case sitting next to the raft.

"Leave it here."

"Seriously?" I'm surprised. "What's in it?"

"I don't know. Preston wouldn't tell me," she says, and then I watch her go to another time and place. I've lost her to some memory she's refusing to share.

My voice snaps her back to the present. "What do you mean—he wouldn't tell you? Why not?"

"I don't know. He just said the briefcase was from his boss."

I can tell she wishes I'd drop the whole subject. Not going to happen. "You can't be serious. We have to open it. What if it's full of money?"

"So what if it is? What are you going to do with money? Oh, wait. You might be able to use it to buy a wife, since your current arrangement isn't going to work out."

She boasts a sly smile, but I don't smile back. She doesn't even feel bad about bursting my bubble. Wow.

"Come on. Aren't you just a little bit curious? Maybe he didn't tell you because he didn't want you to know what was in it. What if there's a—" I stop mid-sentence. "Never mind."

She grits her teeth. "What if there's a *what*? What were you going to say?"

I look at her for a second and debate on telling her my thought, but if the role was reversed, she wouldn't hold back.

"A ring."

I threw the word out like a grenade, and the explosion blasted through her. I feel a little bad about mentioning it now, because it appears that thought never occurred to her the way her mouth is hanging open. She snaps it shut and turns away from me because she must know my assumption is plausible.

"Look. If you want to open it, go ahead. But I don't

want to know what's inside." She peeks up and catches me with a huge grin on my face.

"Sweet!" I pick up my guitar and grab the briefcase with my other hand. "Let's go to the castle. I think I have something there I can use to pick the lock."

Ava chickened out halfway to the castle and said she wanted to wait to open the briefcase. I don't get women at all. I only told her there might be a ring so she'd let me open it, but the way she freaked out kind of makes me feel like an ass for even mentioning it. It's probably full of worthless paperwork and pilot crap anyway. I'll wait until she's ready, but she sure knows how to suck the fun out of a perfectly good day. Doesn't she know that reading material is hard to come by on an island full of illiterate cannibals? Besides, I'm going to need something else to read when I'm done with her journal.

And speaking of freaking out and sucking the fun out of things, what the hell happened on the surfboard? I must be way out of touch with girls because I could have sworn there was a vibe going on, like a, *I really wish he would kiss me right now* vibe. But the second she saw cannibal 'thing 1' and 'thing 2,' she dropped that vibe and it sunk straight to the bottom of the ocean.

And I don't even know who to blame, but if I had one guess, it would be someone whose name starts with a P—who's probably laying at the bottom of the ocean right next to that vibe while I'm up here keeping his girlfriend alive and trying to get her to pay me the least bit of attention in return.

That guy is inked into her brain like a tattoo and the more I read about him in her journal, the more I worry about how permanent the stain may be. She's only known him for a couple of months, but he's managed to become her reason for existing. I'm so screwed. How can I compete with that when all I have to offer is a cave or a tree for a house on an island full of cannibals and coconuts?

Ava went up to her room in the tree house to go to bed early since she wasn't feeling well, so I rushed back here to the beach to retrieve the journal where I hid it under a rock before we went surfing. With the mood I'm in, reading about those two little lovebirds... sitting in a tree... k-i-s-s-i-n-g probably isn't the best idea because first comes love, they've already talked marriage, and everyone knows where it goes from there. It's a risk, but I guess I'll take my chances.

August 9

Things are getting really weird around here. When I got home, I checked the mail and wasn't surprised to find a familiar envelope. The note should have caused me instant worry, but instead, the message made me laugh out loud—

DON'T PUSH YOUR LUCK

Whoever sent this warning doesn't know me very well. My luck ran out on the day I was born. Apparently our vanishing act after the reception must have made someone very angry.

Anyway, I took a long shower until every drop of the hot water ran out and skipped dinner because I wasn't hungry. After throwing some laundry in the washer, I sat on the couch to watch the news. That's when I noticed the library books strewn across the desk. One was even teetering on the edge about to fall to the floor. I thought maybe the stack just fell over, but then I saw the curtains and knew something was definitely wrong. They usually hang neatly with a small gap in the middle but they were pulled together, now overlapping each other in a sloppy fashion. Then it hit me—someone had been in the house.

Many items had been moved and not replaced the way I'd left them, like Friday's mail, which I'd left in a neat stack, was now scattered all over my desk. I honestly don't know why it took me so long to notice. I've failed in my pursuit of being observant.

Everything in my bedroom looked normal until I saw the sleeve of a shirt peeking out from the corner of one drawer. All the drawers had been gone through as if someone had been looking for something. I'm still trying to make sense of this terrifying personal invasion. Nothing appears to be missing, but it's obvious someone went through my things in a hurry, with no attempt to hide the fact that they did.

I thought about calling a non-emergency number at the police department and explaining to the person who answers that I need to report a break-in, but I have a feeling it wouldn't go well. I imagine the entire conversation would go something like this: I'd tell the officer as calmly as I could that I wanted to report a break-in. Then, after jotting down all my info, the conversation would go downhill from there. He'd probably offer to send officers to take pictures of the damage and get fingerprints, telling me to be careful not to disturb any broken glass, and I'd have to tell him that there aren't any signs of forced entry and that the door was locked when I got home. Yeah. Then I'm sure he'd ask the usual questions. Is anything vandalized? No. Missing? No. Do you live alone? Yes. Does anyone have a key? No.

So he might suggest I call the landlord and have the locks changed. I'd be desperate for him to understand the severity of the situation, so I'd add that someone's been following me. "They're outside right now," I'd tell him, and catch myself whispering as if the passengers in the black car could hear me. "Who's outside, ma'am? Are you in danger?" he'd ask with an urgency in his voice that wasn't there before. I'd tell him the car is parked across the street as usual and flinch as the words escape my lips, knowing how ridiculous that must sound. He'd pause for a moment and then say, "Ma'am, I need to ask you something very important," so I'd hang on his every word, hoping he'd have a solution to this problem that has been plaguing me, but next he'd ask if I was currently on any medications.

I saw it in a movie once. Not this exact scenario, but something similar. He'll think I'm schizophrenic or just plain crazy so I'd race through our conversation in my head, trying to figure out what I left out that could change his mind and wouldn't be prepared for his next question. "What's the license plate?" I can picture it perfectly—him at a desk, pen in hand, waiting for my useless "I don't know" response. And there you have it.

I think he might ask if the car had ever threatened harm and since I have no proof that the car at the library was the same one, I'd say 'no'. The conversation would probably end with him reminding me that there are a lot of black Mercedes running around but if anything serious happens, I should call 911 immediately. By serious, he'd mean something that involves proof, then I'd thank him and hang up.

Preston called about ten minutes after the discovery, so I told him everything that happened and was talking so fast I almost didn't hear him interrupt me. "Are you sure someone was in the house? How did they get in?" he asked. His voice sounded gentle but concerned. When I told him I locked the door and it was still locked when I got home, he was silent for a minute before he said, "I know you don't like to be alone, but don't let your imagination get carried away. If the door and windows are locked, no one can get in." For the first time since the Harry Pitts paging incident, I was thoroughly irritated with him for joining the 'Ava's lost her mind' bandwagon. I would expect to get that type of reaction if I called the police but not from him.

But I glanced around the room again and found myself doubting my suspicions, then I agreed with him because the last thing I want to do is scare him away. I told him how much I missed him, and he said, "You have no idea how much I miss you, and it doesn't help that Kirk keeps reminding me of how good you looked at the reception."

Then he laughed and asked if I had any big plans for my birthday. I want more than anything for him to spend it with me because this will be my first birthday without my parents. If Preston's absent too, the day will be almost unbearable. He said he couldn't make any promises he'll be here because he's on Mr. C's schedule, but he told me to keep my fingers crossed. Then he asked if it was bad luck for people with bad luck to cross their fingers. "Never mind," he said. "Leave the finger crossing to me."

He promised to call me tomorrow and after he hung up, I was actually feeling better about the whole situation until I turned to go to my room and something shiny caught my eye. I walked closer and stooped to pick up the crumpled wrapper under the couch. It was an empty package of cigarettes. I have a feeling this will be a very long night with little sleep. I'm really scared.

August 13

Today is my birthday, but it's definitely not happy. After a few restless nights, my sleep returned to normal thanks to Preston and my landlord, who have convinced me that whoever was in my house hadn't meant me any harm. The landlord had the locks changed and was quick to tell me that it was probably the previous tenant's ex-boyfriend, using the lame excuse of the tenant moved out of state as the reason he didn't change them before. Whatever. I've got bigger problems right now.

When I left work, I was relieved Sergio wasn't waiting next to my car—which has become a routine on most Fridays, but I still drove home feeling depressed since Preston told me last night he wasn't sure what day he'd be back. That means he's missing my birthday. And I miss him. The past two weeks seem like two years.

I grabbed a few items and a small cake at the store on the way home. After parking in my driveway, I headed for the door with enthusiasm equal to someone going to the dentist for a root canal. I ignored the Mercedes parked across the street, paused on the steps to get the mail, and then sifted through the envelopes, wishing someone back home might remember my birthday. No such luck.

There was nothing but junk mail, bills, and one envelope from a law firm I'd never heard of. It had been forwarded from my Colorado address. Opening the envelope, I slipped the key in the lock and stepped inside while reading the letter, closing the door behind me without taking my eyes off the professional stationary. I dropped my purse and the bag of groceries on the table next to the door and took a few steps, but then I stopped to continue reading.

The letter notified me of a trust my parents had set up in my name. They arranged for me to receive an income while going to college and saved the lump sum for when I graduated to invest in my own company or venture of my choice. Yet another secret kept by my parents.

The news is life changing. It means Preston and I can leave for Europe sooner than we'd planned, and I can actually go to school there. No more Oceanview Aviation. No more Sergio. No more black cars and mysterious notes. I'll be free to go with Preston and travel the world on my own dime, not his. The best birthday present ever. Not the money itself, but the fact that the only dream I have to look forward to is going to come true. I will soon be able to spend every waking moment with him. This is what I was thinking about when a deep voice from across the room said, "Surprise."

My keys and the mail went flying. My hands flew to my chest as if they would keep my heart from exploding out of my body. I resumed breathing and blinked, then focused on Sergio, who sat on the chair next to my couch. HOLY CREEPINESS!

My photo album was open on the coffee table. My stopping at the store on the way home left him plenty of time to snoop. I wondered with horror what else his serpent fingers had touched? I demanded to know what he was doing in my house and at that point, my anger outweighed my fear. He told me he stopped by to say happy birthday and when I didn't answer, he tried the door and found it unlocked.

Okay, Pinocchio.

"A birthday isn't complete without a surprise, right?" he said, and I just stared. I still don't know how that jerk knows it's my birthday. And where did he come from? I didn't notice his car parked outside. Then it all made sense—the empty cigarette wrapper. He's the one who's been here before. FREAKING STALKER!

I folded my arms to avoid him seeing my trembling hands and contemplated my options. I didn't know if anyone would hear me if I screamed. I could have run out the door and hoped a neighbor was home but instead, like an idiot, my feet seemed cemented to the floor. My keys were MIA since they flew out of my hand with the mail, and my purse was on the entry table just out of reach. There was no way I could get my cell out of my purse to dial 911 before Sergio reached me given my luck and the fact that I'd have to dig for the phone in the bottom of my stupid purse.

I remembered that Preston said Sergio was harmless and opted for the worst plan—tough it out and hope for the best. Not the smartest choice, but definitely the gutsiest. I asked if he always made it a habit to break into people's houses when they weren't home, and he actually shrugged his shoulders. "You know, it really isn't safe to leave the door unlocked. You're not in Kansas anymore, Dorothy," he said with a wink, and his slender finger traced his brow before he said I should be more careful or I might come home to find an unexpected guest in my house. "Or unwanted," I added, and that was an understatement.

Then I told him I didn't leave the door unlocked, but he ignored my comments. With an evil grin smeared across his lips, he delivered his intended speech—something about how he'd thought and thought about what to get me for my birthday, and then it hit him. "I'm the perfect package—what more could you possibly want?" he said, and then, "Damn. I should have wrapped myself up with a big bow." Yuck with a cherry on top. I'm still trying to erase that image from my brain.

I told him what I'd really like for my birthday would be for him to leave. "Now. Before I call the police... or an exterminator," I said bravely, and I bit my lip so it wouldn't have a chance to tremble like my hands. He looked shocked for a moment but then looked up at the ceiling and shook his head, mocking me in disbelief. The slight smile on his face was not an amused one. It was more like a satisfied grin.

He stood up and sauntered towards me, his heavy work boots thudding as loud as my heart when he crossed the tile floor. Instead of turning for the door, he kept coming, and he didn't stop until he was right in front of me—invading my breathing space.

A terrifying panic paralyzed me with fear—my back against the wall—knowing it was too late to run. He placed both hands on the wall at either side of my face and I imagined his serpent tattoo coming to life, slithering right off his arm and onto my neck.

"Why do you have to make everything so difficult?" he asked, and the sweet scent of beer and minty gum on his breath swirled around my face. "You know, I could make all your birthday wishes come true," he told me. Those self-defense moves flashed through my head but for some reason, the only part of my body that would work was my mouth, telling him that when I blow out the candles on my birthday cake, my wish will definitely have something to do with him. "Like... Never. Seeing. You. Again," I said, and my tone was sour but my voice radiated fear.

He studied my face with narrowed eyes—his mouth set in a straight line, and then his eyes fell to my lips. He swooped in, but I jerked my head to the side. He froze with his mouth next to my ear. Under his breath, a laugh escaped, deep and raspy. "Careful what you wish for, baby," he whispered. "Some wishes actually do come true."

I closed my eyes, didn't breathe, and a few excruciating seconds ticked by before he pressed away from the wall and left. When the door slammed shut behind him, I gasped for air and rushed to lock the door before sliding down the wall with my trembling hands covering my face. After I heard him peel away in his car, my emotions boiled over and a flood of tears and sobs poured out of me.

It's been two hours now, and my heart rate has finally returned to normal. He could have harmed me but he didn't, so maybe Preston's right. Sergio might be harmless, but he's definitely all kinds of crazy. Did he really think I would kiss him? Whatever. The thought makes me want to vomit. I should call the police, but I have a feeling it would be my word against Sergio's. Considering how powerful his uncle is, that doesn't give me much confidence. I tried to call Preston, but my call went straight to voice mail. The Sergio incident is something I should probably tell him in person anyway, so for now, I will only hope and pray that our conversation will be in the very near future.

I'm in shock as I storm back to the tree house. How could Preston be so absorbed in straightening his tie and shining his shoes that he couldn't see the danger his own girlfriend was in right under his nose. Idiot! I'm actually thinking it's more of a miracle than I thought that she's even on this island. No wonder she's so attached to him—she's been clinging to his nonchalant *nothing's wrong* attitude with the hope it will keep her alive. What a pathetic pretty boy! I would have done things so much differently had I been there instead of him.

My fist collides with a tree, and I utter a curse between my clenched teeth. Why can't she see he did nothing to protect her? If I ever get off this island, I will hunt Sergio down and make him swallow his teeth, one for every evil thing he said to her, then wrap that serpent around his neck and strangle him with his own arm.

I want answers. I want revenge! I was perfectly content being stuck on this island with Ava, but now I'm more determined than ever to find a way off Lamarai to return home with her because she deserves to be happy, but she also deserves to be safe.

Ava

DAY FOUR: MEMORIES

*L*AST NIGHT I TOLD DAX I WAS GOING TO BED EARLY, but I really just needed time to sort through my thoughts without being distracted by him. I want to pretend what happened on the surfboard never happened at all. And we didn't even kiss. So really the only thing to forget is the fact that I wanted to—the point that has been eating at me since.

Flipping open my sketchpad, I look at the pictures one at a time, stopping at the one of Preston I must have drawn on the plane. I have to admit—the sketch looks exactly like him. Maybe because I've spent so many countless moments studying every aspect of his perfect face—the contours of his jaw, the outline of his soft lips, and the depth of his stunning eyes each time he leaned in to kiss me.

The only color on the page is the green of his irises, blended to create the perfect shade that would captivate the beholder from beneath black lashes. And I succeeded. Bright, seductive eyes stare back at me. His face blurs through my tears, and I turn the page.

I don't remember making this list, but Preston and Kirk have added extra items. I switch back and forth between laughing and crying as I read through it.

TO-DO

1. Give 30-day notice to landlord
2. Get passport and birth certificate from home
3. Shop for good camera
4. Return books to library
5. Look up more info on Aunt Vivianne and mystery man
6. Kiss Preston
7. Go with Preston to get a marriage license
8. Kiss Preston
9. Get a wedding dress
10. ~~Kiss Preston repeatedly~~
10. Check to see if you have a long-lost twin sister for Kirk

Every item, other than kissing Preston and finding a girlfriend for Kirk, involved preparing to leave for Europe. Fate dangled that dream out in front of me, and then cruelly snatched it away. My mother always told me wishes never come true if you say them out loud. But I did, repeatedly, so I guess fate made its final move in the game to make sure I'd never win.

I could hardly wait to tell Preston in person about the trust money, and I didn't have to wait long because he showed up on my doorstep the morning after my birthday to surprise me with a weekend getaway to Catalina Island.

"So how are you planning on getting rid of my shadow?" I had asked him as he pulled away from the curb in a rented convertible Jaguar. The Mercedes jumped in behind us.

"Isn't it a little early for you to be worrying already? Besides, it's your birthday weekend and worrying is against the rules," he told me.

Preston drove to the marina where *Miss April* sat waiting, and after he helped me on the boat, he put my bag in the master stateroom below. He moved quickly and precisely, and as soon as we were unhooked, we drifted away from the slip and into the harbor. I watched him hoist the sails like a pro, and then admired him as he stood at the helm with his shirt unbuttoned halfway down, blowing gently in the breeze and exposing his tan, muscular chest. The black car remained parked in the lot behind us, completely helpless as we sailed away.

Preston had reserved a VIP suite on the top floor of a Mediterranean-style hotel, and nineteen dozen red roses were scattered throughout the entire room. Aside from the roses, the room itself was incredible. The leather couches and chairs were sleek and modern. Just beyond them were large windows boasting a private deck with a small table, coupled with two lounge chairs and a breathtaking view of the ocean. A fireplace, positioned in the middle of the room, separated two doors leading to bedrooms on either side, and to the left sat a small, modern kitchen and eating area. I was utterly speechless.

"I feel terrible you had such a rough week—first the library disaster, and then thinking someone broke into your house. I'm sorry I wasn't there for you. I hope the rest of the week went better," he said with a wink, and then placed his hands gently on either side of my face.

He didn't even know the extent of it.

I told him all about Sergio waiting in my house when I got home the day before, and I also told him I was sure it wasn't the first time. Preston's jaw feathered with irritation so I fast-forwarded to the end because I refused to let Sergio ruin my birthday weekend.

"But I made it clear I wanted him to leave—and I might have said something about blowing out candles on my birthday cake and wishing to never see him again." I bit my lip, holding back a smile.

His expression relaxed into an amused grin.

"Really? Well, that can be arranged. He and I are going to have a little chat." He laughed away his concern. "What's the matter? Satan's not your type?"

I shuddered. "Definitely not."

"Well, Miss April—what exactly is your type?" he asked with a sly lift of his brow, and I couldn't stop the blood from flooding my cheeks. I had walked right into that.

"Uhm—tall, dark, and handsome?"

"So you *do* like Sergio," he said.

"What? No!" My eyes dropped to his chest. "I like serpent free—polite and nice—surfer—piloty types."

"Then I guess it's my lucky day." He waited for me to look up at him to return his smile and then he kissed me again.

He had the entire afternoon planned. We started with the zip line. After lunch we went snorkeling until we were exhausted, and then made our way back to the hotel, stopping in a few shops along the way. I collapsed onto the couch when we walked in the room, but his plans didn't stop there. He stole a single rose from one of the vases and disappeared into my room. After a couple of minutes, he returned and led me to the bathroom where a hot bath was waiting. He'd lit the candles around the Jacuzzi tub, and floating on top of the water were the scattered red rose petals.

But the magic didn't stop there. A candlelight dinner was waiting for me when I re-entered the front room. After dinner, he led me out on the balcony. The sky was dark, and a soft breeze tugged at my hair as I watched the lights twinkle below. Preston handed me a tiny box wrapped in silver paper with a small, red bow on top. Inside was my bracelet covered entirely with emeralds and light green peridots, and in the center of each clover was a diamond. "It's one of a kind, just like you," he told me. "More importantly, it's a symbol of good luck. Definitely something you need." He laughed quietly and lifted the bracelet from the box, then stepped closer to fasten the clasp around my wrist.

"I love it. Thank you."

After he kissed me, he dropped the news that he'd talked to Mr. Caruso about Europe and had offered to help him find a new pilot. He also said Mr. C wanted to hire me as a flight attendant and how he planned to ask me in person on the trip back from Australia. There was something intimidating about Mr. Caruso, making the thought of being alone with him almost terrifying.

"Don't worry. It'll be fine." Preston had sounded convincing, but his expression didn't match the same confidence. "I arranged for a charter plane to pick Mr. C up today and fly him to Australia to meet with someone. *Hotel Charlie*'s in the shop for some scheduled maintenance, and when it's done, Kirk and I will fly to Australia to pick him up. Mr. C wants you to come with us, so he can talk to you on the flight back. So I'll be there—only in the cockpit, not right next to you."

I stared at him, still unsure. Australia was so far away. That meant a long time on the plane. With Mr. Caruso. Awkward. Then I remembered Anna.

"Will Anna be there too?"

He let out a short laugh. "Yes. But she's not much of a talker. Please don't worry. It's not that big of a deal. I promise. Just let him do the talking and act like you're giving it serious consideration, then politely decline and tell him you prefer sailing to flying." He flaunted a mischievous smile. "Unless you want to tell him the truth—that you just want me all to yourself," he said.

My cheeks flushed. There was actually more truth to his sarcasm than I wanted to admit. "Those are both good excuses, but I have one of my own." I leered playfully, and he tilted his head with curiosity. "How about I tell him I'll be going to school in Europe in the spring? It seems I've inherited some money."

A look of shock crossed his face, followed by a look of confusion.

"What do you mean?"

"I got a letter yesterday. My parents set up a trust for me. I haven't called on the exact amount yet, but it must be a lot judging from the monthly distribution amount. I think my parents were going to tell me for my birthday." His shocked expression remained and he listened intently, his eyes fixed on mine. "So the letter said I'd start receiving ten thousand dollars every month following my nineteenth birthday, for four years, and then I'll get the remaining amount in one lump sum."

I'd been so excited to tell him but he sat very still, not seeming to share my same enthusiasm. "Don't you see? I'll have enough money to go to school, and we'll have enough money to leave sooner than we planned—if you want."

His quiet demeanor made me self-conscious, and I worried I'd said something wrong. His silence was maddening. "Preston?"

He seemed to snap out of his trance.

"Wow. That's—awesome," he said. "Maybe I was wrong about your luck. I guess you don't need the bracelet after all," he teased. He reached for my wrist, but I stopped him.

"Are you kidding? Of course I need it. The trust money isn't luck, just good planning on my parent's part. Now I know why they never seemed to be worried about how they'd pay for my college. Anyway, that's a good reason, right? Mr. Caruso can't argue with that."

"Yes, school's a great reason. But just don't mention anything about the trust money, okay? I already told him I was footing the bill."

We danced for a little while and then lay on the couch in front of the fire.

I knew something was bothering him. His mood change was obvious, and I fought to shove this concern to the back of my mind. He ran his fingers through my hair while we listened to the sound of the quiet music.

Soon, I drifted to sleep in his arms and dreamt that we were sailing in the middle of the ocean when a sudden darkness surrounded us. A storm came out of nowhere and rain started to fall, stinging my cheeks from the blustery wind. Preston fought to take down the sails that flapped madly in the gale, struggling to prepare the ship for the sudden hurricane condition that fell upon us. I felt useless, not knowing what to do to help him. Scared and panic stricken, I stood up and squinted through the night, the water trickling down from my hair in a steady stream that almost blurred out my vision entirely. Without warning, the boom swung around violently and hit me in my side, causing me to lose my balance and fall overboard.

My face surfaced and I saw Miss April in front of me, being tossed back and forth in the angry sea. I tried to scream Preston's name but each time I opened my mouth, salt water poured in from the turbulent waves cresting all around me. Finally, I managed a scream, a desperate plea for him to hear. I cleared the water from my eyes long enough to see him walk from the helm to the side rail and look in my direction as if he heard me calling his name. I drifted further away by the second. And I watched in horror as he stood there motionless and did nothing to help me as I floated away.

Preston's arms tightened around me. "Are you okay?"

We were still on the couch, and his eyes were alert, as if he'd been watching me and not sleeping.

"Yes, just another nightmare. I'm sorry. Did I wake you up?"

He shook his head and guided my head back to his chest.

"What time is it?"

"I don't know. Three o'clock last time I checked."

"Why can't you sleep?" I asked, content that he was there next to me, but very aware of the concern in his voice that replaced his usual carefree manner.

"I'm just thinking." He paused. "Let's get you to bed."

He led me to my room, where he turned down the covers and tucked me in, then sat on the edge of the bed.

"Besides your parents, and me, who else knows about the trust money?" he asked, and even in the dark, I could see his serious expression.

"I don't know. No one, I guess. I haven't told anyone but you. Why?"

It wasn't a question I expected him to ask me in the middle of the night. I yawned, struggling to keep my eyes open and on him.

"Never mind. Go back to sleep."

He kissed me on the forehead and started to get up, but I grabbed his hand and gave him an exaggerated pout. Forcing a smile, he crawled on top of the covers to lie on his back beside me. Looking at his profile in the dark, I saw him focused on the ceiling above us. I should have been worried that he didn't answer my question, but I was too tired. I felt content and safe and soon fell back asleep.

The next morning, I slipped out from under Preston's arm and ordered room service. On my way to the balcony, I paused to peek at him. He had rolled over onto his stomach and lay sprawled comfortably across the bed in a fitted T-shirt and plaid pajama pants, looking like a dreamy model in a Hanes' ad.

I'd taken the first bite of my French toast before I noticed him standing in the doorway of my room. He leaned against the frame. His hair looked a bit disheveled, but on his face was my favorite smile.

"Why didn't you wake me up?" he said before sitting down across from me.

"You needed sleep," I told him, "and I need to apologize. If you want to wait until next year to go to Europe, that's fine. I didn't mean to be one of those pushy girls, so concerned with myself that I didn't even stop to think you had reasons to wait until—"

"Ava." He interrupted before I could finish. He stopped eating and set the fork down. "You think I don't want to go with you?" His voice was full of alarm.

My mind raced to reach another conclusion besides the one I'd come up with, but I found none. He reached across the table and grabbed my hand.

"Now I'm worried you got too much sun yesterday and it's affecting your ability to think clearly," he said with a wink, leaning across the table to kiss me. "I'm worried about *you*, not the money," he explained, and I listened intently. "Don't you see? The trust money may be the reason you're being followed. Someone knew you were going to receive it, so they're watching and waiting, possibly thinking they need it more than you." Preston squeezed my hand. "Relax. I have everything worked out in my head. We have at least two weeks before you get the first disbursement, right?"

"We'll go to Australia as planned, kindly decline Mr C.'s offer, and you can give Georgie your two weeks' notice. It'll be close, but that should be enough time for us to get all our supplies and everything together. You can call the investment company and make arrangements for the money to be deposited into a bank account every month, instead of them sending a check. And as soon as I find another pilot for Mr. C, then I'll whisk you away to safety, halfway across the world," he said, flashing me a radiant smile.

I nodded and picked at the remainder of my breakfast, unable to force down more than a couple of bites. He cleared the table and placed the tray in the hall outside the door.

"I'm sorry I worried you. That wasn't my intent," he said, leading me to the couch where he sat down and pulled me onto his lap. "I wanted this weekend to be perfect." I wrapped my arms loosely around his neck and let him hypnotize me with his crystal green eyes. "Let's go to the beach. Please try to forget I said anything. There'll be plenty of time to worry later, but today, you can relax. It's just you and me."

"I don't know if I can," I said with conviction and a playful pout.

"Relax... or forget?" he asked with a sly grin.

"Both."

"Mmm... maybe I can help you with that."

He twisted to flip me onto the couch and leaned into me, kissing me just above my shoulder where my skin was exposed. Following the curve of my neck up to my jaw, he swept his soft lips across my skin and gave me goose bumps.

"What were we talking about?" I said playfully, feeling his warm breath just below my ear. His nose skimmed across my cheek, and then he lifted his head. He waited for our eyes to meet before he began kissing me with more urgency than I was used to. My fingers entwined in his hair and then, unexpectedly, he pulled away and chuckled.

"The beach, remember?" He gloated triumphantly and helped me sit up.

I could barely remember my name.

The beach in front of the hotel was quiet. Wooden lounge chairs covered with cushions were placed neatly in the white sand with canvas umbrellas scattered around them. We spent the morning soaking up rays and taking in the view of the cobalt blue water in front of us. After lunch, we went for a swim and then left our bags at the front desk to go on a jeep tour and a cruise in the glass-bottom boat. It was late afternoon when we finally pulled out of the bay and headed for open water.

He let me steer the sailboat while he stood behind me, kissing my neck and making it difficult to remember the instructions he'd just given me.

"Which way is San Diego?" I asked again with a flirtatious smile.

He pointed to the right.

"Then let's go *that* way." I pointed to the left and started to turn the wheel, but he turned me around to face him, pinning me between himself and the helm.

"You're not really dressed for weather in Alaska."

I giggled. "But I don't want to go home. Forget about San Diego and Mr. Caruso. Let's just leave now and never look back."

"Patience, Miss April," he said, kissing me under the setting sun.

If only I'd tried harder to convince him, we would still be together. Maybe Dax is right, and there is a ring in the briefcase. I wipe away my tears and leave my new room in search of Dax, the one person I can count on to wipe away my sorrow.

He's in the kitchen hut and when I walk in, his feet drop from the table and he shoves something in his pocket.

"Let's go to the castle," I tell him, grabbing the briefcase off the table.

"Yeah, sure." Happiness spreads across his face, and he jumps up from his chair to offer me his hand. "Whatever you want."

Dax

DAY FOUR: REGRETS

OMEN ARE HARDER TO READ THAN A MAP IN THE dark. One minute, Ava's telling me to throw the briefcase back in the ocean and now, she's carrying it to the castle like it contains the secret to the universe. Whatever. I'm sure as hell not going to try and figure that one out.

I almost got busted with her journal in hand but luckily, I heard someone coming and shoved it in my pocket the second before she stormed into the kitchen hut demanding we leave. Before the interruption, I was reading all about her weekend in Catalina Island with Preston, who spared no expense trying to create the perfect birthday getaway. It's not like he needed to impress her; he already had her wrapped around his manicured finger.

"What happened to your hand?" Ava asks quietly.

It takes me a second to catch up to the present.

"I hit a tree."

She's quiet long enough for me to notice the rhythmic sound of her feet crunching through the overgrowth. I really need to teach her to walk quieter.

"Why would you do that?"

I glance back at her feet and wonder if now is the perfect time for that lesson. The last thing I need is to draw attention and have someone follow us to the castle. Getting scolded by Chief Anwai isn't on my list of things to do today.

"I was mad. Here, let me carry the briefcase for a while," I offer, turning to hold out my other hand.

She doesn't hesitate to hand it over, but the distraction didn't work. Now both of her hands are caressing my swollen, scabbed-over knuckles.

"Because I wouldn't let you open the case?" she asks.

"No. It's not that." I turn my head and assure her with a smile, but it doesn't erase the worry creasing her brow. At least her steps are softer behind me. The briefcase must have thrown off her balance. "I was just frustrated and mad that—I can't protect you from everything."

"What? But you have. I wouldn't be alive if it weren't for you."

"Yeah but I wasn't around before to protect you from mystery people who wanted you dead. I'm just lucky they didn't succeed."

She's quiet for a minute, and then she says, "You shouldn't be mad about that. I had Preston to protect me then."

I bite my cheek so hard I can taste blood. Is she serious? I can't stop myself from protesting. "What did he do to protect you exactly? I'm just curious, because it seems he should have helped you figure out who was sending the notes and following you."

I brace myself for the shrapnel of angry words I expect to come flying at my back, but instead she answers in a meek voice.

"You're right. But it's probably my fault. I didn't want to worry him, so I didn't let on how frightened I was. I guess he didn't think I was in danger."

Irritation has caused me to pick up speed, and she's struggling to keep up. I take a deep breath and force myself to slow down.

"Well, it doesn't matter now. The damage is done. We don't get mail here and I haven't seen any black Mercedes on the island, so as long as I can keep you from getting captured by the Lambai tribe or being bit by poisonous snakes, you should be reasonably safe."

I take three more steps before she pulls me to a stop and jerks her hand from mine. Setting the briefcase down, I turn with my hands up in surrender. *Smooth, Dax.* Now she's giving me a look that might actually set me on fire.

"I'm sorry," I tell her. "I didn't mean it. I'm sure Preston thought he was doing everything he could. Just forget that I—"

"I never told you it was a black Mercedes."

My heart jolts at her words and sets off an explosion of curse words inside my head. How could I be so stupid? If I lie, she may never trust me again, and if I tell her the truth, she might take off running into the woods. I vote to take the fifth, but she won't allow it.

"Well? How did you know?"

I open my mouth to tell her, but now confusion slides over her face and her mouth drops open before she says, "Wait. Is this some kind of sick joke? Are you—are you a friend of his? Where is he?" Her voice is laced with anger, and she takes a step towards me to wait for my response.

"*What?* Who?"

"Preston. *Where* is he?" Her eyes fill with tears. "I will never forgive him for this. I know that I'm gullible, naïve, and obviously a complete idiot, but this is the lowest of all pranks. And the cannibals are a nice touch. How much is he paying all of you? How could he?" She bursts out in sobs. "Where are we really? Preston! Preston!"

I'm so shocked by her misinterpretation that it takes me longer than it should to rush forward and silence her. "Shhh. No, Ava. Stop yelling. It's not what you think. Preston had nothing—"

"Liar! Don't touch me!" She rips free from my grasp and takes a step back. "Preston!"

"Ava, look." I pull the journal from my pocket and hold it up. "This is the reason I know. There's no prank. There's no Preston. And the cannibals are very, very real and might make a surprise appearance if you don't stop yelling."

Her face is ashen. She stares at my hand for too many agonizing seconds before she reaches out and takes the journal from my hand.

"Just hear me out," I say. "I found it when you were unconscious and my curiosity got the better of me. I was going to put it back but when I discovered who you were, it made me want to read it even more." Her silence is killing me. She won't look at me, only at the book she's holding in her hand. "I'm sorry. I know it's inexcusable."

"Yes. Yes, it is." Her voice is barely a whisper, and a tear trickles down her cheek. She clutches the journal to her chest. All I want to do is to hold her and take back the hurt I've caused, but when I reach out, she steps away. In her rage, she must have thought Preston was alive in order to pull off such a prank, and now I've ripped that hope from her and betrayed her trust on top of it.

"I didn't read all of it," I tell her, as though it's not a moot point.

"It's fine," she says, but clearly, it's not. "Let's just go."

I pick up the briefcase and continue towards the castle, listening for her steps behind me that have become so quiet I can barely hear her there, as if my actions have ripped out her soul and left an empty shell floating behind me. I feel like the very thing she accused me of yesterday—the biggest jerk on God's green earth.

This is much worse than any wrath Roxy's ever inflicted upon me. If Ava would have slapped me or chewed me out until next week, I would feel better than I do now. But her silent display of disappointment has left an ache in my gut that will never go away unless she decides to forgive me.

"So you know about Sergio?"

Her question catches me off guard, and I'm not sure how to respond. I doubt anything I tell her can make things worse than they already are.

"Yes, I read about Sergio. His face should have been at the other end of my fist instead of a tree." I would give anything to hear her laugh, but she doesn't.

She's quiet again, and I don't dare say a word unless she asks me to. We are less than five minutes away from the castle when she finally speaks again.

"You have an unfair advantage."

Not unless she's racing me straight to hell. "How's that?"

"You know all my secrets, personal thoughts and feelings, and all I know about you is your last name. You've tried so hard to get to know me, and I haven't been very open or done the same for you. I guess I left you no choice but to—"

"But to what? Betray you?" I turn so fast that she almost runs into me. "What are you doing?"

Her compassion is clawing a gigantic rip through my heart. She blinks and starts to speak, but I stop her.

"Don't you dare take the blame for what I did," I tell her. "All I wanted from the moment I found you was to earn your trust, and now I don't even deserve it. Hit me, call me names, something! Be mad, Ava—because that's what I really deserve, but don't give me a free pass to fail like you do for him."

"By him, you mean Preston." She hugs the journal beneath crossed arms. "He may have failed to keep me from ending up on this island, but he never failed to make me feel loved and important."

"But none of that would have mattered if you ended

up dead. He failed to help you and keep you safe. And I'm pissed about that, but I shouldn't be because his failure led you to me. I promise I will keep you safe and do whatever it takes to earn your trust back. Just don't forgive me unless you truly mean it."

"I do mean it," she says, stepping toward me. "I was angry, but I can't stay mad at you for long. You're all I've got left. And I think a little part of me is relieved that you know—well, most of it. I haven't had anyone to talk to since my parents died. I mean, I did talk to Preston, but not about everything. Obviously. It was just different." The color rises in her cheeks, and she looks down. "And just so we're clear, how much did you read?"

I'm not usually one to get embarrassed, but now I'm suddenly uncomfortable in my own skin. She's still blushing. What is she worried I read? Is she embarrassed about kissing Preston or is there more I didn't get to? Guilt and regret are pointing fingers at me like I'm some sort of Peeping Tom, and I want to swat them away.

"Uhm, I stopped at the one about your weekend in Catalina."

Her eyes widen. "I thought you said you didn't read it all!" She delivers a punch to my chest that I know hurts her more than it did me. "That was like—a few days before I wound up here!" She's right. There were only a few entries left. She growls and steps around me to storm in the wrong direction.

"The castle is that way," I tell her, pointing her in the right path. She pivots and stomps off into the trees, which is probably good so she won't see the grin tugging at my lips. This is the feisty Ava I love.

We reach the familiar rock wall and climb over. After she climbs in the canoe, I pull out my coin. I fight back a laugh when she loses the toss.

"Since when do princes make princesses row the boat?"

she asks, and irritation is evident in her tone.

"They don't," I tell her, and I start to row. "I just don't have any other use for this quarter that's been in my pocket for three years. Now that you're here, I finally get to use it for something."

She rolls her eyes right on cue. Folding her arms, she stares across the water to avoid looking me in the eye, but when I glance back in her direction, I catch her staring at me. Her cheeks flush a beautiful shade of red. I can only assume she's still stewing over the fact that I know all her thoughts and intimate details of her time spent with Preston. She needs a diversion.

"So when did you first notice someone was following you?"

She doesn't move. For a second, I wonder if she intends to answer, but then she says, "About a week after I moved to California, I kept getting the feeling someone was watching me, but I thought it was just anxiety from living alone for the first time in my life. When I got the note that said *you're being watched,* and decided it wasn't from Preston, I started being more observant. That isn't really one of my strong suits."

"Really?" I say. "And here I thought you intended to treat yourself to a mud bath in quicksand and make friends with that snake."

She leers playfully, and then seems to remember her genuine annoyance with me.

"Anyway, I came home one day after going to the mall and saw the Mercedes pull up and park in its usual spot across the street. I went inside and peeked through the curtains because I was curious to see who would get out of the car. But the seconds ticked by and turned into minutes. After a long time, still no one got out of the car. The Mercedes seemed to come and go when I did, but I'd never seen anyone getting in or out of the car. That's when I knew for sure I was being watched. I just never knew who or why.

"At one point, I even thought it might have to do with Preston, you know, like a jealous ex-girlfriend trying to threaten my personal pursuit of happiness, but I asked him and he said that wasn't a possibility because he hadn't had any girlfriends before me."

I quirk a brow and start to interject, but I quickly reconsider. We reach the sand on the other side, and I help Ava out of the canoe. "What about the notes? You said you knew who sent them."

"It was my boss, George. And if I had opened the note before I got on the plane, I would have gotten the chance to ask him who he was warning me about. Now I'll never know."

She follows me to stash the canoe and then to the entrance of the castle. I turn and wait for her to look at me before I say, "You can't beat yourself up over 'what ifs' or your whole life will be consumed with regret. I know from personal experience. I believe that all things happen for a reason, and whether we like it or not, we have to find a way to move on."

"You have regrets?" she asks, and I nod.

"If I'd have done things differently, my dad might still be alive."

"What happened?"

"There was a hurricane. The winds were so strong that night they ripped part of the roof right off the chief's house. When Dad woke me to tell me to stay and look after Roxy, I argued fiercely for him to let me come and help him, but he demanded I stay. Thought it was too dangerous. The last thing I ever said to my father was a slew of harsh words meant to express my disproval and undermine his authority.

"He managed to help some of the men from the tribe

secure the wood back on top of the tree house, but then a gust of wind knocked him off balance. I beat myself up thinking that if I hadn't been such an obedient son, I might have been able to change the outcome of that horrible night. Then again, it might have been me that fell sixty feet to my death."

I open the portcullis and then follow her inside.

"I'm so sorry," she says.

"Yeah, me too. But life is short so that you can't sit around and spend all your time pouting and worrying or you waste what little time you have."

23

Ava

LATE AFTERNOON: THE RECKONING

A *FIREWORK OF EMOTIONS—ANGER, DISAPPOINT-*ment, grief, humiliation, and relief all bombarded me until there was nothing left but shock. I'm still not sure how to feel about Dax reading my journal. I can't believe I didn't realize it was missing. I tried to hate him for it, but I can't, because right now, he is all I have left in the world and I can't bear to be alone. So I had to forgive him.

It was easy enough when I thought about all the things I'd like him to know and hadn't told him. But he'd read almost all of my innermost thoughts, even the ones about Preston. I don't know why I care. But I do. I've never hidden my feelings about Preston, but now I find myself wishing a magic eraser would scrub them from Dax's mind.

When he held up my journal, I felt so vulnerable, exposed, like I was standing in front of him with not a stitch of clothing on while he stood confident and comfortable in five layers. What does he think of me now? Does he know I wanted him to kiss me until I remembered how much I wanted to find Preston and kiss him too? And how could I have forgotten Preston in the first place? What is wrong with me?

I can't be angry with Dax for reading my journal when I

am guilty of betrayal myself. I tried to keep up the pouting routine because I know Dax thinks that's what he deserves, but I was too easily distracted by his cut abs and muscular arms, flexing in rhythm as he rowed across the water. And he caught me admiring him. I can't let that happen again. I desperately need to find Preston.

"This is high end," Dax says. He's sitting in his chair to admire the briefcase on the table in front of him. "Genuine Italian leather and obviously airtight and waterproof."

"I'm sure. What makes you think you can even get into it?"

I'm lying on the couch and for being made of wood, it's surprisingly comfortable. "I had a friend in California who taught me a trick. My dad had one similar to this, and we broke into it once just to see if we could," he tells me with a proud look across his face.

"Nice friend. Haven't you ever heard of karma?" I say. "So you ended up stranded on an island... where did he end up? A maximum-security prison?"

I grin, and he leers playfully.

"I have to get something from another room, one that I didn't show you before." He walks behind the counter and then hesitates. "Do you want to see it?"

"I already did, when you left me here alone."

"Are you serious?" His disappointed look almost makes me wish I hadn't told him. He disappears into the tunnel and returns a couple of minutes later with a magnifying glass in his hand.

"Where'd you get all that stuff?" I ask.

He walks back to the table and studies the combination through the magnifying glass.

"A few of the items I found washed up on the beach.... but most of it I got from the chief." He pauses between phrases, deep in concentration. "It's stuff they've found over the years... in their fishing nets.....usually after a big storm.... when the current... drags it up... from the ocean floor." He focuses on the numbers and moves them around. "It's no use to them... so I trade him food... for different items."

I stare up at the ceiling of the cave, lost in thought. What else will wash up on shore from *Hotel Charlie* in the future? Preston's sunglasses? A shoe? The thought sickens me, and I swallow back the lump in my throat. Of all the things to wash up on shore, the briefcase is the last thing I'd expect. And I can't blame Dax for being so curious about what's inside because there was a time I was just as curious.

The night before we left, I laid across Preston's bed to watch him pack. He only owned what would fit in two large suitcases, and he took all but one of his uniforms off the closet rack and placed them in a hanging bag. Then he turned on the flat screen TV that hung on the wall of the bedroom in Mr. Caruso's house before tossing me the remote. I surfed through the channels until I found a cooking show, but studying Preston became much more fascinating than learning how to cook pasta primavera.

He went into the bathroom and returned with a small, black bag of personal items, which he laid in the remaining suitcase, and then removed his T-shirts, jeans, and shorts, from the dresser drawer to place on top of the other clothes. He zipped the suitcase shut and sat it back in the closet between the black briefcase and his other suitcase.

"What's in the briefcase?" I'd asked him.

He climbed on top of the bed next to me and grabbed another remote from the bedside table. Instantly, the lights were dimmed.

"It's from Mr. C," he said, playing with the loose strands of my hair that were casually sprawled across the pillow. I looked at the TV and pretended to be interested in what the man was sautéing until I remembered Preston had dodged my question. I took my eyes off the cooking show to focus on him.

"So what's in it?" I asked again.

He offered a crooked smile and wrapped his arm around my waist to pull me closer. His lips barely touched mine, and then he spoke softly, kissing me gently in between each phrase.

"Well, it contains my next mission... (kiss) should I choose to accept it... (kiss) but it's much too dangerous to talk about..."(kiss). He slid his lips along my jaw until they were right below my ear and whispered. "I could tell you... (kiss) but then I'd have to kill you..."(kiss). His lips made their way to my neck, and his hand on the small of my back pulled me against him.

My heart raced, and I reached up to slide my fingers into his hair as his lips made their way back to my mouth. We lost ourselves in the kiss until I started to feel bad about distracting him from the sleep I knew he'd need for the long flight the next day.

I exhaled quietly. "I should go back to my room; I know you need to get some sleep." Filled with disappointment, I started to get up.

"No. Stay here." He raised both hands in the air. "I'll be on my best behavior, I promise." Rolling onto his back, he patted his chest to mark the spot for me to lay my head. He turned off the TV and the lights and we lay there in the dark for a few minutes before I spoke.

"I'm nervous about talking to Mr. Caruso," I told him, because suddenly, that was all I could think about. Preston had been trying to distract me from those very thoughts until I stopped him.

"I know," he said, and he kissed me lightly on the top of my head. "Stop worrying, Miss April, you'll give yourself nightmares. I'd sing you to sleep, but that would give you nightmares for sure."

"Aren't you worried?" I asked.

"Yes. I'm worried about your excessive worrying—so relax." He laughed, and I remember how his velvet voice put me at ease.

"I've almost got it," Dax says, but it takes little effort to ignore him and go back to my pleasant memory.

***

The next day, Preston picked me up for lunch and took me to my house to get some last-minute things and check the mail. The form I requested from the investment company arrived, so Preston drove me to a bank to have the paper notarized. He took me back to work and then left to mail my form.

By the time five o'clock rolled around, I started to get butterflies. I was about to clock out and head out to the plane when the front desk girls informed me that George wanted to see me. Surprised and a little hesitant, I ascended the stairs to his second-floor office.

George had the blinds pulled closed to block the light of the late afternoon sun that would otherwise blind him as he sat at his desk. The lights were off and the filtered sunlight made for a gloomy feel, especially with all the clutter and un-filed paperwork.

He shuffled through a small stack of papers until he found a white envelope with my name scribbled across the front. The light peering through the slits in the blinds highlighted the dust particles floating through the air, disturbed from his untidy desk.

"No need to sit down," he said, and he handed me the envelope. "I had payroll make out your check early. Thought you might want to have some spending money for your trip." He seemed to force a smile before he picked up a pen and appeared preoccupied, as if he wanted me to hurry and leave, so I shoved the envelope into my purse.

"Thank you, George. I'll see you on Monday."

He nodded in reply.

I hurried outside to find Preston and Kirk. Kirk's hummer and Preston's rental car were pulled up to the plane. Preston unloaded our bags, handed me my backpack, and then parked the rental car in front of the building. I watched him get out with his briefcase in hand and walk into the lobby to leave the car keys at the front desk.

Anna arrived by taxi and wheeled her bag across the ramp. She politely invited me to board and make myself comfortable. The roomy cabin was beautiful. There were many seating areas to choose from, even a sofa on one side facing two chairs. Mr. Caruso's stateroom was positioned behind the main cabin toward the rear of the plane.

I sat down next to a window toward the front of the plane, but since there wasn't a line hostess, I got up and offered to go get a bag of ice. I was grateful that, unlike Kirk, Anna agreed to let me do something.

I passed Preston on my way to the lobby and he said we'd be taking off in five minutes, so I promised not to be late and hurried inside. I grabbed a bag of ice and headed back down the hallway. When I passed the flight room, I noticed Preston's briefcase sitting on the floor next to one of the chairs. He'd forgotten it after making his flight plan, so I grabbed the briefcase and made my way to the lobby, but then I paused by the door that led to the ramp.

Preston was talking to Sergio next to the plane, which would seem normal at first glance to the casual observer—a pilot talking to a mechanic, but I knew better. Preston's body language said it all. His hands were on his hips with his face close enough to Sergio's to kiss him, and Preston was doing all the talking. Preston lifted one hand to point an accusing finger at close range, and my heart picked up speed. Sergio made no movement at all, just stared at Preston without backing down, but I guessed an evil sneer was planted across his face. Apparently satisfied that he'd made his message clear, Preston turned on his heels and headed inside the plane. After a few seconds, Sergio casually strolled away toward the other line techs that were fueling the plane. I stepped outside and ran across the ramp.

I waved at a line tech and almost plowed into Sergio as I came around the fuel truck. Awkward. I skipped the apology but he stopped in his tracks, motioning me forward with his open palm pointing at the steps just a few feet away. Instead of a glare, which I was prepared to return, an uncanny smile was across his face. He watched me walk up the stairs and into the plane.

Everyone looked preoccupied, so I slipped Preston's briefcase into the same cabinet I saw Anna put her bag in, then went to where she stood and handed her the ice. She thanked me, informed Preston I was on board, and then closed the door. I took my seat next to a window and heard the familiar sound of the jet engines start up.

Sergio stood on my side near the front of the plane with wands in his hands. He stared at me while waiting for the signal from Preston, a smug grin plastered to his face that had made me uneasy. He had definitely seemed pleased to see me go, and the feeling was mutual.

"Yes!" Dax says, interrupting my memory. "I got it open."

Great. The briefcase is here because of me. It's fantastic to realize I am the source of my own torture. I already told him I don't want to know what's in it, so I wish he'd stop with the play-by-play. I can only hope Dax gets his fix so we can move on to something else. I keep my eyes closed, not wanting to acknowledge him, because I want to revisit the disturbing thought on the edge of my mind only moments ago.

The realization hits me and my eyes fly open. Sergio had seemed overly happy to see me go. *Sergio!*

I pick up my journal resting on my stomach and flip through the pages until I find the entry I'm looking for. My birthday. Sergio sitting in my chair, in my house, touching my things, breathing the same air, and then trying to touch my lips with his. I scan the page until I see the part that has been jumping up and down in the back of my mind, screaming for attention.

And for some reason, the only part of my body that would work was my mouth, telling him that when I blew out the candles on my birthday cake, my wish would definitely have something to do with him. "Like... Never. Seeing. You. Again," I said.

"Careful what you wish for, baby," he whispered. "Some wishes actually do come true."

Now I remember staring back at him through the small window of *Hotel Charlie* until he finally looked away after receiving the signal from the cockpit. We taxied off the ramp, and he deliberately glanced at me one last time—then flashed me an unfriendly gesture with his serpent tongue finger and mouthed the word—'goodbye'.

One little word. And I couldn't have been cut deeper by that double-edge sword if I'd grabbed the blade with both hands. Sergio knew I wouldn't be coming back.

I gasp and sit up, turning to tell Dax my theory. But his expression catches me off guard. The entire time I've been laying here sorting things out in my head, he's become extremely quiet. His face is full of shock and alarm, and he's studying the contents inside the briefcase like it's a ticking bomb he has to diffuse.

"Dax? What's wrong?"

He snaps out of his trance and looks up at me, but his usual friendly countenance is absent from his face. Curiosity gets the best of me and I get up to see what he found, but as soon as I approach the table, he tosses everything back inside and slams the briefcase shut. I'm so surprised that my feet stop even though I didn't tell them to. He crosses his arms and leans over the closed case.

"You know what? You were right. Pointless to open it. Do you wanna go for a swim?" he says, but his smile is different. He seems nervous.

"What's in it?" I ask, hoping he'll forget my numerous comments earlier about not caring.

"Uhm, well, there's not a ring. But there is some money." He clears his throat. "So, like I said, it was pointless."

He's a bad liar.

"Let me see the case."

I reach over to take the briefcase but he still leans on it with folded arms, looking as though he's prepared to fight me for it.

"What's wrong with you?" I demand. "I think you've gone mad."

"Look. You said earlier you didn't want to know. So let's just leave it at that. Man—it's getting hot in here. Let's go for a swim. Ladies first," he offers, a little too enthusiastically, and gestures to the exit.

I reach for the case again but now he holds on, and I'm beyond irritated. His game playing is infuriating. Time to pull out the heavy artillery.

"I could always tell Roxy about the briefcase, and exactly where to find it."

His eyes narrow and he clenches his jaw. "You wouldn't dare."

I challenge his challenge with a raise of my eyebrows. We stare each other down, but I can see a hint of doubt.

"Ava, please. I'm begging you. Trust me when I say you don't want to know. Let's just forget I opened it and—"

"Give me the briefcase!"

"Fine." He frowns, lets go of the case, and then crosses his arms over his chest. "Don't say I didn't warn you."

He watches me with careful eyes. I slide the case to the opposite end of the table and sit down, then slowly open the lid. A manila envelope is lying on top with a sticky note that says, '*Destroy this*'. I lift the envelope to pull out the contents and suck in a sharp breath when I see what's underneath. The trust letter I got on my birthday is sitting on top of my notebook—the notebook that disappeared from the library. I stare inside the briefcase, trying to convince myself that what I'm seeing isn't really there.

"What are you looking at?" Dax asks impatiently.

"This letter is from my house. And this is my notebook someone stole when I went to the library," I mumble.

"Forget that and just open the envelope," he says. "You aren't going to believe what's inside."

I pull out a stack of 8x10 pictures. The first one is a picture of me at my high school graduation, taken from a spot on the opposite side of the stands from where I know my parents sat. I move the picture to the back of the pile, exposing the next picture of me at the cemetery for my parent's burial, standing next to Mrs. Hansen with her arm wrapped around me. The pictures were taken from a distance. Someone had zoomed in to get the shots.

My mind is spinning with confusion, and I look up at Dax, who is still staring at me intently with his arms folded across his chest.

The next picture is of me getting off the plane in San Diego, and the one behind it is of me sitting at the little café inside the terminal. I swallow back the lump in my throat and continue to the next one.

There's a picture of me coming out of the mall, and another one of me at the library, standing at the curb waiting to cross moments before I'd almost been hit by the car. The picture was taken from behind me to my right, and as I study it, I notice the picture captured the black Mercedes coming into the frame. It *was* the same one that had been following me. My assumption was right.

Now one thing was clear.

My hunch of Preston having something to do with all of this seemed to be dead on. Only, I hadn't in my wildest dreams imagined him on the other side of the spectrum. He was part of the plot. A stabbing pain rips through my chest, and the all-too-familiar lump rises in my throat. How can this be?

"Impossible," I hear myself say, in a voice barely louder than a whisper.

"Uhm, yeah. It looks like your boy Preston wasn't so perfect after all," Dax says. "In fact, it appears he was a freaking stalker! That's just creepy."

I flip through the pictures again, one by one, looking for anything to point to another conclusion than the one Dax is suggesting and the one I fear the most. But my hope dissipates with each photo as I see they all have something in common. The *absence* of Preston.

"It doesn't make sense," I say in denial, more for my benefit and not his. "He loves me." My voice squeaks, and a tear streams down my cheek.

Dax speaks cautiously. "Ava, his mission was to get rid of you."

I look at him in horror before shaking my head. Preston's involvement is obvious, but Dax's new assumption is way out of line.

"Look," Dax says, getting up to walk around the table and stand next to me. He lifts up my notebook to expose a pile of money underneath. Lots of money—bundled stacks of one hundred dollar bills. On top of the money is a handwritten note.

The situation has gotten out of control.
She knows too much, and we already have what we need.
She has become a problem that needs to be eliminated.
You'll get the rest of the money when you find me a new
plane.

I blink and stare in disbelief as the reason for George's final warning hits me. Preston must have left the briefcase on purpose because he didn't want it on the plane. He knew it might be lost. Kirk? Anna? Were they *all* in on it? I let the letter fall from my hand, then fold my arms on the table and bury my face in them, not wanting Dax to see my onslaught of tears. I feel his hand on my back, rubbing gently, trying his best to console me.

"Are you okay? I'm so sorry. It's all my fault. I shouldn't have convinced you to let me open the briefcase." His voice is full of regret.

"It's not your fault," I sob. "If you hadn't opened it, I never would have known."

"That's exactly why—"

"No," I interrupt. "I deserve to know how naïve and gullible I really am. I'm so embarrassed."

He reaches for my arm, lifts me up from the table, then wraps his arms around me and holds me as I weep. I've cried so much since my time on this island that I'm sure Dax probably thinks I'm mentally unstable. I'm beginning to wonder that myself.

He leads me to the bedroom and sits me down on the bed.

"Close your eyes," he says. "Don't open them until I tell you."

I do as he says, but I fight the urge to reach for him as I feel him move away. The briefcase snaps closed in the main room. His footsteps fade away as he leaves to discard of the evidence and main source of my unhappiness. He returns before I have time to panic. Lying next to me, he pulls me into a tight embrace.

"You can open them," he says gently, and when I do, all I see is a blur through my tears that are streaming down his chest. I cling to him, melting into his arms that are trying to subdue my sobs, and then he whispers in my ear.

"I'm so sorry, Ava. I'm so truly sorry."

24
Preston
DAY FOUR: THE MESSAGE

I *WAKE UP FIRST AS PLANNED AND SNEAK OUTSIDE* without making a sound. Kirk won't come exploring with me, but he's definitely not keeping me from doing it. I hurry past the waterfall and don't stop to walk until I reach the outlet that led me to the cliff by the ocean yesterday.

Daylight is barely peeking through the trees, and the quiet of the morning is peaceful and tranquil. I slow down only when I'm a safe distance from being seen if Kirk wakes up.

I'm heading to the cliffs again, but this time, I plan to go below and explore the beach in the opposite direction. I slip my hands in my pockets and my fingers find the tiny box. There's something calming about running my fingers back and forth along the velvet.

The squawk of a bird startles me, and I stop to search the trees above me. A bird that can make that kind of noise must be a decent size. The trees tower above me; some so high I can't see the top. I do a three-sixty to slowly scan the branches, and my eyes fall on a specific tree.

The trunk is wider than the rest of the trees in the forest, but the height doesn't reach more than fifteen feet. The large leaves sprawl out over a huge, flat rock, overgrown with dense, lush moss. Flowers pop up from behind the rock, making the entire scene look like something out of a fairy tale.

I wade across the stream and step onto the rock. Above me, the branches are like a massive umbrella protecting this sanctuary. For a minute, I wonder if the whole thing is manmade. It is the most beautiful and magical place I've ever seen, and I'm suddenly overcome with emotion, wishing Ava were here to see it.

My fingers wrap around the tiny box, and I pull it from my pocket. I lift the lid and take one painful glance at the ring before I close my eyes and imagine her standing in front of me right now, her eyes widening as I drop to one knee. I'd propose just like that, and I couldn't have found a more perfect place if I'd searched the whole world.

I snap it shut and slip the box back in my pocket. But I will never get that chance, and this place will never be ours. The pain inside my chest is almost unbearable. I will never be able to walk past this spot and not think of her.

A thought pops into my head. Reaching into my other pocket for my Montblanc pen, I jump to my feet. I spend minutes moving around the rock, studying the tree from different angles, until I find the perfect spot. Then, with great care and precision I use the pen to carve a message.

I'm not sure how many minutes or hours go by, but when I'm finally finished, I step back to admire my work. A large heart stares back at me from eye level. In the center, it says:

Preston
loves
Ava

Dax

DAY FIVE: LUCKY BREAK

VA CRIED HERSELF TO SLEEP IN MY ARMS, BUT THE peace I see on her face now is doing little to wipe away the guilt I feel for causing her such anguish—first the reading of her journal, and then the insistence to open the briefcase. Some knight in shining armor I've become.

Her cheek is warm nestled against my chest. One of her arms loops around my back and the other drapes up and over my shoulder where her fingers graze the hair at the back of my neck. I reach up to sweep a strand of hair from her face and tuck it behind her ear with a feather light touch. My fingers refrain from skimming along the skin of her delicate arm because I worry she'll wake from my racing heart beneath her ear.

I should be happy that Preston has managed to get himself disqualified from this unspoken competition, but the anger I feel towards him is putting a damper on the celebration. I've always thought he must be lying at the bottom of the ocean, but now drowning seems like too easy a death for him. A traitor like that deserves to be ripped limb from limb and fed to the cannibals.

I need a distraction. If only I hadn't lost the one thing that has kept me occupied for the last few days, I could slip it out of my pocket now and read the last three entries.

Where is the journal? She'd had it when we came in the bedroom, clutched in her hands against her chest, protecting it like it was the last book on earth, but now her hands are both on me. *Her hands are on me.*

My heart skips a beat. I can't think about that.

The journal.

I tilt my head up. There it is. Laying on the end table to my right, open and face down where she must have left it when I left to dispose of the case.

At the nape of my neck, her fingers twitch ever so slightly next to my skin and cause a tickling sensation that ignites every nerve in my being. My slow exhale rustles her hair. I need that damn journal before I lose all self-control.

I reach out and the tip of my middle finger barely brushes the rim of the spine. A mere inch keeps me from being successful. She's tucked up under my other arm so I lean just slightly, bringing her with me, and the move is so slow and minimal she doesn't even flinch. I flip my hand over to tuck my finger under the V of the opening and carefully nudge the book closer to the edge of the table so it becomes within reach.

My hand slips under the pages, and I silently lift the journal off the table and bring it into view. The book is open to the page where she finds Sergio in her house so, with the use of one hand and my mouth, I turn past the Catalina entry to the one where I left off. I peek down at her and then back to the page.

August 16

This morning, Preston drove me to work and dropped me off a few minutes early to talk to George, promising to return to pick me up for lunch before he and Kirk headed to the beach to surf. Ever since I told him about the trust two nights ago, he doesn't seem to want to let me out of his sight.

I made my way upstairs to George's office where he was sitting behind his desk. His office looked the same as I remembered from my interview. The desk was a cluttered, unorganized mess, with stacks of paperwork piled on either side of his workspace.

He motioned for me to sit down in the same chair I occupied just a few months before for my strange interview. He asked what was on my mind while he sifted through some papers directly in front of him. I told him I was there to give my two weeks' notice and caught him completely off guard. I already felt bad considering I've only been there for two months, but he made me feel worse when he said I was one of the best line hostess' he'd ever had.

Then the conversation got really awkward when he asked if I'd found another job in town and instead of just saying no, I suddenly came down with a case of verbal diarrhea and proceeded to tell him I've been dating Preston and that he asked me to go to Europe with him, where I planned to go to school in the fall.

George's face was blank for a moment, and then he slowly leaned back in his chair. He removed his reading glasses, set them on the desk, then rested his elbows on the armrests and placed his hands together, finger to finger in front of his chest. The congratulations I expected were nowhere to be found. Instead, his face creased with worry, or disapproval, I couldn't tell which.

"Is this about money?" he asked. I held my breath, thinking at first that he was referring to the trust money. But then he offered to re-evaluate my pay and give me a wage increase and some more vacation time. Oh, that money. I resumed breathing and almost laughed out loud. I must have looked like a deer in headlights.

Anyway, he forced a nod and didn't wait for me to accept before he told me he'd fill out the forms and send them to personnel. I thanked him but gently reminded him that the best option was for me to go to school. He actually suggested I check out the colleges in San Diego before I make any "rash decisions" I may regret later.

He went on and on about how he'd work around my schedule and even insisted I take the rest of the day off to go check some local colleges out. Then he said we'd talk again next week after I'd had time to look at all my options. He gave me a short smile, then he put his glasses back on and focused his attention back to the papers in front of him.

Obviously, he hadn't heard the part about me dating Preston or he wouldn't have suggested that I stay here and let him leave me behind. Then again, it's probably not good for business to have a calendar girl quit before the year even begins.

I should have argued but the thought of spending the afternoon watching Preston shirtless on top of a gigantic wave overruled my rational thinking so I thanked him and left, figuring I'd just stall for a couple of days and then tell him, but Preston took care of it the minute he found out.

I told Preston what happened when he picked me up for lunch, and he flipped the car around and parked. He made his way through the lobby with me in tow, past the curious stares of the front-desk girls, and then headed up to George's office. Preston tapped lightly on the doorframe, and George looked up from his desk and told us to come in.

I tried to relax as we sat down, but Preston got right to the point. I watched the faint grin disappear from George's round face when Preston told him a local college wouldn't be necessary because Mr. Caruso offered me a job as a flight attendant. He then proceeded to tell George I would need Friday off to fly with him to pick up Mr. C in Australia "so he can extend the offer personally" and added that my two weeks' notice still applied. Preston spoke smoothly and with confidence, but the tongue-lashing I expected to follow his speech was nowhere to be found. George leaned back in his chair, looking very pleased, and glanced between Preston and me.

"Well, I can't argue with that, now, can I? Why didn't you say so, Ava?" he stated in a matter-of-fact manner. Then he rushed on to tell me that Mr. Caruso is a fine employer and he'd certainly miss me, but I made a wise choice considering my other options and he was happy it all worked out and then ended with "That'll be nice for you kids to get to travel together at Mr. Caruso's expense."

Yeah. Wrong thing to say. I started to get up, content with his assumption, but Preston apparently felt the need to clear up the misunderstanding. He reached over to take my hand and said to George, "I said Mr. Caruso offered the job to Ava, but I didn't say she was going to take it. It seems her mind is already made up. I've offered to help Mr. Caruso start looking for another pilot as well."

George shifted uneasily in his chair and paused before he said, "Well, it appears it's too late then, and there's nothing I can do to change your mind." Small beads of sweat formed on his balding forehead. He reached up, tugged at the collar of his dress shirt, and then said, "That's unfortunate. I'm sure Mr. Caruso will be very sorry to lose such a good pilot as you."

He forced a weak smile, stood up, shook Preston's hand, and then glanced at me to wish me the best of luck. If only he knew the truth about the twisted relationship between luck and me, he wouldn't have wasted that wish on me.

August 18

Today Preston picked me up at five when my shift was over and brought me to my house to pack. We barely walked in the front door when my cell phone rang. It was Mrs. Hansen. Her call surprised me because I'd forgotten I gave her my phone number to call me in case of any emergency.

I asked her if everything was okay and put the phone on speaker so Preston could hear the conversation. A cold shiver ran down my spine when she told me someone had broken into my parent's house. She tried to take the blame, worried she hadn't gone over enough to check things out and it didn't help that the police told her whoever it was must have noticed no one was living there.

I assured her she wasn't to blame and asked what was taken, hanging on to a glimmer of hope that it was a random break-in and nothing related to what's been happening since I moved here. But that hope died when she said nothing appeared to be missing and that it looked like they just went through my parents' office. "It's a disaster in there," she said. "They ransacked the desk, and there are papers everywhere. The police thought they might be looking for a safe or some paperwork. You know how popular identity theft has become."

Preston stared at me with eyes as wide as mine, and "Oh" was all I could manage to say because my mind was spinning wildly out of control. She apologized again and told me she started to pick up but decided to wait until after she talked to me.

I asked her how they got in and I can't say I was surprised when she told me there were no signs of forced entry and the doors were locked when she arrived. She wasn't sure when the break-in took place but knew it had to have been within the last week.

Before we said our goodbyes, I told her I'm planning to come home in two weeks and that I'd take care of it then. Preston promises me everything will be fine and even offered to come with me to Colorado so, for now, I will only worry about my dreaded meeting with Mr. C.

The plan is to leave tomorrow at six o'clock after I get off work. Preston says we'll have to stop in Hawaii for fuel and then continue to Australia. That means we'll arrive in Australia early Saturday morning, and Preston hopes to have the rest of Saturday to hang out and surf before Mr. C wants to leave—most likely Sunday morning. I keep telling myself if I can survive those sixteen and a half hours with Mr. C, I'll never have to do it again. I guess it's a small speck of time considering what I hope will be an eternity spent with Preston. I can definitely live with that.

"Dax?"

My blood stops cold in my veins. When I look down, her eyes are still closed. In a panic, I toss the journal on the table and kiss her on the forehead to create a distraction. Her lids flutter open to expose her red, swollen eyes.

"Yes?" I answer.

"I'm so thirsty."

"Yeah, sure. Let me get you some water." She sits up. Slipping out from under her, I ignore the stabbing pain in my lower back from acting as her personal pillow for so long. I get a cup and fill it with water and when I return, she's staring at the journal.

She's so transfixed she doesn't notice the hesitation in my step. I purposely sit facing her and use my body to block the book from her view. Maybe she didn't notice it wasn't the way she left it. I hand her the cup.

"Get rid of it," she says, and then takes a long sip from the cup.

"What?"

"Get rid of the journal. Put it wherever you hid the brief-case or burn it. I don't care."

I must look ridiculous staring at her like she just spoke in a foreign language.

"But—"

"I know you were reading it. It doesn't matter now. Almost the entire thing is based on a lie. Hopes and dreams that will never come true." A tear falls from her eye, and I wonder how it's possible for her to have any tears left. "Please. I don't want it anymore. Just make it go away."

I nod and pick up the leather book. When I get to the door of the room, I turn to see if she'll change her mind, but she's staring back at me with steady resolve.

I can't say I blame her. The fewer reminders of Preston, the better. I crawl through the tunnel to the treasure room and click open the briefcase to toss the journal inside. And I was one entry away from finishing it. My hand rests on the top of the case but refuses to pull it closed. Just one more. She'll never know any different.

The book falls open in my hand and I flip quickly to the last page, but I only read the first two sentences before I shove the book in my pocket and hurry back through the tunnel. Ava is on the couch, lying on her back, staring up at the ceiling. She turns her head when I stumble into the room.

"What is the last thing you remember before you woke

up here?" I ask.

"Why?"

"You said you don't remember anything after getting on the plane. So you don't remember actually flying?"

"No. The last thing I remember is Sergio flipping me the bird right before we taxied away." She swings her legs around and sits up to face me. "Why are you asking me this?"

I swallow and pull her journal from my pocket to hand it to her. "Because you wrote about the flight in your journal."

I'm nervous because I'm holding in my hand the one thing she wants destroyed. Gone. Wiped from her mind like fingerprints with a cloth.

"Just tell me what it says." Her eyes meet mine. I take another step towards her and sit the book in her lap.

"I think you should read it yourself. I know you don't want to, but it might jog your memory and help you figure out what happened. That's what you want, right?"

What she probably wants is to snap her fingers and wake up in her old life. The one with her parents and no memories of Preston, but that life wouldn't include me.

I'm hoping my enthusiasm will spark what little hope she has left for peace and decide maybe I'm right. Because she's refusing to pick it up, like it will burn her skin if she tries, and she stares at it so long that I finally sit beside her and pick it up myself. I wrap my arm around her, kiss her on the temple, and then open the journal to the last page.

"You can do it," I tell her. "I'm right here. We will read it together and if I'm wrong—you can dispose of me along with the book."

A smile tugs at my lips.

"And how would I go about doing that?" she asks, and now I'm a little worried she might take me up on the offer.

"I don't know. I guess you can bury me in the treasure room with all of my treasures. But at least you could read a little first before you start planning my demise."

Her lips twitch to fight back a grin. She sighs and nods her head to begin.

August 19

Kirk is snoring. Preston's in the cockpit by himself because Kirk is asleep on the couch and has been there since we landed in Hawaii for a quick turn about three hours ago. Watching him sleep makes me tired, but I want to stay up to wait for Preston. Kirk's turn to fly is less than an hour away.

This is so much better than flying commercially. As soon as we took off, I reclined my seat and looked out the window at the deep ocean below. The water became a blue blur in the distance, and all I could see were soft, billowing clouds. One hour into the flight, I pulled out my sketchpad, intent on drawing the view, but gave up and decided to make a list of things I need to accomplish in the next three weeks. I was completely surprised when Preston sat down next to me. Anna was absorbed in her book, and she didn't seem the least bit concerned that Preston had wandered out of the cockpit.

"Hey beautiful," he said, reaching over to tuck my hair behind my ear. He smelled as incredible as he looked. I couldn't help asking him if he should be in the cockpit with Kirk, but his soft laugh put me at ease. "Relax," he told me. "Kirk has it under control. Besides, the plane practically flies itself."

He glanced down at my list of things to do and for some reason, I decided it would be a great time to ask about his conversation with Sergio. His lips twitched before a guilty grin emerged. He said he simply made it clear that he's to stay away from me or he'll be wrenching on Hotel Charlie from a wheelchair.

I love that he stood up for me but asked if that was a good idea considering Sergio might tell Mr. C, but Preston said Sergio won't tell because he'll incriminate himself. I'm not sure what he means by that but before I could ask, he distracted me by moving to sit in the seat that faced me. He asked me to draw him and then started striking ridiculous poses to make me laugh. I flipped to a crisp, white page and told him to sit still. "I can do that," he said. "I'll gladly sit here all day if it means I get to look at you."

Him and his flustering comments. I glanced up to see if Anna was listening, but she appeared to be completely oblivious that we were even there. I felt self-conscious as he sat there, smiling with his gaze fixated on me. I was supposed to be studying him, not the other way around.

I was so nervous and started making random comments to distract him like, "don't forget you're flying a plane," and "are you sure you shouldn't go check on Kirk?" and "this drawing won't do me any good if it's floating in the middle of the ocean." That was the only comment that actually got his attention. He cocked an eyebrow and demanded an explanation, so I told him there must be girls willing to pay good money to have a picture of him on their wall. He stifled a laugh before glancing at the paper and then back to me.

I scolded him for moving and he agreed to hold perfectly still, flaunting his incredible smile and charming me with a seductive wink. I wanted to capture that smolder on paper. The trick was to not let him dazzle me to the point I forgot how to draw.

He sat like a statue until I finished, then he reached for the sketchpad and studied the drawing. He looked at me again with an astonished look, and my face got hot in response. Preston shut the sketchpad and told me he needed to go back to the cockpit and give Kirk a break. "But I'm taking this with me," he said, holding up my sketchpad. "Wait until Kirk sees this." Then he kissed me before returning to the front of the plane.

After a few minutes, Kirk came bouncing out of the cockpit to hand me my sketchpad and then stood in front of me, with his hands resting on his hips.

"What gives, Miss April? I don't recall you or Preston ever mentioning anything about you being an artist, especially when we were hanging out in...let me see, where was it... oh yeah, an ART GALLERY!" Anna looked up at the sound of his raised voice, and I snickered as he gawked at me with his contagious grin. He paused, looking pleased that he'd gotten Anna's attention, even for a brief moment, before she went back to reading. (Preston told me Kirk's had a huge crush on Anna since he started flying for Mr. C. and she never pays him any attention.)

Then Kirk told me, "Don't you think that's something you should have made a point of putting in the calendar, kind of more important than—likes rainy days and a good book?" He used his fingers to float quote marks in the air. Putting his hands out, he shrugged his shoulders. "I'm just sayin'."

I giggled and explained I was limited on the number of words, but he gave me the familiar two fingers to his squinted eyes point to let me know he'd be watching me before he sat down across the table from Anna. Kirk is so funny. I still don't understand how Anna managed to sit there and completely ignore him. Neither could he.

She looked up at him briefly before her gaze fell back to the page she was reading, and I pulled my book closer to my face to avoid watching Kirk's useless attempt to get her to pay attention to him.

Kirk asked her what her book was about and she told him "a girl". I could hear a bit of irritation in her voice, which definitely made the situation awkward—at least for me. "Cool. I like girls," Kirk said, and I cringed.

He waited for her to respond, but she didn't, so he invited her to go to the beach with us tomorrow when we get to Australia. He made the offer sound casual and friendly, but I think deep down he was subliminally begging her with his mind. She declined politely without an explanation, so Kirk gave up on asking questions and rambled on about his favorite things to see in Australia.

I couldn't help lower my book to get a glimpse of her expression. She placed a bookmark between the pages and laid the book down on the table, then gave him a polite half-smile and got up as he continued talking. She poured Kirk a soda and then busied herself with preparing dinner. Maybe she hoped he would shut up long enough to drink it.

I think she pretended to be asleep when he came out of the cockpit later to nap, because as soon as he started snoring, she started reading her book again. Poor Kirk. At least those two will keep this tortuously long flight entertaining when Preston's not around.

26

Ava

DAY FIVE: UNLUCKY TRUTH

S I READ THROUGH THE PAGES, IMAGES FLASH through my mind. I can picture Preston sitting across from me, winking and stifling his amusement when he's supposed to hold still, and I see Kirk in front of me with his hands on his hips, questioning me about the sketches. And Anna fingers her necklace with one hand while she holds her book with the other.

"Well?" Dax asks.

I nod my head and close my eyes. "It's working."

I flip through those images again and focus on bringing other parts into view. The entire memory comes flooding over me like a huge tidal wave. Now I can see Kirk sitting across from Anna as she reads, using his hands to describe things he's seen in Australia and wants her to see. She's ignoring him, and then I see her preparing dinner—Kirk taking plates into the cockpit—Kirk sleeping on the couch, and now myself putting my book away in my backpack to pull something else out. An envelope.

I was digging for a piece of gum in my purse and my fingers ran into the envelope from George. I took great pleasure in knowing that the entire paycheck would go towards everything I needed for our trip to Europe. Slipping my finger under the flap, I tore open the envelope to pull out the check to look at the amount. My excitement disintegrated as I unfolded the white paper wrapped neatly around the check, revealing the blatant warning in the center of the paper.

DON'T GET ON THE PLANE

My heart dropped like a cannonball into the pit of my stomach.

I had stared at the note, not wanting to admit what I knew to be true and vividly remember coming to the realization that George had been the one sending the notes. He had my address. His real reason for giving me my check early had been to warn me and stop me from getting on the plane. I thought about all the other warnings. '*I know your secret*', *you're being watched*', and '*don't push your luck*'. George must know everything—who's been following me... who wants the trust money. And he'd acted like he didn't want me to go to Europe. For a few agonizing minutes, I had wondered if his warnings were about Preston.

The cabin spun and nausea filled my stomach, making me regret eating the entire sandwich for dinner. I shoved the paycheck and note into my purse, then jumped up and ran to the bathroom, threw up once, then slid to the floor in the tiny lav and put my head on my knees.

In the small lav on the plane, I had unwillingly contemplated the fact that maybe Preston really wasn't as perfect as he appeared to be. The whole idea seemed absurd. He must have had a background check to be a pilot. So if he wasn't a criminal, then what reason would George have for not wanting me to go with him? He wouldn't go to all the trouble to warn me unless he thought I was in danger. No matter how hard I tried, I couldn't fathom the idea and couldn't imagine Preston wanting to do me any harm. *A ridiculous notion*, I thought, one I tried desperately to shove to the back of my mind.

The tap on the lav door had startled me, and I lifted my head.

"Ava, are you okay?" Preston said from the other side of the door.

"Uhm, just a minute."

Anna must have noticed me bolting for the lav like a maniac. I stood up and turned on the water to splash some on my face. When I finally opened the door, he greeted me with a look of shock.

"Are you sick?"

His face melted into my favorite smile but part of me resented him for looking so incredible when I wasn't sure if I'd have to force myself to hate him in the near future.

"I'm fine now," I lied, and he escorted me to the sofa.

He made the couch into a bed. Kirk must have returned to the cockpit, probably a little early so Preston could check on me. I felt a pang of guilt and a little embarrassment. Preston sat down next to me, and Anna appeared with some ginger ale and a damp cloth, which she handed to him. He lifted my hair to place the cool cloth around my neck and then brushed my hair behind my ears.

"You better add *buy something for motion sickness* to your list of things to do." He chuckled. "I'm a little worried now about dragging you across the ocean."

"It was probably a combo of looking out the window and too much reading."

I had hoped he wouldn't know I was lying. I knew my nerves were the real culprits.

Anna placed a blanket next to me before returning to her seat. I slipped off my tennis shoes and lay down. Preston covered me with the blanket and lay down next to me, then pulled me close. I rested my head on his shoulder, inhaled the sweet scent of his cologne, and wondered if I would have to distance myself and even reconsider sailing across the ocean with him. Deep down, I knew that would be an improbability. I snuggled closer, taking pleasure in the comfort of his warm arms, and my nausea subsided.

I was no different from a lobster in a pot, so content and comfortable, oblivious to any threat of eminent danger the warmness might inflict upon me.

The whole idea of him being a threat sent me into a confused panic, and I was mentally exhausted. I wanted nothing more than to ignore the note and the warnings. I knew I should tell Preston, but I didn't because I wanted to treasure every moment with him, and ignore the fact that those moments might be too good to be true.

I had drifted off in Preston's arms and when I awoke, he was gone so I knew I'd slept longer than five hours. I folded up the blanket, put my shoes on, and walked back to my seat. Anna stood at the entrance to the cockpit, right behind Preston and Kirk.

I picked my purse up off the floor that fell in my haste to run to the bathroom and put it back in my backpack. My empty stomach growled in protest, and I pulled out my phone to check the time. I'd only been asleep for four hours. We would be arriving in Australia in about three and a half hours, and I took pleasure in knowing I would sleep peacefully in the comfort of a hotel bed.

No one noticed that I'd returned to my seat, so I grabbed a magazine and started flipping through the pages, but suddenly Anna's voice got louder. She sounded irritated and was immediately shushed by Preston and Kirk. I glanced toward the cockpit and saw them talking in hushed voices. I couldn't make out what they were arguing about, but I could tell something was wrong. Anna's back was to me, making it impossible to read her lips, and she blocked my entire view of Kirk and Preston.

I returned my attention to my magazine, hoping Preston would fill me in after we landed, but then Anna rushed back into the cabin to sit in her seat. She held the large cross pendant from her necklace in one hand and made the sign of the cross over her chest. I stared at her, confused by the blank expression on her face, but she avoided looking at me.

I leaned over to look in the cockpit and saw Preston and Kirk still absorbed in quiet conversation that appeared to be very intense. Preston got up and walked into the cabin. He gave me the same weak smile that Anna gave me only moments ago.

"Promise me you won't panic." Preston took my hands in his, and my brows furrowed as he leaned closer. I sat motionless, waiting for him to continue. "It seems there's something wrong with the plane, well numerous things actually. There must be a fuel leak because we're dangerously low on fuel. And for some reason, the radios aren't working either."

His next words came out with a sense of urgency, as if he were speaking to a child, trying to make me understand something important.

"We don't have enough fuel to make it to Australia. We aren't even going to make it to New Guinea like I'd hoped. We have no choice but to do an emergency landing."

He paused, and the reality of what he said sunk in. Geography had been my least favorite subject in school, but I knew enough to know that with the exception of a few scattered islands, there wasn't anywhere to land between Hawaii and New Guinea except in the middle of the Atlantic Ocean.

Don't get on the plane.

George knew. Panic overtook me and my breath came faster. "Are we going to crash?" My voice sounded foreign to me, higher pitched and bordering on hysterical.

"Yes."

I could tell he tried to keep his voice as calm as possible. I wanted to tell him about the note, but it didn't matter—it was too late, and before I could say anything else, he let go of my hands and placed his on either side of my face.

"Listen to me. We only have a couple of minutes; this is extremely important. Anna will give you a life vest. Put it on but whatever you do, do not inflate it until you're out of the plane. Do you understand?"

I nodded. Tears streamed down my cheeks between his hands.

Anna dragged a large case marked LIFE RAFT from the rear of the plane and was fastening it securely to the seat next to hers. Next, she grabbed the life vests from a cabinet, handed three of them to Preston, and then slipped one over her head before returning to her seat.

"I'm going to do everything in my power to make sure you survive," Preston assured me. "When I tell you to, put your chest on your thighs, your head between your knees, and wrap your arms around your legs. Tuck your legs under the seat as much as possible. After we cra—land in the water, unfasten the seatbelt and get out of the plane however you can." I followed his eyes to the door. "When you get out—"

"What about you?" I interrupted, terrified of being separated from him.

"When we get out of the plane," he corrected, "I want you to swim as far away from it as possible. I will find you." He leaned in quickly, pressing his lips firmly to mine.

"Ava, you can do this." He let go of my face and slipped the life vest over my head, then fastened my seatbelt and pulled it snug. "Remember—undo your seatbelt, pull this cord when you're outside of the plane, and swim!"

"Preston!" Kirk yelled from the cockpit over a series of beeps and alarms.

Preston jumped up and ran toward the cockpit.

My heart beat triple time. Anna sat in her seat with her seat belt fastened. Her eyes were closed, and she held the large cross from the chain around her neck. Her other hand gripped the armrest.

We descended rapidly, and the plane bounced around through turbulent air. Raindrops clawed at the window, and I pushed the button to lower the shade. My panic turned to alarm. Not only were we going to crash land into the water, but into a storm as well. I closed my eyes.

The turbulence got worse, and I heard the strain of the engines as Preston and Kirk struggled to slow the plane down before it touched the water. My fingers squeezed the armrests. I longed to be with Preston, for him to be next to me holding my hand, talking to me in his calm, velvet voice. I was terrified. But more than I feared dying, I feared the possibility of surviving without him.

And then, before I was ready, I heard him scream with urgency from the cockpit.

"AVA, NOW!"

I leaned over and put my head between my knees. My pulse pounded loudly in my head. I flung my arms around my legs and squeezed tight. Anna had cried and mumbled a prayer over and over between sobs. Kirk screamed a string of profanities that caused my heart to pound faster and louder, barely audible over my rapid, uneven breaths. I squeezed my eyes shut, held my breath, and braced for the impact.

For what seemed like a very long second, it fell completely silent, and then the silence exploded into the deafening sound of metal ripping apart, and my screams muffled Anna's. The force of impact jerked and jolted my body around, and I struggled to keep my grip around my legs. The plane bounced off the water and hit a second time, then rose again only to hit harder the third time and stop abruptly. My body lunged forward against the restraint of the seatbelt. The smell of smoke filled the air and faster than I could think, stillness engulfed the cabin and cool water crept around my ankles.

"Ava!" Preston yelled.

I sat up and saw nothing but darkness around me. My hands shook violently and I fumbled to release the belt, but Preston slid into the seat next to me and released my seatbelt for me as the water rushed in around my legs. The plane must have torn into separate pieces judging from the alarming rate the cabin was filling with water. In a matter of seconds, the water was above my waist. Preston grabbed my hand and jerked me out of my seat, pulling me along behind him. The water rose to my stomach and made it harder to move.

"The life raft is stuck!" Anna screamed.

I could barely see her from the dim lights illuminating the walkway underneath the water. Preston stopped to help her, but Kirk appeared at her side. I remember a trickle of blood ran down his face from a large cut above his right eye.

"I've got it, Preston!" Kirk yelled. "Take care of Ava!"

Anna stood on the seat with her hands braced against the ceiling of the plane to escape the swiftly rising water. Terror consumed her face as Kirk took a big breath and then dove under the water in an attempt to free the life raft.

Preston hesitated for only a second before pulling me towards the exit. The water was up to my chest, and I struggled to stay right behind him. He opened the door and a blast of wind and rain hit my face.

"Take a big breath and jump—then swim away from the plane! I'll be right behind you," he yelled.

The water rose and dropped in front of me in large swells, but I held my breath and jumped. When my lungs started to burn, I knew I was running out of air. I kicked as hard as I could and reached with my free arm to grasp for the air I hoped was waiting close above me. When my face pierced through the surface, I gasped for air, but the choppy water pounded me from every direction.

I choked on some water and turned around to search for Preston in the darkness. I expected him to be right next to me, but I spun around in every direction and he was nowhere to be found. I struggled to tread water and screamed his name, but I could barely hear the sound of my own voice over the pounding rain.

The wind was unforgiving. It created white caps on the swells and blew the salty mist into my face. I blinked, trying to make sense of my surroundings. With my hands still shaking, I felt for the cord under the water and pulled, causing the vest to instantly inflate around my neck. I could barely make out the shape of what was left of the plane, the white paint standing out in contrast to the blackness around it. I swam towards the plane, but then stopped when I became disoriented in the black of the night. He told me to swim away from the wreckage, and I had gone closer.

I screamed for him, but he didn't answer. The rear section of the plane vanished from view, so I turned away from the wreckage and tried to swim back to where I'd been, but it was impossible. I had no bearings. I screamed his name again and again until my voice was hoarse. I stopped swimming and tried to listen for any response, but the rain and wind were so loud that it was all I could hear. The plane was getting farther away at an alarming rate. But I'd stopped swimming. The only explanation for me drifting away so swiftly was that I must have gotten caught in a strong current. I couldn't see the door to the plane with all the water pounding my face, but I knew I had to get closer or Preston would never find me, but the more I tried to swim against the pull, the more tired I got.

My teeth were chattering from the rain, which was colder than the ocean water that engulfed me. I felt a strange movement in the water just below my feet, like a bunch of bubbles forcing their way to the surface of the water, and panic set in. I struggled to lean forward and squinted in the darkness to search the water in front of me.

Before I could react, something shot out of the water like a rocket and collided with my forehead, grazing me just above my left eye. Frightened and stunned, I blinked through the rain and saw a dark shape floating in the water in front of me, then felt something brush past my foot and wrap around my ankle. I screamed, moving my arms and legs in the water, but felt no escape from the object that entrapped my entire leg like long tentacles. I reached for my leg but the strain caused my head to pound at the source of impact. The force of the blow was severe enough that I reached with my other hand to touch my head, expecting to find a large gash. For a split second, I was worried about attracting sharks, so I put my hand an inch in front of my face to look for any signs of blood. Trembling and terrified, I tried to see my fingers, but they were blurry, fuzzy, and then I was unable to find them at all because everything went completely black.

My eyes open to meet Dax's worried stare.

"I remember everything," I tell him, and for the first time since I've known him, he's completely speechless. "I discovered the last note on the plane but said nothing about it to anyone." I shake my head. "I even wondered if George had been warning me about Preston—I actually suspected him—but then talked myself out of it."

Dax scoots closer. "So what happened to the plane? Did it crash?"

"Yeah. Preston and Kirk made an emergency landing in the middle of the Pacific Ocean. We ran out of fuel."

"How did you run out of fuel? I mean, don't take this the wrong way, but shouldn't a good pilot know how much fuel you need to get to Australia?"

Normally, his comment would irritate me, but he has

a valid point. Unless running out of fuel was the plan all along.

"I don't know." I say. "Preston said we should have had enough, but then it was gone all of a sudden, and too late to turn back. And the radios weren't working either."

"So they couldn't even call for help."

"Or they didn't want to."

Dax's eyebrows knit together. "So where are they?"

"Probably at the bottom of the ocean. Preston told me to jump out and said he would follow me, but he didn't. He just let me float away."

"Ava, I'm so sorry. I know you—loved him."

There's such tenderness and genuine sorrow in his voice that I almost feel bad when I tell him, "Don't be. He left me to die." I blink back tears and then laugh bitterly at the irony. "The life raft was stuck in the seat belt. Since it washed up on shore, they must have gotten it free but not in time. Guess their entire plan turned out to be a major fail. Especially since I'm still alive."

Dax takes my hand and gives it a reassuring squeeze. "Let's go back to the tree house and get some food in you, then I'll find something fun for us to do, I promise."

I know he's doing his best to console me, to take my mind off the devastation that has ripped my heart completely apart. I appreciate his efforts, but I know this kind of damage will take a long time to undo. In fact, I'm almost sure it might be permanent.

Dax doesn't pull out the quarter—he must know I won't even watch him flip it, let alone call it in the air. I sit silently as he rows us back to the other side, and then I wait for him to stash the canoe. My feet seem heavier than usual as he pulls me along behind him, and I try to think of nothing other than placing one foot in front of the other.

Dax

MIDDAY: TRAIL OF CLUES

I *DON'T EVEN THINK AVA NOTICES WE'RE AT THE TREE* house until I bring her inside the kitchen hut and sit her down in a chair. I place some sliced fruit in front of her with a cup full of water and then go to the counter to get some pork.

"Seriously?" I'm staring at a naked carcass. "It's not enough that I gave them almost the entire boar, they had to steal some of ours?"

"No one stole any. I ate it," Roxy says, and Ava jumps at the sound of her voice.

I say, "You *ate* it? You expect me to believe you ate an entire butt of a pig?"

"I was starving, okay?" she says with a glare. "It's not like you've been around the last few days so I had to fend for myself, and you know I'm not very good at it."

I hear the accusing tone in her voice, and it strikes a nerve. "Well, you know the saying *you are what you eat?* I guess it's pretty accurate in this case."

"Are you calling me a pig?" she asks, her voice raised one octave.

"I'm just calling it like I see it. Come on, Ava, let's go catch some fish." I walk over to her while keeping Roxy in view to watch for any retaliation.

Ava gives me a weak smile and then says, "I just want

to go up to my room."

Ava walks out of the kitchen, and it's like she's taking half my heart with her. I follow her up the long ladder to my dad's old room, expecting her to ask me to stay with her, but she acts like I'm not even there.

I'm at a loss for words, so I stand in the doorway and watch her sit down in the middle of the floor and dump out the contents of her backpack. I know she's upset and angry, but I don't expect her to fling the sketchpad against the wall where it lands in a crumpled heap at one corner of the room.

I open my mouth to say something, but then stop. She's pulled a photograph out of her wallet and studies it for a few seconds before she stands and wedges the corner of the photo in between a crack in the wood above the sink. She turns her back to me to head for the shower room, pulling her shirt over her head on the way.

My feet are in cement. What I want and what I think she wants are dueling inside my head. I want to stay to make sure she's okay, hold her in my arms, and kiss all her pain away. But maybe she wants to be alone. There are so many reasons for her to be angry with me so I go, ignoring the guilt and the feeling that I'm abandoning her. It's like I helped rip her heart wide open, and now I'm leaving her to bleed to death because I have no idea how to stop the hemorrhaging.

Roxy is sitting near the fire pit, weaving a sun hat from small strips of palm leaves when she hears me approach.

"What's wrong, Prince Charming?" she says, without even a hint of a smile. "Trouble in your little kingdom paradise?"

I want to jab her with a wicked comeback like I always do, but I stop myself. This is a first. Instead, I say, "Ava's really upset and what she probably needs is to talk to another girl. Maybe you could try to remember what it's like to have your heart broken and, you know—give her hug, a sympathetic eye roll, and a few jaw drops before trash talking into oblivion the jerk that did this to her."

"Well, the last part should be easy; I have plenty of nasty things I'm dying to tell her about you." She doesn't look up, but an evil grin contorts her face.

"I'm sure that's true," I say, "but the hard part will be for you not to melt into a pile of green smoke when her tears touch your skin, or there'll be nothing left of you but your pointed hat and broom." I couldn't help it. It slipped out. "And just for the record, I'm only partly to blame for her despair."

Her eyes dart to me then, but they aren't filled with anger. She looks surprised by my confession, as if a small piece of empathy managed to crack its way through her ice-cold heart.

"I'm going to the beach. I'll be back in a while," I tell her. "Please stay here and keep an eye on Ava until I come back. I know you won't do it for me, but maybe you will for her." Then I turn and walk away.

I'm halfway to the beach when I notice the bright spot of yellow on the forest floor. I pick it up and hold it between my fingers. The yellow feather is out of place on this side of the island. This particular Bird of Paradise species is all but extinct on the island because the Lambai tribe uses the tail feathers in their head dresses. I shove it in my pocket and continue to the beach.

The fish are playing a game of hide and seek in my favorite fishing spot, but I wait patiently until one finally appears. Success! I lift the fish out of the water and notice something sparkle in the sand below the surface of the water. I pick it up and examine it for a half a second before my blood turns to ice in my veins. It is Ava's clover bracelet. And there's only one explanation for how it wound up here. This is the perfect place to watch the cave without being seen. I know because it is the exact spot I sat on numerous occasions to read Ava's journal. *Zoron!*

I've never run so fast in my entire life. My heart pounds with every step. I thrash through the forest dodging the trees with ease. How could I leave Ava alone? Roxy won't be able to protect her, and that's assuming she'd even try.

There's no sign of Roxy or Ava in the kitchen hut, so I sprint to the ladder and climb with stealth to the top. Roxy is standing in the doorway to Ava's room with her back to me, so I pause to listen.

"So what's wrong with *you?*" she asks Ava, and I hear Ava respond from inside.

"I just discovered my boyfriend wasn't who I thought he was."

Roxy lets out an insincere laugh. "Well, at least you ended up on an island with another prospect, even if he is annoying most of the time. Maybe not to you—but my brother's cheerful countenance really gets on my nerves. I had to leave a boyfriend behind too, and look at me, what do I have now? That's right—nothing but an annoying stepbrother and a bunch of cannibals without a sense of manners or any concept of hygiene."

Roxy steps into the room and disappears from my sight, but I can still hear what she says to Ava.

"So what's in your safe-deposit box?" she asks. "Not that it really matters. Because it'll be gone if no one pays the yearly fee—while you sit here and rot on this island like me."

"I'm not following you," Ava says, and I imagine Roxy rolling her eyes, completely annoyed. Not many people can follow what Roxy says. The majority of days she's in a sour mood and tends to leave out details of a conversation like she's offering you a riddle that you're not smart enough to solve.

"The key around your neck."

"Oh, it's not real," Ava says, like she's trying to clarify a misunderstanding. "My parents gave this to me as a gift when I was sixteen. They had it engraved with—"

"I saw what it says," Roxy interrupts. "It's a key to a bank safe-deposit box. The number on your key is one off from mine. They're together."

This is startling information. Now I understand Roxy's reaction to Ava's necklace when I introduced them. I'd examined the key closely after I removed the chain from around Ava's neck. On the opposite side of the engraving were five tiny numbers I thought were put there for show. I never got close enough to Roxy to notice she wore a necklace just like it, nor did I care.

"What's in yours?" Ava asks, and I take one step closer to the door.

"Important papers that are pointless now. My mother gave me this key when I turned twelve," Roxy says.

"What kind of papers?"

"I never saw them, but my mother said they're papers proving that my father left me half of his shares to a company. He gave the papers to my mother before he died. So, like I said—pointless. An ocean separates me from this island and my billion dollar fortune. Now I have nothing left but a life of misery."

Well, it's a relief to realize I'm not the only cause of Roxy's misery. She's pissed about her long-lost fortune. Three years together on this island and she's mentioned not so much as a word about it.

My mind is spinning with possibilities, and I'm sure Ava's is too. Finally she asks the question she must think matters most.

"Do you know who your father was?" I can hear the hesitancy in her voice. "Because I was thinking he might also be mine. After my parents died four months ago, I found out I was adopted. I know they adopted me from my aunt, but I haven't been able to figure out who my biological father was. And my aunt died too, right after I was born."

I so do not like where this conversation is going—Ava being related to Roxy. Oh, hell no.

"I never met him because he was killed before I was even born, so I've only seen pictures," Roxy says. "And then my mother made the stupidest decision of her life and married Dax's dad when I was two."

There's a hint of bitterness in her voice that rubs me the wrong way. Really? If it weren't for my dad, she'd have grown up in a motel room, running from town to town. And maybe she wouldn't have ended up here, but let's face it, without me, she'd definitely not be alive to sit here now and dis my dad. Damn. She'd be ungrateful if she were the only girl living in a castle on a planet full of hot guys, where money grew on trees and it rained chocolate.

My breath escapes with a soft whoosh. At least they are having a conversation... a normal conversation... so I turn and retreat back down the ladder, but not before I sneak into Roxy's room and swipe her precious seashell collection.

A quick perusal of the area surrounding the tree house proves useful when I find another yellow feather, confirming my suspicions that Zoron or someone from his tribe has been snooping around. This is not good.

It takes me only a few minutes set a trap made of small vines tied together and wrapped around various trunks six inches off the ground around the entire perimeter of the tree house. I also hang clusters of seashells on the vine to alert me if anyone comes close.

Roxy and Ava look surprised when I appear at the doorway. I pull the chair from the corner and make myself at home close to them. Putting my feet up on the bed, I cross them at the ankles.

"Hey. Just checking to make sure you didn't eat Ava," I say to Roxy with a smirk I know she'll hate. "I know how you like your dessert."

"Very funny," she snaps. "Let it go. Why don't you make yourself useful and go hunt something?"

I laugh quietly and then get up to stroll across the room to pick up Ava's sketchpad from the floor. I set the sketchpad next to the sink and lean over to look at the photo Ava placed there earlier. My heart sucker punches me in the chest.

"What I really want to know," I hear Ava say, "is why I have a key to a safe-deposit box like you, and what's in it."

"Well, I have a better question than that," I say.

"What is it?" asks Roxy. "Let me guess. Would Ava like you better if you could grow a beard?"

Ava snickers and turns to me, probably expecting me to be ready with a good comeback, but instead I say, "No," with all seriousness, and hold up the photo. "I was just wondering why Ava has a picture of your mother?"

Roxy gasps and jumps up from the bed to snatch the photo from my hand.

"Where did you get this?" she demands, and when she turns to Ava, a tear rolls down her cheek.

"You're both mistaken," Ava says with a shake of her head. "That's a picture of my aunt Vivianne, my mom's sister. She died right after I was born so she couldn't be your—"

"You!" Roxy interrupts, taking a step closer to Ava and pointing an accusing finger in her direction. "You're the *something else.*"

Ava and I look at each other with the same confused expression. I make a circle with my finger at the side of my head, and then point to Roxy while her back is still to me.

Roxy plops back down on the hammock bed cross-legged in front of Ava.

"When we left California, I was so upset," she says. "So a few days into our trip, my mom tried to take my mind off leaving by telling me she had something important to tell me. That's when she told me why we were running."

I rush to the chair next to the bed and sit down, eager to hear her story.

"She said my father was business partners with a dangerous man who wanted to buy out my father's share of the company, but my father refused. Then right after my father was killed, my mother found out she was pregnant with me. She suspected the partner had something to do with my father's death and was worried he'd come after her next. She said the partner wanted to eliminate her too, assuming that then he'd have all the shares of the company. So she faked her own death, went into hiding, and started a new life under her new identity."

"What does that have to do with Ava?" I ask, but she ignores me and continues the story.

"She met Dax's father, Jack, and they got married. Everything was fine until one day, we went shopping. For some reason, she thought someone was following us. She freaked out and convinced Jack that we needed to leave California so—"

"I already told her about that," I say. "What about Ava?"

"You're so impatient," Roxy snaps.

"Wait," Ava says. "Was it a black Mercedes that was following you?"

"No way!" I say, but Roxy's eyes widen.

"Yes... but how do you know about the black Mercedes?"

"Because I was being followed by one before I left California," Ava tells her.

Roxy jumps in. "Shortly after my mother thought she was being followed, I began to notice a black Mercedes when I would get out of school, or see it parked down the street when I went to a friend's house. When I told her about it, she panicked and took me out of school. We left right after that."

"Anyway, she told me about the safe-deposit box, and then she said, 'And there's something else I need to tell you'. But she never got to finish because that's when we hit the rocks," Roxy says with sadness in her voice. "So I think the something else was *you*. She was going to tell me I had a sister."

"Are you freaking kidding me?" I say, and then try to stop my brain from exploding.

"Think about it, Ava. They must have been worried about your safety, so they had your parents adopt you. Then, after our father was killed, and Mother knew she was pregnant with me, she decided to run and hide. Your safety-deposit box probably contains papers leaving you the other half of Father's shares. It totally makes sense."

That would explain them having the same keys, and Ava's parents' house being broken into, and more importantly, it would explain why someone would want her dead.

"What was the name of our father's business partner?" Ava asks Roxy.

"I don't remember, Harry something."

"Oh. My. Gosh. Harry Caruso?"

"Yeah, that sounds right," she says, and then turns her head to glare at me because I've leaned closer. They'd been so involved in solving the mystery, I think they actually forgot I was here.

"Sorry," I tell her. "I think I need some air."

28

Ava

LATE AFTERNOON: AIM FOR THE HEART

D AX LEAVES THE ROOM, AND I LOOK AT ROXY. SHE'S staring at the picture in her hands. The baby in the picture isn't me—it's her.

"You can have it if you want," I offer.

"Really?" She looks up in surprise. "Thanks."

I feel the need to hug her given the recent turn of events, but she doesn't seem like the hugging type. All of a sudden, the atmosphere becomes awkward.

"See you later," she says and walks out of the room, leaving me alone with my thoughts.

I lay down on the bed and remember how just last night I'd dreamt of Preston and getting married in a gazebo on a bluff, surrounded by lush, green grass. In front of us was a man dressed in a suit, performing the wedding, and behind him was a magnificent background. Where the grass ended, a cliff tapered down to the beach and vast ocean below. Preston stood in front of me looking overly handsome in a black tux. I had on the dress from the window at Giana's boutique, but instead of a veil, I wore a crown of white flowers. We were holding hands and after the kiss, we turned to our small audience of three people. Kirk, Anna and Giana were sitting together among rows of empty white chairs.

But now the cliff and white chairs disappear from my mind, and Preston and I are walking hand in hand in our swimsuits on a beach of white sand, with *Miss April* anchored just off shore in the distance. Preston leads me to a spot where two palm trees form an arch at the edge of a tropical forest where it is met by the sandy beach. Under the arch, I spy a narrow trail, surrounded on both sides by dense, lush greenery. He leads me down the path for what seems a long time until finally we come to a clearing that opens up to a magnificent waterfall that cascades down to a pool in front of us.

He smiles at me and gently pulls me into the warm, shallow water with him. We walk hand in hand until we are near the base of the waterfall. He holds me close, touching his lips to mine for a long kiss, and I drape my arms around his neck.

"Let's climb to the top," he says, looking up to where the water is spilling over the edge of the rocks many feet above us.

He leads me to the edge of the pool just to the right of the falls, and we step cautiously across the boulders piled at the base of a rock wall to a spot where we can climb to the top. He makes his way up the cliff by placing his hands and feet on various points jutting out, almost as if they are there for that very purpose. I follow closely behind him and copy his every move, trying not to look down at the jagged pile of rocks below. He reaches the top first and leans over the edge to extend his arm out to me.

"It's beautiful, Ava. Come on, you're almost there."

Reaching up, I grab his hand, starting to pull myself up the last few feet to the top when suddenly my foot slips off the rock. I fall into the wall, causing my other foot to slip as well, and now I'm dangling and gripping onto the face of a rock with one hand. Preston holds my other hand tight and supports my weight.

I hang with my face plastered to the side of the rock wall, and my feet flail clumsily to find some footholds unsuccessfully. I wonder why Preston isn't trying to pull me up or give me some encouragement. He isn't saying anything at all. I look down at the rocks below, then up in desperation to where his hand holds mine, and feel my hand start to slip.

I glance first at our hands and realize at once something is wrong. Preston's smooth, strong hands are much larger than they should be, his slender fingers now short and stubby and the reason for me losing my grip. My palm is sweaty and my fingers start to slide down the back of his hand until something stops them, a large, horseshoe ring full of diamonds. I strain my neck to look at the top of the ledge where Preston should have been laying. But peering over the edge instead is Mr. Caruso. An evil grin spreads across his face. Then he laughs a wicked laugh and lets go of my hand.

I jerk awake and stare up at the ceiling of the hut.

Did Preston know the real story about Mr. Caruso's partner? Did he know who I was all along?

This possibility angers me. My entire concept of Preston and his supposed feelings for me must have been a lie. It hurts too much to think about, and I'm tired of feeling sorry for myself. I need something to take Preston off my mind.

Dax.

He said we could do something fun. I grab the orange out of my backpack and hurry to find him.

He's sitting on a stump near a fire pit carving a small piece of wood, so I sit next to him on a different log.

"Hey," he says.

"I have a surprise."

I hold out the orange for him to see and a huge grin spreads across his lips, carving out his perfect dimples. He takes the orange from my hand, peels it with his knife, and then splits it in half. We sit there in silence to enjoy the succulent treat we both know will be the last of its kind.

"Have you recovered yet from the devastating news that you're related to the wicked stepsister?" he asks with a laugh. "Cause I haven't, it's just freaking weird. Don't worry though, I won't hold it against you—'cause I have the same problem."

I smile with him, thankful that Roxy must not be within hearing range.

He shoots me a sideways glance. "So, I guess that kind of makes you my stepsister too. Or does it? Because you were adopted. The whole idea is warping my mind." He shrugs. "It doesn't really matter though, I mean, technically, we aren't related except by marriage, and even though Roxy is totally like a sister because we grew up together, you and I are a completely different story, so—"

"Dax, I know." I interrupt his rambling. "So, what do you want to do?"

I see his face light up with excitement. "Really? Are you feeling up to it? 'Cause I wasn't sure after the whole briefcase ordeal."

I narrow my eyes playfully. "I'm fine," I lie. "But I don't really want to talk about it—I just want to do something fun. You promised, remember?"

"Sure, right." He jumps up and shoves the piece of wood in his pocket. After replacing his knife and grabbing the bow and quiver, he holds out his hand. "Let's go."

He takes off into the trees on a mission. His hands are strong, but his skin is rough in comparison to Preston's. I think of Preston holding my hand so many times during our walks on the beach and can't help but think it meant nothing to him. A nagging emptiness rises in my chest. I squeeze Dax's hand in response to my pain, and he turns his head to comfort me with a wink.

Deep in the forest, he stops near a small clearing where the ground is covered with flat rocks smothered in green moss. Across the clearing from where we are is a large tree.

"Want to learn how to shoot a bow and arrow?" Dax asks, and then gives me a wink. "Or if knives are your thing, I could teach you how to throw it. Then next time, you could kill the snake on your own."

I hesitate. "I'll try whatever's easier."

He contemplates my answer. Pulling out his knife, he walks over to the tree. He carves a large bull's-eye in the trunk, walks back to where I am, takes off his quiver, and lays it on the ground beside him, then hands me his bow.

"Are you right handed?" he asks, and I nod in response. "Good. Then hold the bow up with your left hand and pull back on the bowstring with your right."

I feel awkward but do as he tells me and lift the bow. He walks behind me and grabs my arms to turn me slightly so my left shoulder points toward the bull's-eye. Then he uses his foot to slide my right foot out, walking back around to my front to examine my position.

"Perfect."

He looks pleased and reaches down to fetch an arrow from the quiver. After he shows me where to place the arrow and how to hold it steady, he tells me to give it a try. I lift the bow and pull back on the drawstring, then try to hold it there while I squint through one eye to focus on the target. My arm begins to shake from the resistance of the bowstring so I hold my breath to try and steady it, but it's no use. I let go suddenly and the arrow goes shooting past the intended target, missing the entire tree. I sigh, knowing my cheeks are bright red. Shooting the bow is much harder than I thought it would be.

Dax's expression is one of surprise. "Ohhhkay," he says in mock disbelief.

He grabs another arrow, hands it to me, and then readjusts my stance. I lift the bow and aim again, this time leaving both eyes open. At the last second, my grip slips and the arrow arches upward, landing somewhere in the bushes to the left of the tree.

I exhale loudly. "Maybe I should try the knife."

He shakes his head and grins. "You just need to relax."

I watch him grab another arrow, and then walk around to stand behind me. He wraps his arm around my waist and places his hand on my stomach, pulling me against him. His left hand closes around mine where I grip the bow, and then his right hand interlocks with the fingers of my right hand, holding the arrow in place. I try to relax, but his close proximity is not helping. With one smooth motion, he raises the bow in my arms while drawing the bowstring back—farther than I was able to before. He places his face next to mine and then whispers softly in my ear.

"Relax."

I'm sure he's smiling. I should be looking at the target, but I can't take my eyes off the muscles flexing in his arm as it rests against mine. I can feel his warm breath on my neck, and my stupid heart starts to race. He slides his mouth next to my ear.

"Keep your eye on the target. Take a deep breath."

I inhale deeply.

"Good," he says softly, "Now slowly exhale and let go."

He slides his left hand down my arm, stopping at my elbow to steady me. I exhale at his command and let the arrow slip from my grasp. The arrow lands with a muted thud just to the right of the bull's-eye.

"Sweet!" Dax exclaims. "I knew you could do it."

He spins me around and wraps his strong arms around me, pulling me in tight for a big hug. I hesitate for a moment before letting my arms fall around him too, resting my head on his bare chest. He's so warm, and his skin has a sweet scent, not like Preston's cologne, but more like the smell of fresh-cut wood. I wonder why I didn't notice before when he hid us inside the tree. I thought he would have let me go by now but his arms are still around me, and he's very still.

"Should I try it again?" I ask, and then make the mistake of looking up at him when he doesn't answer.

He shows off his innocent dimples. I marvel at the color of his eyes, so vibrant blue they almost look unreal, and I'm suddenly lost in them, unwilling to move.

I force myself to look away from his intense gaze and allow my eyes to fall to his mouth. He does the unthinkable. He lowers his head to kiss me, but the moment his lips touch mine, I drop the bow and push him away, taking a step back at the same time. Rage sweeps over me until I see the hurt on his face. Instantly, my anger melts away.

"I'm—sorry." My eyes drop to the bow lying on the ground. "You took me by surprise; I just—wasn't expecting that." I reach down and pick up the bow.

What was he thinking? No. I know what he was thinking, what was I thinking? I was just staring at his lips. Of course he tried to kiss me—and I panicked.

"My bad," he says humbly and rests his hands on his hips. "I got a little carried away."

A slow smile returns to his face, and I exhale a sigh of relief. I've been holding my breath and waiting for those dimples to appear.

He quietly clears his throat. "I'm not going to apologize for it though, because I'm not sorry." I don't miss his sly smirk. "Go ahead; try the bow again."

He hands me another arrow. An overwhelming urge comes over me to shoot perfectly, knowing my failure might land me in the same precarious position as before, with him pressed up against me and his mouth next to my ear. I can still feel where his hand rested on my stomach, and I swallow before sliding the arrow into place. I hold the bow up and simultaneously pull back, concentrating on inhaling and then letting my breath out slowly. My release of the arrow sends it flying straight, just to the left of the center of the bull's-eye.

I look at him for approval, but he's eyeing me with suspicion.

"Nice one." I see a small dimple appear on one side of his mouth. "So, were you just holding out on me or were you deathly afraid I might help you again?"

I can't stop my cheeks from reddening. "No, you're just a great teacher," I say and try to sound convincing, but I know that's only part of the reason and I'm guilty as charged.

"Let's find the other arrows, and then we'll look for something you can kill." He slings the quiver over his shoulder.

Kill?

"I don't know if I can do that," I say, following him towards the tree. He pulls out both of the arrows that are stuck in the bark and puts them away.

"Sure you can." He lets out a laugh. "Just pretend the target is me."

His laughter is contagious. "Very funny."

He grabs one of the arrows from the forest floor and then turns to look at me, his face serious.

"I want you to know how to defend yourself. There's a chance I might not always be around to protect you," he says, but he smiles to soften the blow of his words.

He walks a few feet ahead and searches the bushes for the last missing arrow, but I stay frozen in place. His words terrify me. Why does he say things like that? I can't fathom the possibility of being stuck on this island without him. Alone, Roxy and I wouldn't stand a chance of surviving, whether from starvation or an attack from any of the cannibals. These thoughts worry me. But mostly, I just don't like the idea of him not being around.

Dax finds the last arrow, slides it into the quiver, and then holds out his hand. He motions with one finger to his lips for me to be quiet, and then we walk further into the woods. He stops and holds up his hand, signaling me to stop too, and then very slowly points up in the trees in front of us. On a branch, a beige- and brown-colored bird sits. Dax silently hands me the bow, and then, just as noiselessly, he pulls an arrow from the quiver on his back.

I ready myself and aim at the bird, aiming first with one eye and then with two. But Dax stands behind me and rests his hand on the small of my back for moral support, and now I can't stop thinking about our almost kiss— and my un-loyal heart that raced in response to his close proximity. What is wrong with me? I love Preston. But I shouldn't, because he isn't real and he didn't love me.

Dax steps closer and tenderly brushes the hair back from my face. This shot needs to be perfect and I have to hurry before his hand slides to my waist—or to that spot on my stomach to pull me against him when he decides I need more help.

But I'm too late. His hand just moved to my waist and the other hand has found my arm to gently guide my elbow higher. My breath hitches and my heart speeds up as if he's controlling it with an imaginary gas pedal. I can't concentrate because he's too close, and my head is reminding me of that with every shaky breath.

29

Dax

LATE DAY: A SHOT IN THE DARK

AVA'S FINGERS RELEASE THE ARROW. THE BIRD MAKES a high-pitched squawk, but it doesn't fly away as the arrow whizzes past its head and into the thick forest.

She hands me the bow in frustration, and I'm trying not to boast an amused smile. She seems relieved that it's over but a little irritated, and I can't help but wonder if it's because her attraction to me is so obvious. I wink before raising the bow in one fluid motion and make quick work of shooting the bird.

"Nice shot," she mumbles.

"Thanks," I reply. "As long as we don't show it to Roxy, we'll have something to eat for dinner tonight."

I replace the bow on my shoulder. Holding the bird in one hand and her hand in the other, we head back towards the Anwai village. When we get back to the tree house, Roxy isn't around again. Ava fails at hiding her disappointment. She watches me remove the feathers in preparation to cook the large bird.

"Where do you think Roxy is?" she finally asks, probably wondering if this is her usual routine.

"I'm not sure. I told you she usually avoids me, but now that I'm cooking food, she'll show up." I wink at her and then place the bird on the spit over the fire.

After discovering there's no fruit left in the kitchen hut, we set off to gather some bananas and papaya fruit, and then some berries like the ones I gave her the first day she woke up in the cave. Just as I predicted, Roxy is sitting by the fire when we return, staring into the flames. Ava sits down beside her.

"So if you're not busy tomorrow, you should come hang out with Dax and me," Ava offers.

I throw her a discouraging glance in hopes of reminding her that two's company and three's a crowd.

"Thanks, but I've got plans," Roxy says flatly, without taking her eyes off the flames. I dramatically brush my forehead in relief while standing behind Roxy, and Ava scolds me with a slight shake of her head.

"So, what kind of things did you like to do back home?" Ava asks Roxy, trying to pull some info out of her, but her vibe is making that extremely difficult. "Did you play any sports?"

"Not really."

"What sports did you play, Ava?" I ask loudly, hinting at Roxy and attempting to help Ava out.

"I played soccer and volleyball mostly, but I liked basketball too," she says, but there's still no acknowledgement from Roxy.

"Sweet! Me too," I say with a huge grin. "Well, not basketball, but I played soccer and beach volleyball. If I can figure out how to make us a soccer ball, we can have ourselves a little one on one."

Ava stares at Roxy, who remains inattentive and deep in thought. Her lack of attention only eggs me on.

"Roxy's hobbies were kissing boys and going to the mall with her friends." I let out a short laugh, but they don't join me. The atmosphere is suddenly awkward.

"So what was our mother like?" Ava asks, trying to change the subject.

Roxy pauses before answering.

"Well, obviously she was good at keeping secrets, ruining people's lives, and abandoning her children," she snaps, and then shoots her a sideways glance.

"My parents didn't tell me either," Ava says in a gentle voice. "But I know they did it to protect me. I'm sure our mother did the same for you."

I pass around some sliced papaya and bananas on a palm leaf. Pulling the bird from the fire, I divide the meat between us.

"So one bird is all you could manage?" Roxy frowns at me. "Maybe if you spent less time drooling over Ava, you could do a better job of taking care of me like you promised Dad."

She thinks I'll be hurt by her comment, but I'm amused. "You're just jealous that I have something to drool over other than dinner," I say, and then watch Ava's face flush. "Besides, I was teaching Ava how to hunt."

Roxy looks surprised. "Great. Well, it seems you two were made for each other." She wraps up her share of the bird in a palm leaf with a large portion of the papaya, then grabs some bananas and gets up to leave. "I'm outta here."

"Don't leave," Ava says out of desperation. "Stay and eat with us. If you want, tomorrow I'll show you what Dax taught me. We can shoot the bow together."

"Thanks, but I'm not really into it," she replies, and then strolls off into the trees.

Ava looks disheartened.

"Cheer up," I tell her. "You'll get used to it. That's how she always is."

I pour us some water, and we eat in silence for a minute or two.

"I just thought she'd want to hang out and get to know me a little," she says.

"Give her some time. She doesn't handle change well."

I smile gently. "We better clean this up and go inside. It's getting dark."

She nods and helps me extinguish the fire.

"What about Roxy? Will she be okay in the dark?"

"She's fine. She's off to her secret place. There's a cave there, so sometimes she stays all night."

We place the remaining fruit in the wooden bowl in the kitchen, and then I follow her up the long ladder and down the walkway to her room.

"Goodnight. I'll be dreaming of ways to create us a soccer ball," I announce with a wink. She tells me goodnight, and I head to my room.

The song I've been forming in my head begs to be played, so I grab my guitar from the corner and start to play. After a few times, I switch to playing some songs my dad taught me. When I finally stop playing and lay in bed, my worried thoughts take hold. Will I hear someone snooping around below in the middle of the night?

I fight the urge to go back to Ava's room and sit in the chair in the corner to keep guard. Maybe I will when I'm sure she's asleep. I stare at the ceiling even though it's too dark to see it and focus on every sound outside. I'm used to the normal sounds so anything out of the ordinary should stand out.

A thump quickens my heart, and I freeze. I didn't hear the seashells, but I could swear I just heard footsteps outside. I sit up and strain to listen. Definitely footsteps. *Damn it!* The sound of soft footsteps is getting close.

I spring to my feet, grab my bow, load an arrow, and turn to the door just in time to see a faint blue glow and then a silhouette as someone launches themselves in the room. The figure creeps toward my bed. I aim my arrow at the back of the person's head but when she leans down, I see her long hair fall forward over the bed.

"Ava?"

She inhales a sharp breath and flings around to see me standing in the corner with my bow and arrow drawn. I drop them on the floor to run to her, and she flings her arms around my neck.

"Are you all right?" I let out a short laugh. "What are you doing? What's wrong?"

She holds her grip around me. "I'm scared. I heard a noise, well, a lot of noises, and it's so dark. Please don't leave me alone. I can't stand it," she says. She must be relieved that she made it to my room without falling prey to the imaginary dangers lurking outside her room that she's certain are looming in the trees. I don't want to tell her that she's not that far off.

"Shhh, it's okay," I say, putting my hand on the back of her head. "I'm sorry; I forgot how frightening the darkness is. I guess I'm just used to it. Come on, I'll come back to your room and stay until you fall asleep."

"No. You can't leave me," she says in a panic.

My heart leaps in my chest. I reach up to gently release her grip from around my neck. "Okay, whatever you want. Let me get my bow."

She holds the light up for me to pick up the bow and arrow, and then I grab the quiver from where it hangs on the chair. I take her by the hand and lead her back to her room.

"There was a noise over there." She points to the wall near the entrance to the shower.

"It's just a bat," I say calmly. "It won't hurt you. Come on, lay down."

She lies down on the bed, and I join her.

"You better turn that off. It may come in handy sometime," I tell her.

She powers the phone off and drops it on the floor, then rolls over to face me. I can barely see her.

"Dax?" she whispers.

"What?"

"I can't see you. Give me your hand."

I lift my hand in response to her request and she gropes until she finds it in the dark. I interlock my fingers with hers and squeeze tightly. She pulls our hands to her chest. Maybe holding my hand there will put a temporary stop to the hemorrhaging hole inside her heart.

"Relax. I'm not going anywhere," I assure her. "You know... if you need me to, I could always kiss you to sleep," I say, and I laugh quietly. "But only if you ask really nice... and beg."

"Don't hold your breath," she says with obvious sarcasm. "But I do have a favor."

"Name it," I say a little too quickly. "Your wish is my command."

"Sing to me."

I wasn't expecting that, and I don't say anything for a few seconds. "I don't have my guitar," I tell her. "Besides—I can kiss better than I can sing."

My mind wanders where it shouldn't, but she is not so easily distracted.

"Please? I heard you earlier, and your voice is amazing."

My dad had a good voice, and sometimes I'd sing with him, but this is something new for me and I'm nervous. I've never sung in front of anyone before, and now silence fills the room from my indecisiveness. Why does she want me to sing? I'd rather use my mouth for a different activity.

She tucks her head into my shoulder, and my heart rate picks up speed. I enjoy the moment until one of her tears falls onto my skin.

"Please?" she says again, in barely more than a whisper, and I know, without a doubt, I will do anything in the world for this girl. I want her to be happy. I sing until I lull us both to sleep.

I wake before she does but refuse to move. I didn't even

move last night except to comfort her when she jerked in her sleep and I was sure she'd had a nightmare. She kept our entwined hands tight to her chest, so I squeezed hers gently and kissed the top of her head before drifting back to sleep. Not exactly the best protection plan. Zoron could have snuck in and slit all our throats easily, and I wouldn't have heard him coming, but at least I would have died a happy man with Ava by my side.

I've been laying here for an hour, and now the shrill call of a bird causes her to jerk awake. She smiles up at me. "Can I have my hand back now?" I tease. "You haven't let me move it all night, and I'm afraid there may be permanent damage."

She lets go of my hand. I roll over and groan, part legit and the other part exaggeration because I want to see her blush. I flex my arm to get the blood flowing.

"So what was that song you sang to me last night?" she asks, apparently doing her best to distract us both from the situation she finds awkward.

"It's a song my dad used to sing to me when I was little. It always put me to sleep. He taught me to play it on the guitar a few weeks before he died." The memory makes me smile. "Dad traded Chief Anwai his waterlogged watch for that guitar. Originally, it belonged to some poor, adventurous soul who made the mistake of exploring Lamarai Island and wound up being dinner." I climb out of the hammock bed and pick up my bow and arrow. "I'm going back to my room now. I'll see you downstairs."

"Dax?"

I peek my head back in the doorway.

"Thank you."

"Anytime," I say, and with any luck, it will be *every* time.

DAY TWELVE: TRUTH OR DARE

*D*AX AND I WERE RIDING WHITE HORSES ON A BEACH along the water's edge, laughing as the wind blew through our hair. I clung to the reins, wearing a long, princess dress, and Dax looked striking in his royal robes fit for a prince. Our horses raced up a hill to a flat field of green grass that overlooked the ocean. We left the horses to graze and walked hand in hand to a tree near the ledge of the cliff.

He bent down and picked a handful of wildflowers that grew in a small patch. Handing them to me with a smile, he wrapped his arms around my waist. We admired the view for a long time before I looked into his azure blue eyes. A gentle breeze tugged at my hair.

"I missed you," he said, "But I've finally found you, and I'll never lose you again." Then he kissed me with passion like I belonged only to him. He took my hand in his to lead me back to the waiting horses.

"I'll race you back," he taunted and helped me onto my horse.

"You'll lose," I told him, waiting for his dimples to appear.

I nudged my horse to go as soon as Dax climbed on his, and we raced down the path to the beach. We rode side by side and headed for a castle on the beach in the distance, with a long drawbridge leading to the entrance. Finally, I took the lead and looked back to throw him a triumphant grin.

But as I turned back around, a black horse with a rider appeared out of nowhere. The ominous intruder cut me off a few feet away, and I was thrown to the sand when my horse stopped short and reared up. The bouquet of wild flowers I held in one hand littered the ground around me. The mysterious rider in armor raised the visor of his helmet to reveal his identity.

Preston looked down at me from on top of his black stallion.

The call of a bird startled me awake that morning after Dax had spent the night in my room, and I was happy for the rude awakening that saved me from a troublesome ending to my dream. I contemplated my strange dream before I shoved it to the usual spot in the back of my mind. That was the second time I'd dreamt of Dax.

The morning sun peered in through the doorway. Dax was lying beside me with his eyes open. He'd asked me if he could have his hand back, and warmth spread in my cheeks. But the fact that I'd clung to him all night like a teddy bear wasn't the only reason I'd been blushing. I sat up, desperately hoping he didn't have a clue I'd just been dreaming about him. About us *together*. Kissing.

He politely excused himself, and I thanked him before he slipped out of my room.

I'd been so sad the night before after Dax first walked me to my room. But he had no idea that leaving me alone would cause me to start missing Preston, regardless of what the briefcase exposed.

That night, I hadn't wanted to think of how Preston knew he'd have to kill me, I only wanted to remember his flawless smile that centered between his smooth chiseled jaw, his playful yet seductive laugh, his green eyes sparkling with excitement every time he looked into mine. And the smell of him, that heavenly scent I'd have given my soul for just to get a whiff when he wasn't around. I missed the way he looked, polished and perfect, with his designer silk shirts that clung to his muscular chest.

My mind had flashed through all of our time spent together, wandering through each magical moment of our dates that seemed so over the top. Our drives down the coast, candlelight dinners, and walks on the beach followed by my birthday getaway on Catalina Island. I was tortured by the idea that everything had been too good to be true, especially him. As if the pain of him being gone wasn't enough, the pain of his betrayal had piled on top.

I had tried to shove Preston out of my mind to focus on Roxy and think of ways to make her want to spend more time with me. That's when I heard music coming from Dax's room—the same catchy melody I heard him playing on his guitar when I woke up on the beach.

Dax started to sing and his voice was amazing—smooth and relaxing, and the thought of him trying to kiss me popped into my head along with the memory of his hand on my stomach. I squeezed my lids shut and tried to focus on the words of the song, but Preston's face just kept appearing like a spreading infection in my mind.

But then the vision of the contents in the briefcase clouded those memories like a large blob of black ink, the stain bleeding and blending together to ruin the purity of the past and the picture-perfect images I had clung to. The blow of his deceit was far worse than the first day on the island when I discovered he was gone.

My hand muffled my sobbing because I knew if I didn't that Dax would hear me, since there was nothing separating us but a few feet and thin, wooden walls. The tears rolled out in a steady stream.

I felt abandoned and betrayed, and the worst kind of loneliness engulfed me as realization hit hard. Preston left me alone intentionally, and now there will be no wedding, no traveling the world, and no going to college. If I'd made different choices, my path would have led me to a very different place. Then, without much effort, a new emotion sprung up to block out the hurt he caused me. I was angry.

Somewhere during all that stewing, I had dozed off, until something awoke me and I found myself in utter darkness. Without a full moon or the light from the fire in the cave, nighttime on the island is almost pitch black. Dax had stopped playing, and the sounds of the forest and the creatures living in it were loud. My imagination ran wild. My chest tightened, and it was hard to breathe. My breathing accelerated as I panicked.

Despite being frozen with fear, I forced myself to roll over and felt around for my purse next to the bed. My fingers found my cell phone and with trembling hands, I pushed the power button. Relief poured over me when the screen came to life and a bluish glow lit up the room. I put the phone on my chest to illuminate the ceiling above me and listened to the silence.

But the quiet was shattered by a flapping noise that came from outside of my wall. My heart pounded, and I jerked my head to the left to stare where I thought it came from. I lay absolutely still, afraid to make a sound. Another noise startled me, and I whipped my head to the right.

In that moment of terror, I wondered if Zoron had come back to get me. Dax said it was dangerous to be out after dark, but I hadn't asked why. Something smacked into the wall behind me and the need to be with Dax became overwhelming.

I had sprinted to Dax's room.

My face flames with embarrassment every time I think about it. I'd thrown myself at him and begged him to stay with me, then begged him again to sing me asleep. And then I had wrapped myself around his arm like a clinging vine. Oh my.

After I'd taken a shower to distract myself from the humiliation, I found him sitting on a log near the fire pit, cleverly crafting a soccer ball using fresh twigs and tying them together to form a sphere. I plopped down next to him to eat a bowl of fruit and watched him stuff the core with moss, and then wrap the outside with some dried out animal skin he saved from the wild pig. Finally, he stitched the seams together with fine strips of bark.

He juggled his new toy in front of me.

"I'm impressed," I said, and I truly was.

"Let's go to the beach and try it out," he had said with his contagious enthusiasm. He pulled me up from the log, and we'd gone to the beach to try it out.

That was over a week ago.

Without a doubt, life is cruel, unfair. But today, I want to change my destiny—I want the life I dreamt about with Preston. I want someone to love me, to protect me, and to make me laugh. And most importantly, I don't want to be alone.

The last few days have merged together. Dax and I have spent the mornings hanging out at the castle or playing soccer at the beach, jumping in the water to swim when we get too hot. Our afternoons have been consumed with hunting, which I know takes longer than usual because Dax lets me do the shooting. I'm still terrible, so sometimes he takes over to leave us more time to play.

Staying busy has made it possible for me to keep my memories with Preston contained in a file in the back of my mind. As long as I'm with Dax, I can cope. Together, we've created things. He helped me make a toothbrush from the course-haired skin of an animal, and he even made me a comb out of sticks he carved and wove together. And each night after dinner, Dax plays his guitar and sings, while I listen to his soothing voice. Sometimes, the memories of Preston creep up again, causing the ache to rise in my chest, until Dax lies down beside me and gives me his hand, singing me his familiar lullaby until I fall asleep.

Life without Roxy has become a pattern too. She shows up to get food and then leaves again, and each time Dax complains about her taking more than her share. It seems like she wants to completely avoid me, as if getting to know me is at the bottom of her list of things she wants to do.

"We don't see much of Roxy," I said last night as Dax and I laid together in the darkness.

"Yeah. That's been nice," Dax said with a laugh, and I punched him in the dark.

"Seriously. I can't help thinking it's because of me. She never accepts my offer to hang out with us, and she hasn't slept here since I have."

"Well, I hope you're not losing any sleep over it, because I can think of a much better way to miss out on sleep, and it definitely doesn't include Roxy. Would you like me to show you?"

I punched him a little harder and tried not to think too hard about his suggestion. "That won't be necessary."

I let go of his hand to touch his face, feeling the dimples carved above his mouth. He took my hand back and kissed my palm before lacing his fingers through mine. We've become an inseparable team, and I depend on him like a drug. I feel like he's a necessary part of me.

"But she never sticks around," I also said. "We're always alone."

"Maybe that's the point," Dax had replied. "In fact... maybe she doesn't dislike you as much as you think. She might believe she's doing us a favor. Maybe... we shouldn't be *wasting* all this alone time."

"Oh. My. Gosh."

He laughed, and I felt his warm breath next to my ear. I turned away from him onto my side and pulled his arm around me since I still had a hold of his hand. My eyes flew open when he planted a sweet kiss on my cheek.

"Goodnight, Ava."

"Night," I had said, and squeezed his hand before he started singing me a quiet lullaby.

But this morning, I woke up alone, and I'm wondering how Dax managed to escape with his hand. I'd wrapped his arm around me and held on tight last night, ignoring his multiple suggestions of how we could intimately pass the time. But thanks to his good night kiss on my cheek, the visual of us kissing in my dream wedged itself inside my head and kept me up long after he fell asleep. I sigh, remembering how the touch of his lips on my skin did funny, happy things to my stomach.

I hurry through my usual morning routine, and find him waiting for me in the kitchen hut with a big smile and an animal skin bag strung over his shoulder next to his bow and quiver.

"Come on," he says in his cheerful morning voice. "We're going somewhere else to eat breakfast."

He holds out his hand like he always does, and then takes off in a different direction than the day before. My hand feels at home in his, giving me a sense of security I desperately need. He makes me feel safe, and I know he'll protect me at any cost, causing a wealth of happiness to cover the hurt Preston left to accumulate in my chest, smothering the pain almost completely.

We reach the beach and walk along the shoreline to where the land carves in a bit, forming a small cove-like area below a sheer cliff. The waves crash into the rock wall and bounce back, leaving a film of white froth floating on top of the water. This spot looks vaguely familiar from the morning we walked the beach in search of Preston, but I'd been so concerned with finding him that I missed the beautiful scenery surrounding this part of the beach.

We walk until the sand turns into rocks, and then take off along a path that leads to the top of the bluff. The flattop is covered with soft green ground cover and some bushes, and a few feet back is a line of trees marking the entrance to the forest.

"Wow." I look at the ocean below us in awe. "This view is incredible."

"Yeah. I love to come up here," he says. "It's a great place to get away and clear your mind, but actually, I need a couple of minutes to set things up. You can go wander around over there, and I'll come get you when I'm ready." He smiles mischievously and points into the trees directly behind us. "Just don't wander too far or you might run into Roxy. Her special place is near that small point of rock."

I quirk a brow, and he winks.

"Stay close to the stream. You'll be fine."

I nod and head for the trees, surprised that he's giving me permission to wander around without him. I step into the tree line, follow the sound of gurgling water, and veer to my left until I find it. I follow the stream deeper into the forest, stopping to admire all the different flowers growing near the water's edge.

I spot a bright yellow, exotic-looking flower and decide it would make a nice centerpiece for our breakfast, so I maneuver my way across the stream to the other side to get it. I pluck it from its stem and turn to cross back when something catches my eye.

A tree much smaller and different from the rest sits nestled in among the giant trees further down the stream. I blink twice to make sure I'm really seeing what I think I see. It looks as though someone has carved a message into the bark midway up. I can't get a good visual on it from this side of the water, so I hop from rock to rock to get back to the other side. One step away from reaching it, my foot slips and I fall in the water.

Luckily, I managed to save the flower at the expense of not catching myself with both hands, and now my shorts are soaked. Figures. I giggle and pull myself up before remembering the tree. I turn around and find it, but the carving is still indiscernible.

I take a few steps forward and spot a rock that I can stand on to get a better view. Before I can reach it, I hear Dax calling.

"Ava."

He slows down as he gets closer. Was he panicking?

"Geez. Didn't think you would wander off so far," he says playfully. "Come on, everything's ready and I'm starving."

He holds out his hand and notices the flower I'm holding.

"Nice."

"Yeah. I crossed the stream to get it, and that's when I saw something cool." I turned to point to the tree. "It looks like someone carved a message into a heart on the bark of that tree. I can't quite make out what it says without getting closer."

"Well, let me save you the trouble," Dax says. "We are dangerously close to Roxy territory. I'm sure it says 'I hate Dax'. Let's go. If you really want to check it out, we can come back after breakfast."

His dimples make the carving seem trivial.

"Okay."

He leads me back to the cliff where he had put great effort into setting up. He had wooden bowls and fruit and coconut arranged on a wooden tray. He takes my yellow flower and adds it to the bouquet he had in one of the cups.

We sit down and leaned against a large rock that juts out of the ground near the edge of the bluff. We stare out at the ocean while we eat the array of fruit. When we are done eating, I scoot closer to him and rest my head on his shoulder.

"Let's play Truth or Dare?" he suggests, and I don't have to look at him to know that he's boasting a big grin.

There's never an end to his games. Truth or Dare isn't a fun game for worriers like me, and it reminds me too much of the five-question game I played with Preston over dinner.

I lift my head and groan. "That game's not my favorite."

"Oh. Well... we could play spin the bottle instead." He flashes a mischievous grin. "I have plenty of bottles back at the castle."

I roll my eyes. "I'm just not very good at this game."

"What?" He laughs. "No one is *good* at Truth or Dare. It's just fun. You need to stop worrying so much and relax—live on the edge a little."

"I *am* on the edge. Literally. And only because you're here with me. I'm not a huge fan of heights," I remind him.

"Really? How about blond, blue-eyed, non cannibal types? Are you a fan of those?"

Yeah, I could see where this was going. The heat in my cheeks answered the question for me. The more time we'd spent together, the bigger fan I'd become.

"Okay, Truth or Dare it is," I say, not missing his triumphant grin. "Who's going first?"

"Ladies, of course," he says slyly. "Truth or dare?"

I stare at him for a moment, hesitant to choose. "Truth, I guess."

"So do you remember the day on the beach when we were eight?"

I nod, wondering where he's going with this. So many

possibilities.

"When it was time to go, you started to cry."

Uh, oh.

"Why were you crying?"

His alluring eyes search mine. I know the kind of answer he's waiting for, but I stall before answering. "I didn't think I'd ever see the castle again."

"Are you seriously going to cheat?"

He looks disgruntled. Apparently, I'm a bad liar too.

"I wasn't finished." I pause. "And... I was worried I'd never see you again." I can feel myself blushing, and I turn my head to look in the other direction, away from his steady gaze. "Truth or dare?" I ask.

"Truth."

I turn back to see a smug grin plastered to his face, and I eye him curiously before asking my question. "If you found a genie in a bottle and he gave you three wishes, what would they be?"

He laughs before answering.

"It's funny you should ask, because I've actually thought about that before. Two of those wishes have already come true. Now that you're here, and I found a surfboard, the only thing missing is a pizza. A meat lover's with thick crust and extra cheese." He catches me blushing again. "Your turn."

"Truth," I say, hoping for the best.

He leans closer, and my heart starts to race.

"If you had the choice to leave here today and go back to your old life, or stay here with me... which would you choose?"

Cheater. Totally unfair. He knows I have nothing to go back to. Which raises the question, what would I do? Preston's gone and nothing more than a scam, plus now I know Mr. Curuso wants me dead. So that leaves only one option.

"Uhm, I guess I'd stay here with you. You and Roxy are my only family now."

His face radiates happiness, but I'm filled with worry. Exactly why I hate this game.

"Dare," he says, before I can offer him the choice.

His eyes are focused on my lips. I'm quick to look away and notice a small rock balancing on top of a larger one on a point, about a hundred yards to the right of where we sit.

"I dare you to shoot that small rock off the large one with your bow and arrow," I say, pointing it out to him.

"Seriously?' he says. "You really are bad at this game, aren't you?"

I giggle and watch him get up to retrieve his bow and one arrow from the quiver. He stands directly in front of me to raise and draw the bow, flexing his strong arms while I admire his smooth, chiseled chest behind the drawstring pulled tight across it. He lets go, and I turn my head just in time to see the arrow and small rock disappear from view, down the other side of the cliff.

"That was—awesome," I tell him. He returns to sit by me, and I internally cringe because it's my turn. "Truth."

"What's wrong? Are you scared of a little dare?" he taunts.

"No, I'm not scared." I am, but the competitive part of me takes over. "Fine. Dare."

A satisfied grin pulls at the corners his mouth and then he takes my hand in his, lacing his fingers with mine. He shifts closer, and now he's staring at my lips again. *Oh, no.* My bravery comes to a screeching halt, and my heart starts beating double time.

"I dare you to kiss me."

I stare back at him. That was a dirty trick, and I walked right into it. I look at his cheek and start to lean towards it, but he pulls back.

"No. A real kiss."

He's looking into my eyes with intent, and those dimples are disarming. I look down and smile shyly, knowing I've been defeated. I've dreamt of kissing him, and now my insides are flitting wildly as that dream flashes through my mind. My heart's racing and my stomach's doing somersaults. I'm scared. Terrified. Not of kissing him, but afraid I might actually like it.

Before I finish debating with myself, his fingers find my cheek, grazing my skin as if I'm made of paper-thin glass and he thinks I might shatter. He leans in to kiss me and his lips are so soft, warm, and inviting, as they move across mine ever so smoothly. My eyes close and I hesitate, holding back a little, but then I realize how much I *do* like kissing him—more than I want to admit.

He deepens the kiss, and I open my eyes to meet his vibrant blue irises that match the vast sky behind him. His fingers slide through my hair to rest behind my neck with his thumbs at my cheeks. He holds me there and kisses me like he never wants to stop. Every ounce of worry, loneliness, and rejection I've felt is absorbed by him and replaced by pure bliss, leaving me feeling so light and weightless I think I might float away. Then he pulls away slowly, gently tugging at my bottom lip.

"It's my turn," he says through a satisfied grin. "And I choose dare."

"Kiss me again," I say in a breathy whisper, surprised at my own forwardness, but I *want* him to kiss me again. The words barely escape my mouth before he presses his lips against mine with more urgency than before. And this time is different. He's relishing kissing me, like I am the last piece of triple-layer caramel chocolate fudge cake on earth and he's never tasted anything so good.

There's not even time to be nervous, and no room inside my body for that emotion, because I am consumed with everything warm and fuzzy, bursting inside like the sunrise spilling over the mountains on a summer day. This kiss is longer, so much better than I imagined in my dream, and I feel a sense of happiness that I haven't felt since being on Lamarai. His kisses are closing the hole in my heart one stitch at a time.

"Truth or dare?" he asks softly against my mouth.

I know he'd love for the kissing routine to go back and forth all day, and part of me longs for the same. There's something tempting about being on an island, virtually alone without anyone watching, that makes me want to continue kissing him, welcoming the relief of my sorrow. His kiss is like a drug that creates a numbing effect on my pain. He waits anxiously for me to make my choice, his soft, full lips ready to pounce less than an inch from mine.

"Truth," I say, expecting his face to be filled with disappointment, but a sly smirk creeps across his irresistibly kissable mouth.

"Okay." He looks into my eyes and now I'm starting to regret my choice of action. "Ava Starr, you're amazing, beautiful, perfect, and all I've ever wanted. I've dreamt of you since the first day we met. I waited a long time to find you, and by some miracle—here you are. So my question is... if I asked you to be my princess, and live happily ever after with me forever... would you say yes?"

I lean away, shocked by his question. My mouth opens to say something, but words fail me. I'm utterly speechless—but he's just getting started.

"I just happen to know a chief," he pauses, "that can make things happen." He glances down at our intertwined fingers, then squeezes my hand and clears his throat quietly. "You know, like a marriage ceremony for example. Not now, of course, but when you're ready. I would marry you in a heartbeat, but there's no rush. We have all the time in the world."

He studies me and waits for my answer, sheer joy radiating from the dimples on his adorable face. I blink, pausing, as visions of a future with Dax swirl through my mind. The thoughts are pleasant—exciting, perfect images of happiness so vivid I can almost touch them. Dax is real. He loves me—and he's mine for the taking. I smile back at him, knowing only one little word stands between the two of us, and our perfect fairy-tale ending.

An internal battle rages in my mind. My pulse is racing, and the word he wants to hear is on the tip of my tongue, begging to be released. But is he out of his mind? We just kissed. Only weeks ago, I'd been ready to marry Preston on a moment's whim. And now Dax sits in front of me, asking me to spend the rest of my life with him.

It seems inevitable—the only choice being whether to spend it with him as a friend, or his wife. He's already my best friend, but I can't deny my deeper feelings for him. I know I could be completely happy by his side, but it will take time. And this is the cause for my uncertainty—not knowing exactly how long the shattered dream of my first love will continue to haunt me.

Before I can answer, he gets up and walks to the edge of the cliff before turning to face me.

I gasp. "Dax! Get away from the edge; you're making me nervous."

"Come on. Live a little. Come and get me—then tell me you'll marry me." His eyes are so alluring. "Or would you rather I jump?"

"What?" I say. "Don't be ridiculous. I'm serious; come back from the edge."

"That's not an answer. One," he says, holding his arms out to the side. "Two."

I narrow my eyes. "You wouldn't dare."

"Three."

He leans back and is gone.

"Dax!"

I crawl to the edge just in time to see him hit the water feet first after an elegant backwards dive. I hold my breath until I see him surface, and then bite my tongue to keep from swearing. I'm not sure over the sound of the wind, but I think I hear him laughing. He waves at me, and then gestures for me to follow his lead. Yeah, right.

"Show off," I mutter, and then stand to brush the moss and dirt from the front of my shirt.

"Ava?"

Ice slips through my veins. I know this voice. It's the same one that begged for my time, borrowed my love, and stole my heart, and it is now threatening to crush my chance for a happy ever after.

I spin around and see Preston standing a few feet behind me. He lets out a relieved sigh and falls to his knees, but cold fear rushes over me. Am I dreaming? I blink twice. My heart starts to race and I'm consumed with mixed emotions, so I stand perfectly still and wait for him to say something.

"Thank goodness you're alive. I thought you were dead," he says, his voice strained.

My feet are frozen in place, and I stare at him with unbelieving eyes. He looks as gorgeous as ever, the only difference is the three weeks' worth of stubble that covers his perfect face. My legs want to run to him—my arms want to fling themselves around his neck and my lips want desperately to collide with his, but I refrain while my mind and heart duel in a fierce battle. All I wanted from the moment I woke up on this island was to find him alive, but now that I have, the reality of it seems like sheer torture.

He seems troubled by my silence, standing up to take a step towards me, but I take a step back in response.

"Ava, it's me."

"Stay back," I order, ignoring the stabbing pain shooting through my heart at the sound of my own words, words that cause his expression to become one of concern.

Kirk and Anna break through the tree line and run up behind him. They are out of breath as if they've been running to catch up to him. My eyes flicker to their faces and then fall lower. They're holding hands.

I quickly glance to my right, but there's no sign of Dax. I'm outnumbered in a big way.

"Oh my gosh! Ava?" Kirk says with a huge grin, but I narrow my eyes at him.

"Something's wrong," Preston says to Kirk, and then says to me, "What happened to your head?"

Dax told me the lump on my head has all but disappeared, leaving only a greenish-blue bruise in its place.

Preston starts to take another step towards me and I step backwards again, my heel resting over the very edge of the cliff. Sand and pebbles slip from beneath my foot, and I know Dax must be watching me from the water. I'm terrified to jump but also terrified of the person standing in front of me.

A look of fear crosses Preston's face. "Ava, please come away from the edge. It's me. Preston."

Kirk jumps in. "Seriously, you're freakin' me out right now. Get back from the edge before I come over there and get you myself." He orders me towards him with his hand, but Anna says nothing.

"I'm warning you—all of you! Stay back or I'll jump," I tell them, hoping they won't make me keep my promise. They're probably planning to push me anyway.

"Ava, please. Let me help you," Preston begs. "I've missed you so much."

His eyes fill with tears, but I refuse to fall for his acting this time. I swallow, trying to hold back the onslaught of tears I know are coming.

"You left me to die," I say. "How could you? I loved you."

Kirk and Anna's expressions are both one of shock,

but on Preston's face is an undeniable expression of horror. He shakes his head and opens his mouth to speak, but then he closes it.

He lunges forward to grab me, but I'm faster. I turn in an instant and scream as I leap off the edge to the frothy waters below.

Acknowledgements

I would like to thank the amazing team at Clean Teen for making my dream become a reality. You are my superheroes. Thank you Marya, for the best cover ever; Rebecca, for loving Wicked Luck from the start; Cynthia, for your expert editing skills; Courtney, for working your magic; and every one of you for your help, patience, hard work, friendly reminders, and enthusiasm. You guys rock.

A special thanks to my family, who puts up with my writing and never complains, even when you have to eat cereal for dinner, or pizza...again. I love you! Thanks also to the best parents a daughter could have, who have always loved and encouraged me to follow my dreams. Thanks for believing in me.

Thank you to all my wonderful friends who are my biggest fans and support group and who stick with me even when I'm on a writing binge and become a recluse. I appreciate all the times you let me pick your brain, every word of encouragement, and for being excited right along with me. Laurey and Jennifer, thanks for your photography skills that save me from being invisible to the world. Also, an extra big thanks to Dawnee for your willingness to read every single rewrite, for all your fabulous suggestions, for all the laughs and tears along the way.

And last but not least, infinite thanks to every reader who picks up this book to go on a wicked adventure of luck and love. I'm your biggest fan.

About the Author

Shannon Maynard lives in Colorado with her five girls where she is a legal assistant by day and an author by night. In between working and writing she can be found driving kids to soccer, folding mountains of pink laundry, or eating her weight in chocolate. Other addictions include shoe shopping, reading YA, and Australian and British accents (which may be partly to blame for her massive crush on Thor). If she had one wish it would be for more hours in the day to spend enjoying all of the above. Okay, everything except the laundry.

Shannon studied art and criminology before getting a license in cosmetology, but eventually wound up an expert daydreamer; a skill that occasionally leads to getting lost while driving, but has been a huge asset to her love for writing. Her debut novel WICKED LUCK is the first book in the Wicked Luck Trilogy.

CPSIA information can be obtained at www.ICGtesting.com
Printed in the USA
LVOW12s0231300515

440388LV00006B/7/P

9 781634 220668